Dare To Dream

By

Emma Carney

The right of Michael Parker to be identified as the Author of this Work using the pseudonym, Emma Carney, has been asserted by Michael Parker in accordance with the Copyright, Designs and Patents Act 1998.

Copyright © Michael Parker 2024

All characters in this publication are fictitious and resemblance to real persons, living or dead is purely coincidental.

All rights reserved. No part of this publication may be reproduced, stored in a retrieval system, or transmitted, in any form or by any means without the prior permission of the publisher, nor be otherwise circulated in any form of binding or cover other than that in which it is published and without similar condition being imposed on the subsequent purchaser. Any person who does so may be liable to criminal prosecution and civil claims for damages.

Chapter 1

The five girls were sitting in an alcove on a curved, red quilted lounger. In front of them was the low table where their drinks were plus their bags and mobile phones. The mobile phones had to be instantly available because the girls were always on alert, ready for any text messages or the opportunity to take a photo that could be instantly uploaded to their Instagram followers and other diverse social media accounts! The noise in the club was already at maximum crescendo level as the DJ, known as Disco Dave, pumped out hits accompanied by his own vocal interruptions which were supposed to encourage everyone to get up and dance and to help keep the party going. He looked like he was having fun anyway.

Although there were plenty of dancers enjoying themselves on the dance floor, arms held up in the air, waving and swinging like paper streamers in a flow of swift rising air, none of the girls were paying a lot of attention. They were in high spirits, talking (shouting more like because of the noise) and just enjoying the thought of no more studying because those days had come to an end; college was history, and this was supposed to be their 'Prom' night. They were all reminiscing about their time there, the boys they'd fancied and how close they'd come to giving in to those fumbling, adolescent advances. Some were planning ahead, some not, but for now their futures were not really on their minds; they were just living for the now and enjoying their evening.

Although they were all equal, there was an underlying acceptance that Alesia Merriman was Queen of the bunch; the Ice Queen as she was often referred to behind her back. Alesia was smart, attractive and aware of her own sexual charisma, which she never deliberately flaunted — not that she needed to. She wore her hair, which was blonde, in a ponytail, *a la* Sandy in the film, Grease. It was the way she liked it. She had lovely hazel eyes, which seemed to sparkle whenever her face lit up in a smile or whenever she laughed.

Alesia was the one that her friends expected to do well in life; the one who would always make the right choices, choose the right husband, have an ideal family. She was always being chased by the boys, none of whom had managed to break down her resistance. She would always insist to her friends that she was saving herself for the right one; the man who would tick all her boxes and push all her buttons.

Alesia took a sip of the latest wine, Prosecco, they were all drinking and tried not to spill it as she laughed at something her best friend, Denny, had said to her. She loved Denny like a sister. They'd grown up together, practically lived in each other's houses when they were kids, and never imagined their lives would change much as they emerged into the real world away from the cocoon of adolescence.

Denny was an attractive girl, but with a slightly lighter complexion to Alesia. She was a brunette, but she kept her hair straight. She had brown eyes and a small, button nose above a generous mouth, when she smiled she somehow manage to show practically all her teeth — all perfectly straight.

Sitting beside Denny was Sylvia who had become one of the group when she moved into the town a few years earlier. Sylvia was of mixed race. Her father was Jamaican, her mother, English, This gave Sylvia a lovely olive complexion, which made her a magnet for the boys. She was also well endowed; another charm that the boys liked. She had been fairly free with her favours to the boys but never more than a clumsy grope with most of them. Secretly, Alesia and Denny were surprised, and pleased, that Sylvia had managed to get this far without getting pregnant. She had a pleasant, fun loving approach to life and simply enjoyed living and being chased by the boys.

Sitting either side of Sylvia were Pam and Heather who complemented the group in looks, humour and sense of fun. Pam was the more studious looking, and always correct in her manner and speech. Heather on the other hand, was the opposite: she was slightly built, thin faced but pretty. Not very tall though. Both had been friends with Alesia and Denny for a few years but never as close as they may have liked to have been. The overall make up of this pretty bunch though was one of joyous and outrageous friendship that nothing could dissemble or destroy.

Denny was leaning across the table saying something to Heather when she caught sight of Simeon Grant walking towards them. She sat up straight as Simeon reached the table. He immediately dropped into a crouch.

"Hello, ladies. Enjoying yourselves?"

Simeon was the boy that most of the senior girls at college fancied, including Alesia. He had an underlying charm that always made it easy and effortless to break down any initial resistance a girl might offer. But he never took advantage of that because he was aware of the risks when getting too close to someone of the opposite sex. But he was always friendly, easy to talk to and just lovely to have around.

Alesia couldn't take her eyes off him. She felt her pulse rate go up a notch and felt a slight restriction in her throat as she tried to say hello. She took a mouthful of wine before she was able to speak.

"Hi, Simeon," she called over the table. "We're good. And you and your mates?"

Simeon glanced back over his shoulder. "They could do with a few firecrackers under the table to get them going." He looked back at Alesia. "Or a few more beers."

"Who have you got with you?" Denny asked.

He half closed his eyes and lifted his chin a little in pretence of thinking hard. "Erm... Clive Dean, Wally Henderson, Mitch Johnson and Scott Jones."

"What, Chicken George?" shrieked Heather. "What's he doing here?"

Simeon laughed, showing his lovely white teeth. It gave Alesia another tingling moment.

"We forced Scott to come," he told them. "He didn't have a choice really. I went round his house and asked him in front of his dad."

Heather leaned forward, her face breaking into a conspiratorial expression. "So, he had to do what his dad told him, right? Pretty crafty that, Simeon."

He grinned. "Probably not, but at least we got him here. I'm sure he'll enjoy himself once he's had a few."

Scott Jones was the one Heather had called Chicken George. It was a nickname he'd been stuck with because he helped his chicken farmer dad on the farm at weekends and other non-school days. Few people called him that to his face, probably through cowardice. Although he was something of a quiet lad, he had a self confidence that was immediately evident whenever he was spoken to. And he was an accomplished guitar player, a talent he was blessed with.

He was a big lad too and not afraid of anyone. Despite that, he would rarely use his fists when challenged by those ignorant enough to call him out. Scott would almost always walk away and let the epithets fall off him like water off a duck's back. It brought him a few secret admirers, particularly one or two girls who had managed to get close to him.

"Has he had a dance yet?" Heather asked.

Simeon shook his head. "Not yet. Why? You want to dance with him?"

Heather laughed and rocked backwards. "No thank you very much."

The other girls laughed with her, clearly of the same opinion.

"Well," Simeon said, "that's one of the reasons I've come over."

They all stopped laughing and allowed themselves to settle down so Simeon could explain.

"Are you up for a challenge?"

Denny glared at him. "Challenge? If it's drinking you're on about, Simeon, you'd be on a loser; you know you would. You boys would all be on your knees before we'd had a chance to get warmed up."

He held his hand up. "Of course we would, but I'm not talking about knocking back shots."

"So, what is it?"

"There are five of us and five of you, and in about ten minutes, Disco Dave will be putting on a couple of slow numbers. He always does. So, the challenge is that we draw lots for partners while the slow stuff is on."

"We can't all leave our tables," Heather pointed out, knowing that there was no way they could get up and leave their personal gear unattended. "And we can't carry all our stuff on to the dance floor." She shook her head. "Won't work."

Simeon winked at her, which gave her a funny feeling in her tummy. "I know, so here's the thing. We draw lots for partners and for the table minders."

"Well, that's easy," Heather interrupted. "I'll stay here; then at least I won't have to dance with Chicken George."

Simeon touched her briefly on her arm sending another tremor coursing through her body. "If it's a challenge, we all have to be in." He looked at the others. "Right girls?"

Heather was about to argue, but the girls started protesting. "Come on, Heather; it'll be a laugh," said Pam. "I don't mind dancing with any of them." She looked at Simeon. "Just for the slow stuff, right?" she asked.

He smiled, melting another heart. "You can spend all night with your partner after that if you want."

Pam and Heather were not the only girls imagining being picked to dance with Simeon and spending more than just a few minutes on the dance floor with him.

"Okay, Simeon," Alesia said. "We're in. How you going to work it?"

"We draw the names. First boy and girl picked out will mind the tables, then the other eight get to dance with those they have drawn."

"That's not much of a challenge," Sylvia put in, shaking her head. "I thought it would include shots."

"Dancing and drinking shots might not be a challenge for you, Syl," Simeon said, "but it is for a couple of the lads."

She clamped her lips together and nodded.

Simeon stood up. "I'll be back," he said and walked away.

Immediately the girls all got their heads together giggling and talking about which boy they wouldn't mind dancing with. Simeon was top of the list, while Scott Jones was definitely bottom. They all agreed it would be magic if he was picked to keep an eye on the boys' table.

The music seemed to get louder, almost as a precursor to the challenge that was to come. Presently, Simeon came back. He crouched down at the table again.

"Right, here we go." He then laid out ten pieces of paper, each with their names on. He laid five in front of Alesia, and another five in front of Heather. "Those, he said, tapping the pieces in front of Alesia, "are you girls. These," he tapped those on front of Heather, "are us boys." He then turned the pieces face down and then started shuffling them around, making sure to keep the girls separate from the boys.

"Right. Pick one from each pile." He looked at Alesia. "You first, Alesia. But don't show them yet."

Alesia picked out two and held them in her fingers. Then Heather. Her hands were shaking as she picked out two more. She was followed by the other girls.

"Right," he said when it was done. "Let's see who we'll be dancing with and who will be minding the tables."

Alesia had picked first so she laid hers on the table. "Heather and Wally."

Heather leaned back and clapped her hands. "Yes!" It meant she would be sitting the dances out and not finding herself trapped with Scott Jones.

Pam turned hers over. "Clive and Denny."

Denny felt a degree of disappointment because she had a soft spot for Mitch Johnson, not that she'd ever admitted it anyone, and was hoping the draw would have been kind to her. She turned hers over.

"Simeon and Sylvia."

Sylvia clenched her fists together and let out an audible sigh of relief; she'd managed to snag the pick of the boys.

Four names left and the tension was building.

Heather looked at Alesia and raised her eyebrows as she turned hers over. "Pam and Mitch," she said as Pam clapped her hands softly and whispered something inaudible.

They all looked at Alesia because they knew who was left.

She turned hers over. "Alesia and Scott." She didn't say anything, but her expression said it all.

Simeon stood up. "Great." He scooped up the pieces of paper. "See you all on the dance floor. Have fun girls."

And with that he walked away.

***

If it was possible for five young women enjoying a night out to be silent, this was the moment. It was brief though; Heather put her hand to her mouth to stifle a giggle but couldn't stop herself. In her mind was a vision of Alesia, the Ice Queen, in the hands of Chicken George and doing her level best to keep her face turned away because she couldn't stand the smell of chickens. It was nonsense of course, but such was Heather's incorrigible imagination, it served to turn a harmless piece of fun into a huge joke. She tried desperately to smother the laughter but failed miserably.

"I'm sorry," she said to Alesia, shaking her head and wiping her eyes. "But you should have seen your face."

The other girls were grinning too. Even though they wouldn't want to admit it, they could see the irony in Alesia, who they all believed was class, being paired with Scott Jones who, in truth, had nothing going for him and was at best a non-entity in the vacuous college league of boys they were willing to sleep with. Not that they were in reality going to jump into bed with any of them. Well, maybe Sylvia would.

Alesia picked up her drink, took a mouthful and stood up. "It will be painless," she said and shrugged. "After all, it isn't serious; it's only a laugh." She put her glass down and declared that she was going for a pee. She picked up her small bag from the table and disappeared through the gyrating crowd of dancers who were all blissfully unaware of the silly drama being played out at the Ice Queen's table.

Denny, who was feeling sorry for her friend, looked over at Heather. "I think you're being mean," she said, having to shout to get her voice across the table.

Heather started giggling and no longer tried to stifle it. "Oh, come on, Denny; you know Alesia can be a bit stuck up at times. I know she doesn't mean to, but this will spoil her image, won't it? It's a good thing we don't have to be back in class anymore; she'd never live it down."

Denny turned to Sylvia. "You creamed in there with Simeon you lucky sod."

Sylvia affected a kind of hug, shaking herself a little. "Gorgeous Simeon," she said. "I bet Alesia's pissed off about that."

"Make the most of it, Syl; you won't get another chance; not once Alesia has finished her dance with Chicken George. She'll be all over Simeon, you watch."

Suddenly the blaring music gave way to the Disco Dave's voice coming over the speaker system bringing the music to an end before the moment when lovers could smooch to some unbelievably romantic music. The girls turned the heads in unison and looked over to where the boys were sitting. Simeon said something to them, and they got up and started ambling across the dance floor affecting a nonchalance just for that macho effect..

As the boys crossed the floor, they could see some giggling going on with the girls, and whispered asides with their hands over their mouths. Scott felt uncomfortable as it was, being forced into something he wasn't sure he wanted to do. He knew what was exercising the girls' minds, which was why he was feeling reluctant. Being a figure of fun, particularly among members of the opposite sex, did little for his credibility and self-esteem. But he'd agreed and hoped he could get through it without any drama.

Denny looked over to where Alesia had disappeared and wondered for a moment if she'd done a runner. But then she saw her come through a door and head back over to the table.

The boys stopped at the table. By now all of them, boys and girls, were looking a bit sheepish, except Heather who had a smile fixed to her face. They each paired up. Only Sylvia looked as though she'd won the lottery as she gazed up into Simeon's face like a star struck teenager, which she was of course. Scott hung back until his friends were heading away to the sounds of Moonlight Serenade, the classic Glen Miller song, filling the room with its sensuous sounds.

Alesia looked at Scott as he held his hands out towards her. She took a deep breath, brushed the front of her skirt down and took one of his hands. He smiled briefly and led her out on to the dance floor. Then he turned towards her, lifted her hand up and placed his other hand around her back.

Alesia thought she was going to flinch, but the touch of his hand was completely unexpected. It was firm without being too strong, and she could feel a comfortable warmth where his hand pressed gently into her back. The hand he had held as he led her on to the dance floor was not that of a pimply eighteen-year-old college boy either, but the hand of a man, one that offered unspoken security. When he smiled at her, Alesia felt a shock ripple down her spine and into her legs threatening to weaken her knees. The effect was startling, and it made her tighten her grip on his shoulder.

She looked into his face and was seeing someone she'd never seen before despite having walked past him so many times at college and had never taken any notice of him. His hair was not straight but tumbled loosely in waves. She could see it was natural. It was too dark to determine the colour of his eyes, but she couldn't stop looking into them.

As the haunting melody filled the room, he moved her over the dance floor like a man who knew how a woman had to be held and guided as they danced in unison to the song. He didn't clinch her too tightly or try to get close, but Alesia suddenly wanted to feel his body against hers, to feel his strength and to experience a pleasure she never imagined possible.

The music stopped. Alesia blinked and shook her head. "Wow, already?"

He smiled. "Thank you, Alesia. I'll let you go now."

Her mouth fell open in disappointment as Disco Dave brought the sound of Errol Garner's classic song, Misty, flooding in over the speakers.

"I thought we agreed to do two songs," she managed to blurt out. "Don't you want…"

He stopped her — they hadn't agreed anything about the number of dances, but he was quite happy to go again.

"Of course."

They started dancing again. "Are you okay?" he asked, looking directly into her eyes.

Alesia, surprisingly, couldn't be happier; she wanted this to go on all night. "Yes, I'm fine."

"There's a but though, isn't there?"

"No," she said quickly and tried to get closer to him, which was just about impossible. "No, this is good." She was fumbling her words, trying very hard not to say what had been on her mind when she'd drawn the short straw and picked his name as a partner. "You dance well," she said. "Where did you learn?" It was an attempt to get him to talk so she wouldn't have to stammer and stutter and spoil what she thought was such a lovely moment.

"I went to dance classes with my mate. We were about sixteen at the time. Three months. It was fun."

He turned her round gently, holding her securely, blending his body movement with hers.

Alesia's eyes were sparkling, her face a picture of pure pleasure. She was miles away, blissfully unaware of the wide-eyed stares from the girls who couldn't believe what they were seeing. What they could see though was two young people in complete harmony with each other and looking absolutely perfect.

And then the music stopped. Alesia felt disappointment flooding through her.

Scott stepped back and held her with both hands on her upper arms. She didn't want him to let go. He smiled and took one hand away. He touched the corner of his mouth.

"You have a smudge of lipstick there," he said. "You'd better wipe it away before your friends see it; you wouldn't want them to think you'd been kissing Chicken George, would you?"

Alesia's face dropped and suddenly she felt ashamed of herself. He would have known what they had been saying about him. Their body language when he came over at the beginning of the dance was enough to give the game away.

She looked up at him. "Scott."

He didn't answer but walked her back to the table like a perfect gentleman. "I enjoyed dancing with you, Alesia; it was really nice. Thank you." He turned and walked away leaving her standing there with her mind all over the place.

***

Alesia leaned up against the sink in the ladies' room and gently removed the smudge of lipstick. Then she studied her face in the mirror, trying to make sense of what she'd just experienced. Her heart rate had settled, but she still had an unusual feeling in her tummy as the memory of the last ten minutes burned fresh in her mind. She felt as though she was alone in a bubble despite other girls being in the room talking and fixing their makeup. Some were chatting through the doors of the toilets while a friend stood listening and responding. Others were busy on their mobile phones, fingers tapping away to send whatever vital message needed to be uploaded on to their Social Media accounts. It was all noise, but for Alesia, there was no-one else in the room.

She leaned forward against the sink and stared at herself in the mirror. She knew about nicknames: the Ice Queen. She sighed and shook her head gently. Her nickname was complimentary, despite implying a sense of detachment from mere mortals. It was a term she could live with, but Scott's nickname was nothing but a derogatory term that harked back to Alex Haley's novel, Roots.

She saw her friend Denny in the mirror coming through the open door. She turned at that moment as Denny spotted her. She came running over, her expression already displaying the question that had to come. She grabbed hold of Alesia's hand.

"Oh my God!" she gasped. "How was it? Are you okay now?"

Alesia leaned back against the sink. She shook her head slowly. "Denny, I've never felt so humiliated in my life."

Denny's grip tightened. "Really? Was it that bad? Did he say anything?"

"No, it was the exact opposite." A wry smile touched the edges of Alesia's mouth and broadened into a wide grin. She looked directly at Denny. "I loved it. Absolutely loved it."

Denny frowned. "We are talking about Scott Jones here, aren't we?"

Alesia put her hand on Denny's shoulder. "Oh my God; he knew how to dance. Properly, I mean. As soon as I was in his arms, I just got lost. I couldn't believe it. I wanted it to go on." She shrugged. "I couldn't help it. It was ..." She lifted her head in thought, trying to find the right words — words that would convey the way she felt when she was in Scott's arms. Then she lowered her head, shaking it gently. "Oh, I don't know. I can't explain it, Denny."

"So why do you feel humiliated?"

She dropped her hand away from Denny's shoulder and folded her arms across her stomach. "He told me I had a smudge of lipstick." She touched her lip. "Here. Then he said I should wipe it away before going back to the table because I wouldn't want you lot to think I'd been kissing Chicken George." She rubbed her hands over her eyes as the tears started. "He knew what we'd been saying about him." She shook her head quickly. "I felt so embarrassed. It was awful."

Denny's face was now a picture of horror. "So, what did you say to him?"

Alesia sniffed back the tears and took a deep breath. "I said his name, Scott, and he stopped me. Then he thanked me for the dance, said he'd really enjoyed it and walked away."

Denny was now shaking her head slowly. "Didn't you call him back?"

Alesia shook her head. "What for? More humiliation?" She sniffed and pulled a tissue from a dispenser and dried her eyes. When she'd finished she asked Denny not to tell anyone. "If they see I've been crying, I'll just tell them I tripped and fell in here."

"Of course; I won't say anything. But what about Scott? Do you think you'd want to see him again?"

Alesia managed to chuckle. "No point; he made it perfectly clear what he thought about me, and I don't blame him." She straightened up. "Still, it's done, it's over. Let's go back and get dancing."

"Who with, now Scott is out of the question?"

Alesia's smile broadened. "Simeon," she said. "Just a few minutes with him and Scott will be history."

They linked arms and started laughing, no more thoughts other than looking ahead and making the most of what remained of the evening.

Chapter 2

Alesia woke up the following morning with a major hangover. She sat up in bed and squinted at the clock on her bedside table. Nine o'clock. Bloody hell, she thought, and put her hand to her head. Then she swung her feet out of bed and made her way to the bathroom to empty her bladder which was full to bursting.

She heard a hammering on her bedroom door. "You awake in there yet?"

It was her mother.

"Yes, mum."

"I've brought you a cup of tea. I'm off to the shops," she called out. "Do you want anything?"

Packet of condoms would be good, she muttered. "No thanks, mum; I'm fine. See you when you get back."

She heard her mother come into the bedroom and then leave. She finished off emptying her bladder and went back into the bedroom, sat on the bed and picked up the mug of tea.

And started thinking.

God, she could have done with those condoms last night, she thought grimly. Simeon had brought her home in his car, and what started out as a goodnight peck on the cheek became several minutes of passion where neither of them wanted to stop. But it was Alesia who had to stop them; she knew that if either of them had protection, she would have gone all the way.

She smiled and shook her head from side to side thinking how close she'd come to losing her virginity. And at that moment she didn't care. Although in the cold light of day she knew that she would not surrender that easy.

But she promised herself she would buy some condoms, just in case.

She got herself showered and dressed and then went downstairs for a bowl of cereal and another cup of tea. Then, while she was scooping the cornflakes into her mouth, she checked her phone for messages, hoping to get an email from the university to which she applied. There was nothing there, so she turned the phone off. Within seconds it buzzed at her: a message from Denny telling her to meet at the Haven Tea Shop in the marketplace at ten o'clock. She tapped in the thumbs-up icon and pressed send.

She smiled to herself because she knew exactly why Denny wanted to see her.

Denny was already in the tea shop when Alesia walked in. She was drinking a latte at the counter and chatting to the lady who owned the café. She said something to the woman, then came over to the table where Alesia was now removing her coat.

"I've ordered you a coffee," she said, and sat down. "Well?"

Alesia put on a querulous expression as she settled into the chair. "Well, what?"

"Oh, come on, Alesia. How did it go last night?"

"I nearly gave in," she admitted.

Denny's face dropped. "No, I don't believe it. Seriously?"

Alesia held her hand up and brought her finger and thumb together without actually touching. "We were this close," she admitted. "And God, I wanted to, but I couldn't let it happen."

Denny leaned closer, almost halfway across the table. "With Simeon? Why not?"

Alesia's eyebrows lifted and she shrugged. "No condoms."

Denny sat upright. "Oh, otherwise you would have done."

Alesia nodded. "I think so. Yes." The waitress brought over her coffee and put it front of her. Alesia waited until she was out of earshot. "Let's face it, Denny; it's going to happen one day, and I'd sooner it be with someone like Simeon."

"Or Scott," Denny said mischievously.

Alesia laughed and took a sip of her coffee. She put the glass down and wiped the foam from her top lip. "That will never happen, Denny, you know it won't."

Denny moved her shoulders in a small shrug. "I know nothing," she said. "But you never know. The way you were last night, nothing would surprise me."

"He didn't stay at the prom last night, you know. Scott," she added.

"Why not?"

Alesia shook her head. "I don't know. Maybe he was too upset with us calling him Chicken George."

Denny looked thoughtful for a moment. "That's a shame; after all, it was only a bit of fun."

"Heather didn't seem to think so," Alesia reminded her. "And we all shared the joke quite happily." She sniffed. "Anyway, I've got a lot of running around to do." She looked at her watch. "I'll be off in a minute. And I'm meeting Simeon for lunch, by the way."

Denny grinned conspiratorially. "Lucky you. But be careful, Alesia; you've got your whole future ahead of you. Don't bugger it up because you're pumping out all those pheromones."

"I won't, Denny; I've promised myself."

Denny reached over the table and put her hand on Alesia's. "Right, you go off and have yourself an uneventful day, while I get busy in my dad's studio."

Denny's father owned a gallery and studio in the town. It was Denny's ambition to run the gallery and contribute as a professional photographer. It was something she wanted to study at university: that and fashion, and preferably at one of the top universities, which usually meant France or Italy.

"More photo work?"

Denny nodded. "We're doing a kind of living history: a compilation of shots from the beginning of the Second World War. Should be good. And he's promised to give me a driving lesson this afternoon."

Alesia drained her latte and got up. "Must go. Have fun. Love you, Denny."

Denny smiled. "Love you too." She paid for the coffees after Alesia had gone and left the tea shop. The weather was good and bringing people out to shop in the market square.

Denny was happy — no more college, university to look forward to and then, hopefully, a career building her father's business and eventually taking it over.

She negotiated the market square when she caught sight of Alesia's mother. She was sitting on the steps of the Council Chambers looking out of sorts. Denny frowned and went over to her. She could see immediately there was something wrong. She crouched down beside her and took hold of her hands.

"Hello, Mrs M. Are you okay?"

Mrs M. shook her head. "I've had one of my turns, Denny. I don't feel too good."

Denny knew that Alesia's mother had a heart condition. She was sixty years old and looked seventy. "Have you taken a tablet?"

Mrs M. shook her head. "I left them at home." Her eyes hooded over.

Denny turned round and looked at the pedestrians passing by as though by some miracle one of them might stop and help. She realised that was unlikely to happen, so she got her phone out of her bag and called her dad. He picked up almost immediately.

"Hello, Denny. What's up?"

"I was on my way to the studio, dad, and I've found Alesia's mum having a turn in the street. It's her heart, dad and she doesn't have her pills with her."

"What's her complexion like? Is there any colour in her face?"

Denny shook her head. "No dad; she's quite grey."

"Where are you?"

"We're on the steps by the Council Chambers."

"Right, wait there. I'll lock up and come and get you."

Denny breathed a sigh of relief. "Thanks, dad. What are you going to do though?"

"A&E," he said. "It's all we can do. Is Alesia there?"

Denny shook her head. "No. I'd better call her though; tell her to get up to the hospital."

"Good."

The phone went dead. Denny turned hers off and put it into her pocket. "My dad's coming, Mrs M. He's going to take you up to A&E."

Mrs M. immediately put her hand up to protest, but Denny simply took hold of it and forced it back into her lap.

"I'm going to phone Alesia now," Denny told her. "She needs to know what's happening."

Mrs M. drew in a tired, slow breath and simply nodded her head.

Thirty minutes later and they were at A&E waiting to be called by the Triage nurse. Alesia was on her way. Denny's dad made sure she didn't need anything before heading back to the studio. He slipped a twenty-pound note into her hand for a taxi home. He took Mrs M.'s hand and wished her all the best, gave Denny a kiss and left them sitting there telling them he hoped they wouldn't have too long to wait.

Denny looked around the room, which was packed. Some hope, she thought to herself. And what a way to start your first day of freedom — stuck in A&E.

Alesia arrived, flustered naturally, and found her mother being checked by a doctor having negotiated the Triage and the interminable wait that usually follows. Denny left Alesia with her mother but said she would wait until they knew the outcome of the doctor's examination. For Alesia, she was worried for her mother's sake but also disappointed because she'd had to phone Simeon and cancel the lunch date. They couldn't plan their next meeting until Alesia knew how her mother would be.

Then the blow fell when the doctor said they would have to admit her mother to monitor her condition, run a few tests and make a decision, if that was necessary, on any treatment she might need.

While her mother was being helped into a ward and being prepared, Alesia went through to the waiting area to tell Denny what was happening and to buy each of them a coffee from the machine.

"I didn't realise your mum was so ill," Denny said to her. "I knew she had a heart problem but…" she shrugged and shook her head. "God, you just don't know, do you?"

"You know why she's like that?" Denny shook her head. Alesia took a mouthful of coffee. She blew air out of her mouth, held the cup on her leg and told Denny how it happened.

"My mother wanted to give my father the gift of a child. Son or daughter; it didn't matter." She looked down at the cup and blinked her tears away. "They both knew that dad might not live much longer because of his cancer. Mum was forty and the doctors said getting pregnant at her age could be disastrous. A real problem is what they actually told her. And the only way was IVF. And being private, Mum and dad's money was as good as anyone's." She sighed deeply, took another mouthful of coffee. "The IVF was successful, and I was born." She looked at Denny. "Can you imagine the sheer joy and pleasure they got from that?" She sat back on the seat and stared up at the ceiling reflectively. "But it cost mum; her heart was damaged because of her age and the C section they had to perform. They said she would be okay but would have to take heart pills for the rest of her life. But they were happy. Mum had given dad the best present he could have hoped for." She lowered her head. "He died a year later."

Denny's expression was quite forlorn. "I didn't know any of this, Alesia. I'm so sorry. I knew your mum had a heart condition, but she hid it so well."

Alesia smiled. "That's mum."

"And you lost your dad."

"I never knew him, did I? I was only twelve months old when he died."

Denny sighed. "Well, let's hope your mum gets through this," she said. "She must be a pretty tough woman to have coped with all that."

Alesia nodded. "She is." She drained her cup and looked at Denny. "You might as well go home now. I'll be here all night. And thanks for helping mum."

"No need to thank me; I'm sure you would have done the same if it was my mum."

Alesia grinned. "Of course. Now get yourself home. I'll phone you as soon as I know anything."

Denny leaned closer and kissed Alesia on the cheek. "See you soon. Love you."

Alesia blew her a kiss. "Love you too."

Chapter 3

Alesia managed to grab some sleep, but sleeping on a hospital chair just didn't help. She stirred and went to the drinks machine, bought a coffee and went up to the nurses' station to ask if she could see her mother. But was told she would have to wait until the doctor had finished his rounds. She took that as a sign that there was no need to worry too much about her mum because she was sure they would have told her if there had been anything seriously wrong. She made her way to the toilets, taking her coffee with her, and managed to refresh and tidy herself up. Then it was back to the ward to sit and wait in the corridor where she nodded off again.

"Miss Merriman?" Alesia opened her eyes. It was the doctor. He sat down beside her. "We can let your mother go home now, but I think you have to understand that she will need a reasonable amount of care and attention for a while. Is there anyone else at home besides yourself?"

Alesia shook her head. "No, just me."

He looked thoughtful for a moment. "If you can afford a Carer, that would be tremendously helpful."

"I can do that; no need to get a Carer in," she said.

"Well, that's fine, but you have to remember you have a life too. Full time caring is what it implies: it's hands on twenty-four hours." He lifted a hand. "But in time, your mother should improve and become reasonably independent. Do you understand that?" Alesia said she did. "Fine. You can go through to the ward now. I'll arrange for your mother to be taken down to the main entrance."

"I can go now?" Alesia asked.

He looked at his watch. "Yes. The porter will have her prescription with him. He'll give that to you when he gets to the ward." He stood up. "Good luck then. I'm sure things will work out for you. Goodbye."

She thanked him and hurried along to the ward. Her mother smiled brightly when she saw her. Alesia kissed her, wiped away her mother's tears and then her own. Eventually the porter appeared with the wheelchair and prescription. Then it was over, and they were on their way home.

The drive home was quiet. Alesia wanted to ask a ton of questions but thought it would better to wait until they were home. Her mother didn't have much to say. Alesia didn't try to push her either.

When they arrived at the house, Alesia had to help her mother get out of the taxi. It was more because Alesia felt the need to make sure her mother couldn't fall. She looked unsteady on her feet, which gave Alesia some concern. Her mother told her not to fuss, but in truth she felt safer with Alesia holding on to her.

Alesia opened the front door and used her feet to push the junk mail aside that had been posted through the letter box. Then she helped her mother into the front room and settled her into an armchair.

"I'll make us a cup of tea, mum," she said, "and then we'll figure out how we're going to deal with this."

She went back into the hallway, picked up the mail and closed the front door.

As she walked into the kitchen, she tossed the mail on to the worktop. The envelopes slid over the smooth surface, separating in a long line. That was when she saw the University's unmistakable coat of arms on one of the envelopes. Her heart almost did a double beat as she picked it up, turned it over and dropped it back on top of the others, not sure if she was really prepared for what was in it.

She made tea for them both and went through to the front room. She handed one to her mother very carefully because she noticed her mother's hand was shaking a little as she took the cup.

Her mother looked up at her. "Thank you, my darling." She took a sip, then moved her arm to put the cup on the small table beside her. Alesia took it from her and put it down.

"How are you feeling, mum?"

Her mother lifted her eyes. "Truth? Lousy; but not lousy enough to think I'm going to die. Not just yet anyway."

"Well, maybe that cup of tea will help, then we can figure something out."

"Like what?"

"How I'm going to look after you of course."

Her mother tried to pick up her cup, but Alesia got there first and handed it to her.

"You're more nervous than me," her mother joked, taking the cup. "But I think I would like to lie down for a while; get my strength back."

"Well, once you've finished your tea, I'll get you settled down."

It was almost thirty minutes later when Alesia walked into the kitchen and picked up the envelope from the University. She opened it, unfolded the single sheet and started reading. She read it through once, then read it through it again. Then she sat down on the breakfast stool and started crying softly. She had been accepted as a student but needed to reply by the end of the month, ten days away now, otherwise her place would be reallocated etc., etc.

She glanced up at the ceiling imagining her mother in the bedroom where she had settled her. She would be sleeping by now and totally dependent on Alesia.

She looked back at the envelope and knew there was no way she could go to university — not now and probably not ever.

***

Two weeks later, Alesia walked into Denny's studio. It was just for a chat. She'd managed to come up with a routine for her mother and knew when, and for how long she could leave her. Her mother was a lot stronger now; the medication seemed to be helping, which was a blessing for Alesia for obvious reasons.

She gave Denny a kiss on the cheek and sat down at the counter, which Denny liked to call a reception desk. She felt it added a little more to the ambience of the gallery, which was also how she preferred the studio to be called.

Alesia dropped her bag on to the countertop and sat down on the stool, which was always there, to one side, for customers to park their backsides if they so wished.

"What are you up to?" Alesia asked.

Denny was scrolling through pages of photographs, selecting some and deleting others. "Sorting out the wheat from the chaff," she said. "How's your mum by the way?"

"Not too bad," Alesia said cheerfully. "It's good now that I can leave her from time to time."

"Have you discussed your future with her yet?"

Alesia shrugged her shoulders. "How can I do that, Denny? I can't leave her, and we can't afford to pay for people to come in and look after her; not if I'm out all day at work."

Denny knew that Alesia had deliberately lied to her mother and said the university had rejected her. It was a shattering blow to her friend knowing that she had to make that choice, a choice that would impact her future and destroy all her hopes and dreams, but it was a sacrifice she had to make.

"Will you be able to take on any work? Part time maybe?"

"It would depend on how close it is, what the hours were." She screwed her face up. "But it's pointless thinking about it, not yet anyway."

"Have you seen Simeon?"

Alesia's face brightened. "Yes, he's been round a few times."

Denny peered at her. And?"

Alesia gave her a stern look. "No," she growled. "Not while my mum's in the house."

"So, you still have an unopened packet of condoms in your purse?"

Alesia laughed. "Afraid so. Perhaps I can get you to babysit my mum so me and Simeon can go out on a date."

Denny nodded thoughtfully. "I could do that for you," she said. "It might help you to get your end away and cheer you up."

They both started laughing and as the laughter died down, Denny opened a drawer and pulled a memory stick out.

"Oh, I want you to see these." She plugged the memory stick into the laptop she been using to scroll through the other photographs and opened the file she wanted to show Alesia.

"I've been picking out various shots of us as we've gone through college, choosing the good ones and throwing out the not so good ones."

"Thrown all mine out, have you?"

Denny smiled. "No way, Alesia; you're the pick of the bunch, you know you are." She stopped scrolling and selected two photographs, putting them up side by side. "That's the boys at the prom night." She tapped the screen. "And that's us," she said, tapping the screen again.

Alesia leaned in a little closer. "Wow. They're good."

Denny began ticking off each one. "Clive, Wally, Mitch, Simeon and Scott." She pulled her hand away. "And one of them has gone already."

Alesia frowned, a little startled. "Gone. What…"

"Scott," Denny said, and for a moment Alesia's heart sank.

"He's not…?"

Denny chuckled. "No, not that. He's gone to live in America."

And suddenly, for some inexplicable reason, Alesia felt really downcast. "For good?"

"Apparently. It's something he's wanted to do for some time. Seems he had it all planned. And with his father's blessing too."

She then ticked off the girls. "Me, you, Heather, Pam and Sylvia." She turned her face towards Alesia. "And I suppose you could say another one has gone."

"Meaning me?"

Denny nodded. "When we were at college, we all had our plans, our hopes and our dreams." She sighed. "And we're barely out of school and already two of those ten are no more."

"God, you make it sound so morbid," Alesia groaned.

"Denny smiled. "I do, don't I? But I wonder where we'll all be in, say, fifteen years' time."

Chapter 4

Fifteen years later

Alesia parked her battered Vauxhall Corsa Estate at the fresh fish business she worked for at Kings Lynn docks, delivering fresh fish to trade customers, and locked it. She straightened up and eased the discomfort from her backside with a quick rub of her hands and then walked in through the open office door. Sitting at the desk tapping away on her computer was Jeanette, who had become quite a friend to Alesia.

"Morning, Alesia," she trilled in her sing-song voice as Alesia came into the office. "Bit blowy out there today."

Alesia agreed. "Yeah. I'm glad I don't have to go far to catch the fish."

Jeanette laughed and pulled a sheet of paper from a tray and handed it to her. "There you go my darling— your deliveries for the day."

Alesia took the sheet, studied it briefly. They were her usual deliveries, which meant she shouldn't run over her scheduled time and would get home in time to take her son, Alex, to football training.

She walked through into the factory, which was more of a huge preparation area. There were several women in there working at flat tables prepping raw fish, filleting, gutting or throwing the kind of monstrosities away that needed to be filleted with a hand grenade. A fork truck was bringing pallets of fresh fish straight from the boats and carrying them through automatic doors into a large freezer room. The smell was overpowering but to be expected. Somewhere a loudspeaker system punched out music from a local radio station, although it was difficult to make sense of what was being played because of the noise.

Alesia went into a changing area and pulled on a white coat, a hair net and a hard hat, pulled a pair of Wellington boots on and then put on a rubber apron. Once she was suitably dressed, she made her way over to a huge, walk-in refrigerator, stopping to have a quick chat with some of the women.

She pulled a sack truck away from a row, opened the fridge door and dragged the truck in behind her. She found the shelf allocated to her and started piling the boxes on to the sack truck. There were only so many she could handle at any one time, so it was a case of wheeling the truck out into the yard and over to the van, which she would load up with the fish, and then back to the fridge for another load.

It was while Alesia trudged back and forth that she often thought back to how her life had turned out, and how different it might have been had it not been for her mother's illness. She'd married Simeon of course: a match made in heaven some people called it, but for Alesia it was a match made in hell. It started to fall apart when she told him she was pregnant. Simeon wanted her to abort the baby, but she refused. And that was the beginning of the downward spiral until they divorced, and Alesia was left as a single mother with no financial support at all from Simeon.

It had taken Alesia a few years before she could look back on those early, head spinning times without feeling a huge disappointment. Now she could think and talk of them with a philosophical shrug and be thankful that Simeon had at least given her a treasure no-one could take away from her, and that was her son. She'd continued to live with her mother until the end came. It had been inevitable in a way, and for a short while, Alesia thought she would be able to enjoy a lot more freedom now there was just her and Alex.

But it was not to be — her mother died just about penniless. She had no money to speak of and the house still had a mortgage on it. She had other debts too on which she had defaulted, which meant the house was taken from her by the bank to cover the outstanding debts. Alesia moved into a rented flat with Alex and had to ask for benefits while she looked for work. One small piece of good fortune that did come her way was that her lifelong friend, Denny, had paid for her to have driving lessons. She said it would help if she had at least that string to her bow. And that was how she ended up delivering fresh fish to trades people in the area, because she could drive.

Alesia was just loading the last of the day's orders into the van when Jeanette came running into the yard carrying a plastic bag.

"Alesia! I've got another drop for you. Just come in. It's at Monk's Farm out Fakenham way."

Alesia stopped dragging the empty sack truck behind her as Jeanette pulled up beside her. She was quite breathless.

"Sorry about this, but it's on the end of your route." She held up the plastic bag. "The order's in there along with the address and Post Code." She handed the bag to Alesia who lifted it up and looked at it quite disdainfully.

"Two bloody fish," she said. "Who orders two bloody fish? The delivery charge will be worth more than the fish themselves."

Jeanette touched her on the arm. "I think it's a friend of the boss," she said. "A favour I think."

Alesia grunted. "Well, let's hope whoever it is doesn't plan to make a habit of it."

Jeanette thanked her and took off back to the safety of her warm office. Alesia shook her head and dragged the sack truck back to where they were stacked and then back to the van to begin her round robin of deliveries, ending up at Monk's Farm.

***

Denny arrived at the gallery, which was already open. Her business acumen and her gift for photography had turned what used to be a high street photo and art studio into a very successful business with customers all over the United Kingdom. As the years had gone by, so Denny's on-line business had grown, which was the reason her sales were always at a high level. And along with that she had developed other avenues of design, including creative art for writers and video game producers. And it was this excellence that had brought her a contract with a video game production company. Denny was certainly going places.

The reason the gallery was open when Denny arrived was because she had two young women working for her. One, Isabel, was a graduate like herself, while the other, April, was a local girl, which gave Denny the small satisfaction of knowing she employed at least one member of the community. Denny had tried desperately to find a way of offering Alesia some form of employment, but it was a non-starter really, but she was happy that Alesia did at least have a job, despite it being a smelly one.

Denny called out a greeting as she swept into the shop. April appeared from the back room and asked if she wanted coffee, to which Denny said yes. Then she slid into the chair behind the reception desk and unlocked one of the drawers. She opened a small box and took a memory stick from it, loaded it into a laptop which had already been booted up by April, and began scrolling through a long file of photos from which she would be compiling a box set for a customer.

As Denny scrolled through the list of files, it was inevitable that she would come across the file that contained the photos she'd taken fifteen years earlier at the Prom night. She didn't know how many times she'd looked at them, but it was almost impossible for her to avoid them.

Isabel came through with Denny's coffee and put it on the counter. "Morning, Denny. April made this for you."

Denny thanked her without looking away from the screen.

"What are you doing?" Isabel asked.

Denny sat up a little straighter. "I'm supposed to be working but each time I go through this particular folder, I can't help stopping, even if it's for a few minutes. Just memories," she said. Then she started to reminisce about that night and how each of them ended up; those that she knew of anyway.

"It was our Prom Night at Kings Lynn College. We were all good mates. That's Clive and Pam," she said, pointing at two faces. "Clive joined the RAF and a year later they married. Clive transferred to the Royal

Australian Air Force, and they were never to be heard of again, apart from the odd rumour that filtered through from their respective relatives. None of us saw that coming."

"Heather and Wally." She chuckled softly. "Heather loved Wally really, but no-one knew that, not even Wally. He's in prison now. Heather is a single mum. She has a little girl called Christine. I just hope she's happy."

"Alesia and Simeon." She made a sharp hissing noise. "Waste of space, that one. They got married, had a kid and then got divorced. "Bloody shame. Poor Alesia ended up as a single mum as well as looking after a baby and a sick mother. Her mum died penniless. The bank repossessed the house leaving Alesia homeless."

Isabel put her hand to her mouth. "Oh my God, how awful. What's she doing now?"

"Delivering fish."

She then moved the slides over and drew Isabel's attention to what was probably her favourite photograph and memory of that night. It was a photo of Alesia and Scott Jones. Denny had snapped them with her camera like all the other shots, but this one said something special. It was the way Scott was holding Alesia and how he was looking at her. And more to the point; how Alesia was looking at him. The lighting in the room was subdued, but somehow enough had filtered through to soften and enhance the image.

Isabel leaned forward and gently touched the screen with the tip of her finger. "What a gorgeous photo," she said softly. "Oh my God; they're so in love."

Denny nodded slowly. "And they didn't know it. That's Alesia, who married Simeon, dancing with Scott Jones. He went to America shortly after that shot was taken and no-one has heard anything of him since." She sat up. "Such a shame."

"Where are you, Denny?"

Denny laughed. "Oh, I'm there." She pulled the girls up. "That's me, pretty as a picture and still single."

"Didn't you fancy any of those boys?"

Denny nodded. "One of them." She pulled the boys up. "This one. His name's Mitch — Mitch Johnson." She said nothing for a while, just thought about how she didn't just fancy Mitch, she was besotted with him. But, like so many missed opportunities, she never made anything of it. "He went his own way. Worked up in London, I think. Still there as far as I know." She drew a deep breath and sighed. "But there you go, and now it's over and I have work to do."

She picked up her coffee and started on the task she had meant to do fifteen minutes earlier. Isabel left her to it and disappeared into the art gallery where she had her own work to do.

And that was the moment the door opened and a smartly dressed, good looking guy walked into the shop.

"Ah, good morning. Is Denny Brown about?"

It was Mitch Johnson.

Chapter 5

Alesia was still annoyed about the stupid delivery she had to make to Monk's Farm when the Satnav indicated her destination was barely a mile away. She thought she might give Mr. Monk a piece of advice about ordering two cod fillets to be delivered. At least that way he, or she, might take the hint and not order again.

She slowed at the side road showing on the Satnav and turned into what could best be described as nothing more than a lane. There were distinct tyre impressions running the entire length of the lane, and grass growing between the tracks. The wheel bucked in her hand as the deep ruts basically took over control of the van while she was simply a passenger. This annoyed her even more; so much so that she knew she'd be wound up when she took Alex football training, and that was never a good thing.

As she reached the end of the lane, it opened into a wide area in which were two buildings. One was an industrial size unit, maybe not as big as those found on industrial estates, but a fair size anyway. The other building was what Alesia could only describe as a cottage, although it was a small house with upstairs windows. There was no garden or picket fence around the house, just land. She wondered if anybody actually lived there. The cottage was thatched, which did rather date it. She could see some other buildings beyond the cottage. They were more like cattle sheds or barns but looked old and dilapidated.

She brought the van to a halt close to a door at the corner of the building. There were two cars parked there. She looked at them and decided, scornfully, that must be one piece of cod each for the two owners of the cars.

She got out of the van and went to the rear doors, pulled one open and stepped into the very cold refrigerated interior. The shelves were empty save for one carrier bag containing the two pieces of fish. She lifted the bag off the shelf, and climbed out of the van, pushing the doors hard to make sure they were closed. She didn't have to lock them because the van was now empty.

She glanced along the building, more out of curiosity than anything else, wondering why the place was called a farm. There were no stables, no tractors or combined harvesters. No cows, no sheep. Nothing. Then her imagination started playing tricks on her and she suddenly felt just a little uncomfortable. Perhaps she'd been lured here under false pretences? Maybe there was a serial killer hiding inside waiting for her.

She tutted and clutched the carrier bag like holding something by the scruff of the neck, just in case. Then she walked up to the door at the corner and opened it.

The first thing she saw was a tiny room that was no more than a basic kitchen. There was a worktop, a sink and a gas hob. A tea towel hung from a hook close by the sink. There were two dirty cups in the sink. Above that was a cupboard. Alesia was tempted to peer into it but ignored the temptation.

She stood there for a while, half expecting someone to come through. She couldn't hear any machinery running, which made it all very creepy because of the silence.

Tentatively, she walked through the small kitchen to the door at the far end and pushed it open.

And at very moment, someone came walking over with his hand up. He made a pushing movement with his hand, which Alesia took to mean that she should not walk in but to go back into the kitchen. She did this and waited until he came through the door, which he closed behind him.

He stood there, just looking at Alesia, and saying nothing. He was wearing overalls, rather like a mechanic would wear. He had a hard hat on with an indistinguishable logo on it.

Alesia thought she recognised him but dismissed the idea. She frowned and held up the carrier bag. "Mr. Monk, your order. I think you should realise…"

He put his hand up to stop her. Then he smiled and touched the corner of his mouth. "You have a smudge of lipstick, just here," he said.

Alesia automatically put her hand to her mouth, and then stopped. "But I'm not wearing…"

He smiled again.

Alesia felt a little breathless as her heart started beating harder beneath her ribs.

"Scott? Scott Jones?"

His smile grew broader, and he took step towards her. "Hello, Alesia."

Alesia's mouth fell open in amazement. Then, inexplicably, her heart rate increased, and she threw herself forward and wrapped her arms around him in a massive hug.

"Scott, it's so lovely to see you." Then she realised what she was doing and pulled away quickly. "I'm sorry," she said, quite flustered. "That was a bit presumptuous of me. I'm sorry." She stepped back. She was still clutching the carrier bag, which she lifted up. "Oh, your fish order."

He looked at the carrier bag in her hands. "Yes, sorry about the small order, but it was the only way I could think of to get you here so I could see you."

Her heart rate was still high but beginning to slow down. "What do you mean?"

He shook his head. "Oh, nothing really." He shrugged. "I just wanted to see you without, you know, people around."

She tipped her head to one side. "Well, I'm here, so your plan worked."

He looked at the dirty cup in the sink. "Would you like a cup of tea and a chat?"

Alesia would have loved more than just a cup of tea. She shook her head. "I'm sorry, but I need to get back; I have to take my son football training."

"Your son? So, you're married?"

Alesia thought he looked disappointed, but then, why should he be, she wondered. "No, divorced. I'm a single mum now."

He nodded his head slowly. "Okay then, I won't keep you seeing as you need to get back for your boy. Perhaps we can meet up another time?" He grinned. "Maybe if I order more fish?"

Alesia laughed softly at that. "I could always meet you in town for a drink," she said. "If you want." For the first time in a very long time, Alesia felt apprehensive contemplating what could loosely be described as a 'date'.

"I'll give you a call," said. "Let me have your number."

Alesia took her phone from her pocket and handed it to him. "Ring your phone," she said.

Scott did that, which now meant they had each other's number on their phones. They simply had to save and add an ID.

"I'm sorry I can't stay," she said, putting her phone back in her pocket. She looked up, not sure how to say goodbye after so short a time. "I'd better go," she said finally, a shade of disappointment in her voice.

"Yes." Then he stepped closer and opened his arms. Alesia closed the gap and hugged him. And as she pressed in and felt his arms around her, her mind went back all those years to the moment she knew she was in love with him but was too scared to admit it.

She let him go. "Goodbye, Scott. See you soon?"

He nodded once. "You bet. 'Bye, Alesia."

***

Denny did a double take when she recognised Mitch Johnson standing at the half open door. He was wearing a suit with a white shirt and tie. His shoes were leather and looked highly polished. And he still had that Italian look about him, one that many of the girls at college commented on. His hair was almost jet black with a slight curl to it. Denny used to think he was very much like the Hollywood actor Dean Martin. But not now; he was just gorgeous and no longer that eighteen-year-old teenager who hadn't quite filled out. She closed the laptop; slid out from behind the counter and went over to him.

He closed the door and took a step forward. "Well, Denny, how are you?"

She took his hands in hers and held them as she reached up and kissed him on the cheek. "What are you doing here?" she asked as she settled back on her heels. She didn't let go of his hands either; she just stood there looking up into his blue eyes.

"Here in this shop?" he said, looking down at his feet. "Or here in town?"

"Well, here in town I suppose," she said. "I thought you'd moved to London. No-one has seen you in what, fifteen years?" She stood back a little, still holding his hands and looked him up and down. "And looking so smart, too."

He smiled. "It's my job to look smart. When I'm working," he added.

"Working? Here?"

"I'm the manager Lafayette's."

Denny's jaw dropped. Lafayette's was like a mini Harrod's. It was what most people referred to as the poshest shop north of London. A touch of class was often the expression used as well. And it did have class along with some fairly high prices. She was speechless.

"Can we talk?" he asked.

Denny snapped out of her trance-like state. "Of course, of course." She pointed behind her. "My office," she said. "It's private."

Mitch allowed himself to be taken to Denny's office. He had little choice because she had hold of his hand. She called out to April to let her know she had a customer and would be in the office, and then offered Mitch a seat as she closed the door.

She sat down facing him, her mind still racing. She couldn't think of anything to say. Mitch could see she was struggling. He thought it was simply the shock of seeing him after all these years, so he started the conversation off for her.

"You're right, Denny," he began. "I moved to London and started a kind of apprenticeship at Harrod's. It was a stroke of good fortune really; not something I ever envisaged as a career. But it proved to be something of a turning point for me. I loved the job and gradually worked my way up the ladder until Lafayette came after me?"

Denny looked puzzled. "Head hunted? Really?"

He smiled. "Believe it or not, that's exactly what happened."

"So how long have you been here?"

"Couple of months now."

Her heart lifted. "Permanent?"

He nodded. "I'm not going anywhere."

"Are you living in town?"

He pointed back over the top of his shoulder. "I'm living with April."

For a microsecond, Denny's heart did a flip, thinking he'd moved in with a woman. Not that it had anything to do with her. Then she realised he was talking about her assistant. "April? My April who works here?"

He nodded. "She's my sister."

Her eyes brightened. "Of course. April often mentioned her brother, but I never twigged." She laughed softly and shook her head. "Is that a permanent arrangement?"

Mitch frowned. "Goodness, no; I need my own space, obviously. I'm actually looking at a new build on the edge of town. Lovelock Gardens?"

"Wow." They weren't cheap. "Sounds lovely."

Just then there was a knock on the door an April came into the office. She saw Mitch and brightened immediately. "Hello bro, fancy seeing you here."

He turned and offered his cheek as April kissed him. Then she looked at Denny. "Surprise, surprise."

Denny nodded. "You could say that. Can you bring a couple of coffees, please April?" She glanced at Mitch. "Oh, sorry, Mitch. Do you want coffee?"

"He'll want tea," April said. "Won't you bro?"

Mitch looked at Denny, held his hands up and shrugged as April left the office. She was singing too.

"Right," Denny said with a deep sigh. "To what do I owe the pleasure?"

"April has told me a lot about the work you do here, including the portfolios you compile for individual customers covering all manner of things — weddings, birthdays, christenings, wartime memories, that kind of thing. Well, Lafayette will be celebrating one hundred years in business come Christmas, and we want to put on an exhibition summarising our time here in town. The idea is to basically turn over one of our departments to a kind of Christmas gala night with music, dancing, and a complete exhibition of Lafayette down the years. We do have a whole range of photographs gathering dust in our storeroom, but there's a wealth of history there, both of the town and Lafayette's." He paused there letting it all sink in. "And we would like to commission you to take it on."

Denny's mind moved up a gear from the dawdle it had enjoyed just watching him as he sat opposite her talking about his time in London and subsequent move here. She realised that a commission like this would mean she would have to spend time at Lafayette's, which meant spending time in Mitch's company. Even without thinking of contracts and costings etc., she just wanted to say yes straight away, and it was taking all her will power to not leap over the desk and kiss him.

She cleared her throat. "It will need a lot of work, of course, and Christmas is only six weeks away. I might need to spend time at Lafayette's just to get the…"

Mitch held up his hand. "Why don't you have dinner with me so we can talk and put some kind of plan into place?"

She definitely wanted to leap over the desk and kiss him now. She closed her mind to that kind of exhibition and cleared her throat again. "That would be lovely, Mitch. When and where?"

"Porters," he said. "Tomorrow night. Eight o'clock."

Denny had been there a couple of times. It was a small, well-appointed restaurant in the heart of town where the meals and service were always good. "That would be lovely," she said.

And then April walked in with a tray and their hot drinks. She put it on the desk and looked at Denny but couldn't know why her boss was looking so starry eyed and why her brother had a smug look on his face.

Chapter 6

Alesia arrived home a little after noon, parked her car in the street where she lived, which was never easy, but she normally found somewhere. The furthest she'd ever had to park was about one hundred yards away from the house. She checked the pigeonholes in the main hallway for her mail, and then opened the door of her ground floor flat.

Alesia had an arrangement with her old college friend, Heather, who lived at the Fiddler pub, which her parents owned, to look after her son whenever he wasn't at school. Today being Saturday meant that Alex would be with Heather at the pub. She did often wonder it that was the right place for a ten-year-old to spend his spare time, but it was convenient and free; Heather wouldn't take any money for it despite being nearly broke herself.

Sometimes, Heather would take Alex down to the allotment she had (it was her dad's really) where she would spend hours cultivating, cutting and talking (there was plenty of chat to be had among the growers). Heather nursed an ambition to work in something that meant she was up to her knees in fruit and veg. She would often take her produce to the local market, but she had to share a stall with her friend, Alison, who had a flower shop. It meant their stall would always be busy: flowers one end, vegetables the other.

Heather had her own kid too: a little girl named Christine. She was four years old. Heather had never told anyone who the father was, not even her parents, which caused a major problem with her dad. She confided with

Alesia at the time that she thought her dad was going to throw her out onto the street. Alesia promised her that she could come and live at her place until she got everything settled. Fortunately, her dad relented after enormous pressure from Heather's mother. Heather eventually gave birth to little Christine. Naturally, her dad loved the little tot immediately and became a doting grandfather.

Alesia had a quick shower to get rid of the smell of fish, which always seemed to cling to her no matter how well covered she was when working. She microwaved a ready meal, washed it down with a cup of tea and then hurried off to the Fiddler.

Once upon a time, Alesia would never have gone out of the house without making sure she looked her best, but that was when she was with Simeon. Now that the reality of her life was well and truly established, and the gilt had come off the gingerbread so to speak, she was no longer the Ice Queen and had little time for making herself attractive, but she did at least make sure she was tidy.

She locked the car, hurried round to the rear entrance and pushed open the door. Heather's dad was moving some empties into a bin. He looked up and pointed upstairs.

"He's ready for you, Alesia. Got his gear on already."

"Thank you Mr. Bough. Heather there?"

She didn't wait to hear the answer but carried on up the stairs to the flat above the pub. She couldn't wait to tell Heather her news. Alex was wearing his football kit and watching some children's programme on TV. He jumped up when Alesia came in and gave her a hug.

"I'm going to be Harry Kane today, mum," he said. "Score lots of goals."

She gave him a smacker of a kiss and hugged him tightly. "Good for you, Alex." She let him go. "I won't be a minute," she said, "I've just got to tell Auntie Heather something."

"Tell me what?" Heather called from the kitchen.

Alesia hurried through to where Heather was washing up. She let Alesia give her a quick peck on the cheek.

"You'll never guess who I saw today," she said to Heather.

"Who?"

"Scott Jones."

Heather stopped and took her hands out of the sink. She turned and faced Alesia, her eyes wide open and a shocked expression on her face.

"What, Chicken George?"

Alesia pulled a face. "Please don't call him that, Heather; that was a long time ago."

"Yeah, you're right. So, what a surprise, eh? Has he changed?"

"Well, it's been fifteen years now. He's changed a bit like all of us."

Heather pulled off her Marigold gloves and dropped them on to the draining board. "So, what's he like? I want to hear everything about him, what he's been up to, what he's doing now and…" she gave a little shake of her shoulders, "…when you're going to see him again?"

"I only spoke to him for a minute or two," Alesia said a little exasperated. "I couldn't get much out of him in that short space of time."

"But your woman's intuition would have told you a great deal. Where did you see him?"

"Place called Monk's Farm. I had to deliver two pieces of fish there. I was bloody furious."

"Why?"

"I'm used to delivering boxes to the trade, not two bits of cod as a personal favour to my boss. She knew I always take Alex to football training on a Saturday."

"A personal favour?"

Alesia nodded. "Seems Scott knows the boss and so he asked for this so he could see me. Away from the crowds, he told me."

Heather gave an agreeable murmur. "Hmm; that's interesting. So, if he wanted to see you away from the madding crowd, how come it only lasted a couple of minutes?"

Alesia sighed. "As soon as he knew I needed to take Alex to football training, he said he would see me some other time, so we swapped phone numbers. I'm going to meet up with him for a drink."

Heather pulled a face. "What was he doing at this farm?"

Alesia shrugged. "I don't know. He was wearing overalls, so I guess he's a mechanic or something. Probably there to fix a tractor."

Heather laughed. "God, you haven't seen him in fifteen years and then bang; it's all over in two minutes." She gave Alesia a curious look. "Were you disappointed then? I mean, you don't really have a soft spot him, surely? Not after all these years."

Alesia couldn't tell her the truth, that seeing Scott again like that rekindled that feeling she discovered within herself that night at the Prom.

Heather pressed her chin into her neck as she gave Alesia a weird look. Then she pointed at her. "Bloody hell, you do! You still have a soft spot for him." She lifted her head and almost did a pirouette around the kitchen. "God, you kept that secret. None of us knew."

"Denny did."

"Really?"

Alesia nodded. "But listen, don't you dare tell anyone. It's done, it's in the past and we've all moved on. Okay?"

"Okay love, you go off to your football training. I'll see you later."

Alesia kissed Heather on the cheek. "Thanks for keeping an eye on Alex. Tarra!"

Twenty minutes later, Alesia drove into the car park of the local football club. She turned the engine off and turned to give some pointless instructions to Alex, but he was already leaping out of the car and hurrying into the club changings rooms. She tutted and held her hands up.

"Always the same, never listens," she muttered to herself.

She got out of the car, making sure she was tucked up against the chill that was in the air and hurried out to the touchline where she could watch all the action and see Alex pretend he was Harry Kane. She said hello to a few of the mums and dads that were there; faces that were familiar to her, but names that were not. But they were all singing from the same hymn sheet; being there for the benefit and, hopefully, the advancement of their kids,

The training session appeared to go well and then the boys and girls were finally divided into two mixed teams for the start of a thirty-minute match, which was when the parents became vociferous, including Alesia. And it was as she was bawling encouragement at Alex when she heard a voice behind her.

"So, this is what you get up to at football training."

She spun round. Scott was standing there, a smile on his face.

"Scott?" She screwed her face up. "What are you doing here?"

"I've come to apologise," he said.

"Apologise? What for?"

"Letting you go so easily."

She shook her head. "No apology necessary, Scott. At least I didn't have to make excuses — to leave you standing, I mean."

Like I did to you that night at the Prom, he thought to himself. He reflected on that briefly. Then he pointed towards the kids. "Look, why don't you carry on shouting at your son, and we can talk later." He gave Alesia such a lovely smile that it took her a while to turn round and search for Alex. She felt Scott move beside her.

"Erm, Scott."

"Watch your son, Alesia; I'll still be here when the game's over. Why not point him out to me so I can have someone to cheer for?"

She stuck an arm out. "The boy wearing a number nine shirt with Kane on it."

"Thank you." He didn't start shouting immediately but after a while he began to get involved and was calling out all kinds of encouragement to the lad.

When the session had finished, the boys and girls all disappeared into the changing rooms.

"What now?" he asked Alesia.

"We wait outside the changing rooms until they're ready. Come on."

He walked beside her until she stopped and leaned her back up against the handrail that fronted the walkway around the large hut. Scott did the same.

Alesia folded her arms across her chest. "It was really nice to see you, Scott," she said. "Quite a shock too after all these years."

"I expect it was."

"So, what did you do in America?"

He looked down at his feet. "I'll tell you about if you have dinner with me tonight."

She gave him a sideways glance. "Really? I thought we would be meeting over a cup of coffee."

"Don't you fancy it then?"

Alesia wanted to tell him she fancied it like mad, but there was no way she wanted to overwhelm him by revealing the feelings surfacing inside her like a hot underground geyser that had been lying dormant for years.

"Of course I do; I just need to check with Heather, see if she'll have Alex for me."

"You do that then," he said, "and let me know, but don't leave it too long, will you?"

At that moment, Alex came hurtling out of the hut and up to his mum. "What did you think, Mum?" he asked breathlessly.

She smiled down at him and tousled his hair. Then she reached down and kissed him on the top of the head. "You definitely remind me of Harry Kane," she lied. "One day you'll be playing for England."

Then suddenly he was gone, dashing off to talk to some of the other kids.

"Does this always happen?" Scott asked.

Alesia tipped her head towards a few of the youngsters who were huddled together. "Alex likes little Mandy there. He won't admit it, but I think he would sooner spend his time with her than some of the other boys."

"It happens at that age as well then, does it?"

She frowned at him. "Does what?"

"Being too embarrassed to admit you have a soft spot for someone."

Scott was referring to the time he last saw Alesia fifteen years ago at the Prom, and wondered if she would pick up on that. Hoped more than wondered though.

And then Alex came running back. "Mum, can I have a sleepover at Mandy's tonight please? Please?"

She gave a surrendering sigh and rubbed his hair again. "I suppose so. What time."

"Thanks, I'll find out." And he was off again.

"Sleepover?" Scott asked.

Alesia nodded. Yeah, they get on really well, and Mandy's mum is lovely. Dad too." She pushed herself up from the handrail. "Right, back home and get him looking half decent for his date." She started walking and Scott fell into step beside her,

"What about our date?" he asked.

Alesia stopped and turned towards him. "Oh, yes, of course." It was a stuttering response, which showed how surprised and unsure she was. "At least I won't have to ask Heather to babysit Alex for me. What time?"

"Well, if you give me your address, I'll pick you up at, say, eight o'clock?"

"Okay then; that will give me time to take Alex over to Mandy's." She then had a thought. "You're not thinking of nywhere posh, are you? I don't have much to wear these days."

He shook his head. "Chinese, Indian, Pizza, fish and chips." He stopped talking abruptly. "No, on second thoughts we'll forget the idea of fish and chips, eh?" They laughed together. "You choose," he said. Then he took his phone out and turned it on. "Text me your address."

They reached the car as Alex came running up.

"All sorted," he said to his mother. "Mandy's mum said she'll do tea."

Alesia laughed softly. "That's what I love about her," she told him. "She feeds you too."

They got into the car. Alesia started the engine and put the window down. "I'll see you tonight then," she said to Scott.

He blew her a kiss. "Looking forward to it. 'Bye."

Alesia reversed away from the parking spot.

"Who was that?" Alex asked.

"Nobody," she said. "Just an old friend who I haven't seen for years."

She drove away from the training ground feeling a brightness growing inside her. She thought of Heather pulling her leg about the way she must have thought of Scott all those years ago and the smile on her face just got wider.

Chapter 7

Heather was staring out of the window thinking of Alesia telling her how she saw Scott at Monk's Farm. She felt sorry for her friend and the way her life had panned out. No glittering career or enviable marriage for the Ice Queen; just the life of a single mum destined to deliver fish for a living.

She smiled, turned away from the window and then thought about the conversation she'd had with her parents that morning. She had dreaded it and had put it off for a long time. In some ways her life had mirrored that of Alesia's, but in a bizarrely different kind of way. She'd chosen to speak to her mum and dad at the breakfast table because that was the quietest time of the day before her father got busy with running the pub.

"There's something I have to talk to you two about," she said. "And it has to be now,"

Her father was about to shove a piece of toast into his mouth. He stopped, holding the toast halfway. "Sounds serious," he said.

"Something on your mind, love?" her mother asked.

Heather took a deep breath, sighed heavily, and began. "There has been a reason why I've never told you who Christine's father is." She took another breath and could feel her heart thudding beneath her ribs. "It was a decision we both took at the time because he's in prison."

Her dad dropped his toast on to his plate. Her mother was just finishing off her cup of tea. They both looked stunned.

"And he's being released on parole next week."

Her mother was the first to speak. "It's Wally Henderson, isn't it?"

Heather glanced at her and nodded briefly. "Yes."

There was a further period of silence. Then her dad spoke. "Why are you telling us now when you've kept quiet all this time?" He looked at his wife and then back at Heather. "I think we've known all along it was Wally, but you were so adamant about not saying anything that we assumed it was an accident you'd had with another bloke."

Heather gave a sheepish grin. "So did half the town, I think." She stared at her empty plate, a wistful look on her face. "The reason I'm telling you is because he's being released on Monday and I'm going up to Wandsworth to meet him."

"And you want us to look after Christine, is that it?" her mother asked.

Heather looked at her and shook her head. "No, mum; I'm taking her with me."

Her dad sat up stiffly. "What, to meet a bloody ex con?"

Heather gave him a piercing look. "He's Christine's father, dad."

Her mother reached across the table and touched her husband on the arm. "Bert, it's alright. Let Heather explain."

Heather picked up on her mother's cue. "The thing is, I've been looking for somewhere to rent, but I'm having trouble finding somewhere suitable."

"Why do you want somewhere to rent? Isn't there some kind of halfway house for ex-cons?"

Heather gasped. "Dad!"

He looked at his wife, realising he'd said something stupid. "What?"

"And you want Wally to stay here?" her mother asked. "Is that it?"

Heather nodded. "Until we can find somewhere, I promise you."

Her dad was about to say something but was stopped by his wife.

"Bert, you love little Christine, don't you?" she said to him.

He frowned. "Of course I do," he said. "But what's that got to do with anything?"

"Neither of us know Wally or what he's like, but it's obvious Heather still loves him, despite him being a criminal. If you refuse to let Wally stay here until they've found somewhere, he might hold that against you and refuse to let you have anything to do with your granddaughter. Do you realise that?"

His face was a picture when it was put to him like that. He loved little Christine like she was his own daughter, and the thought of being deprived of her was like a stake through his heart. He looked over at Heather.

"Would you let him do that?" he asked.

"I can't speak for Wally," she said honestly. "But mum could be right."

"He'll have to help out in the pub," he told her grudgingly. "No lounging about in the bar, and no bringing his mates in either. And certainly not up here."

Heather smiled at him, got up from the chair and walked round the table to him. She put her arms around him and wanted to call him an old softy. She looked over at her mum and winked. Then she kissed him. "Thank you, dad. I promise you Wally will be no problem. Hopefully he'll get a job back on the lorries. He still has a valid HGV licence."

"That would be a big help," her dad said. "But wasn't that the reason he got four years in the nick? Carrying stolen goods up and down half the motorways in England?"

"That's behind him now, dad. And once we've got our own place, I'll be able to keep an eye on him."

She kissed him again and went back into the kitchen, her mind on the coming Monday and having Wally in her arms again.

And mentally keeping her fingers crossed.

***

Alesia couldn't take her mind of the day she'd just been through, meeting Scott at the farm and then at the football training. And here she was waiting nervously for him to arrive and take her out to dinner. Heather had come over earlier to tell Alesia all about her conversation with her mum and dad that morning, and how excited she was knowing she would be with Wally on the Monday.

Alesia was so pleased for her. She already knew that Wally was little Christine's father, and she also knew that Heather had made secret trips up to London to visit Wally. She knew this because it was with her connivance that Heather was able to invent a reason for disappearing most of the day. She didn't stay long because he knew Alesia was going out that evening with Scott.

The call button on the front of the house sounded in Alesia's flat making her jump. She paused, breathed in, calmed down and went to the front door.

Scott was standing there. He smiled. "Hello, Alesia." He looked her up and down and whistled softly. "You look lovely. As always," he added.

She stepped out on to the porch and closed the door behind her. Then she leaned close and gave Scott a peck on the cheek. "You're looking good yourself, Scott."

He half turned and held his arm out. "Shall we go then?"

It only took ten minutes to drive into town. Being evening there was little traffic on the road. There wasn't much conversation between the two of them; just a chat about how they were. Small talk really. Scott parked in the main car park and used his phone app to pay. Alesia was standing by the car when he'd finished. He walked over, offered his arm, which she took, and five minutes later they were sitting at a table in the Chinese restaurant Scott had booked earlier.

"Do you want wine, Alesia?" he asked.

"I guess so," she answered, "but what about you?"

"I'll stick to sparkling water," he said. "Driving," he explained.

"I'll have a glass of house wine then,"

The waiter left them looking over the menu while he went off to fetch their drinks.

Alesia struggled to make a choice, not having been to a Chinese for ages. "Will you choose please Scott? I can't make up my mind."

He nodded; his eyes fixed on the menu. Alesia watched him, trying to see if there was any change to the face she remembered from the night at the Prom. She let her hand wander up to her mouth where she touched the corner of her lip, a smile growing as she recalled that moment.

The waiter returned with their drinks and took the order. Scott handed him the menu cards and watched him go. Then he looked at Alesia.

"Delivering fish then. How did that happen?"

She grimaced and gave a small shrug. "Life happened I suppose. I ended up as a single mum, broke, needing a job just to make ends meet and the fish job came my way." She looked at him, an implacable expression on her face. "The man I married was, well, a complete waste of space."

"Is there any chance you might get married again?"

She shook her head — a quick shake.

"Haven't you met anyone who you might…" He tried to find the right words. "Who you could, well, who you might want to marry?"

She looked directly at him. "I would have to love someone before I could think of marrying again, Scott."

"And you've never met anyone who…"

"There was someone," she admitted. "But he was out of reach." She tipped her head to one side and shrugged. "It was never going to happen."

He guessed that she'd fallen in love with a married man, but he was reluctant to ask her if that was the case. And he could tell by the look on her face that she didn't want to talk about it.

She reached for her wine and lifted the glass. "Now, can we talk about you?"

He sighed and relaxed. "What do you want to know?"

She put the glass down. "Come on, Scott, don't make it difficult. You bugger off to America and no-one hears anything about you. Then suddenly you turn up at Monk's Farm with that ridiculous order for two fish." She laughed softly. "I could have brained you."

"I got into music," he said. "I went over to the States because I wanted to get into Country music, and Nashville was the place to go."

"You make it sound as easy as falling off a log."

He laughed. "Well, cliché girl, it wasn't that easy. I had to convince my dad that I wanted nothing to do with the chicken business and wanted to make my own decisions about my life."

She pulled a face. "What did he say?"

"Told me I'd be back in six months with my tail between my legs like the Prodigal son begging to be taken back into the family business."

"Well, obviously it didn't work out like that, so what happened?"

"I started doing session music. There was always a need for a guitarist or keyboard player. I got myself an agent and..." he shrugged. "...it kind of took off from there. I played for some of the big bands: Guns n Roses, Queen, Fleetwood Mac." He shook his head and chuckled. "It was manic, Alesia. Bloody madness."

She peered at him. "Did you get into drugs and all that?"

He didn't give a straightforward answer, but simply raised his eyebrows.

"Women?"

He grinned. "There were a few, but I was never interested in marrying or anything like that, which was basically what most of them were after."

By now Alesia's mouth was hanging open. "So why did you give all that up and come back?"

"My dad's health was letting him down. He told me he would have to sell the business before it killed him but wanted to give me a chance to come home and take it on; see if I could make a success of it."

"And you did, despite the lifestyle you were living."

He looked round briefly as though he was looking to see if anyone was in hearing distance, but considering the noise in there, it was difficult to have a decent conversation across the table.

"Alesia, I made a shed load of money over there, but I never had much time to spend it. I also earned royalties from some of the songs I wrote. It was a good time to take stock of my life, where I wanted to be and to at least get some time with my dad before…" He left it there for a moment.

"And that was the reason you came back?"

He said, "There was another reason, which I can't talk about. It's a little personal," he added.

Alesia felt an empathy with him, and although she wanted to know what this 'other reason' was, she would never ask him.

Their meals arrived, which meant the conversation changed from the facts of life to the food they were eating. Scott was able to talk about the kind of food he basically lived on while touring and the kind of restaurants that he enjoyed when he wasn't on the road.

"Have you told anyone about America? You know; what you did and all that?"

He cocked his head to one side and gave a rueful smile. "And who would have believed me? I told my dad I played guitar in a band and that's all he ever told anyone else."

Alesia found herself looking at a guy who had kind of transformed himself from an unfairly ridiculed college boy to a man who had turned himself into something of a paradox. She could understand how most of his former peers at school would have scoffed and ridiculed the idea that Scott, Chicken George, could have made such a phenomenal success of his life.

She knew her feelings for him had grown stronger as she sat there listening to him, but his admission that he was never interested in marrying or anything like that made her wonder if he preferred the single life. If that was the case, Alesia knew there was little chance of them becoming an item. And after her experience with Simeon, she'd already admitted to him that it had soured any thoughts or inclinations she might have about another relationship. She decided to change tack.

"So, what now, Scott? Your dad's business?"

He forked a roll of noodle into his mouth and had trouble answering her for a moment. "Sorry about that," he said when he'd managed to deal with it. "I really don't know, Alesia. I'm not a businessman. I don't think there's any room in my head for that kind of stuff." He shrugged. "I guess I'll make an attempt at helping dad, but I think he will probably have to sell up."

"That would be a shame," she said to him, meaning it would be a shame because he would have nothing to keep him in England and would probably go back to the States.

He screwed his face up. "Not really. He'll make a lot of money and could afford to retire." He laughed softly. "Probably buy himself a villa in Spain."

"And you, Scott?"

He shook his head. "No, I don't see my future in Spain. And I'm not planning to go back to the States yet either."

Alesia felt an immediate lift in her spirits but had to smother the inclination to say how pleased she was to hear him say that.

"Well, in that case, Scott; I hope you'll find something that will fulfil you."

He forked another roll of noodle into his mouth and winked at her. "I will, Alesia" he said. "I will."

Chapter 8

Scott was back at Monk's Farm the following morning, working on a bag stitcher inside the bagging shed. It was Sunday, but in his current station in life, weekends meant very little. There was work to be done and he needed to get on with it.

He was thinking pleasant thoughts about the previous evening with Alesia when the phone vibrated in his pocket. He dusted his hands down on his overalls and reached inside for the phone. He pulled it out, looked at the caller number which he didn't recognise, shrugged and accepted the call.

"Hello."

"Is that you, Scott?" a woman's voice asked.

He recognised the American accent, and his face brightened. "Joanna?"

"Oh, thank God I found you. How are you my darling? Have you missed me?"

He shook his head slowly trying to take it in. "Where are you?"

"I'm in a café in the square at Kings Lynn."

"Tuesday Market?"

"Is that what you call it?"

"Yes, Tuesday Market Place, actually. But what are you doing in UK?"

"I've come to see you."

He turned round and started walking over to the small kitchen where he could sit down. "How did you get my number?"

"Your dad."

"My dad?" That was a total surprise to him. He pushed open the kitchen door and sat down on the only chair in there. "How did you find him."

She chuckled down the phone. Her voice sounded sultry. He loved the sound of it.

"Don't you remember?" she said. "When your dad paid us a flying visit last year, he gave me his business card and made me promise to look him up if I was ever in England. So here I am, and I'm dying to see you again."

Scott recalled how he'd been a little vague with Alesia the night before when he told her he had little to do with women over in the States; but Joanna was the closest he'd come to a lifetime commitment. He'd proposed to Joanna one evening when he'd been drunk but hadn't put a ring on her finger. Whether that was the reason Joanna had gone cold on their relationship, he wasn't sure, but he did retain the notion that they were still engaged. He thought they were getting back on terms when his father asked him to come back to England. It was a while before he made the return trip, and he believed Joanna was seeing someone else because of his plans to return to the UK. He promised himself that he would never get involved with a woman again, yet here he was listening to Joanna's voice and allowing those familiar feelings to surface once more.

"Well?" she said, breaking his train of thought and prompting him to answer.

He snapped out of it and sat up. "Oh, yes, I would love that. Where and when?" He looked at his watch. "I'm working at the moment, but I should be finished in an hour. Meet you at the Dukes Head?"

"What?"

He smiled. "Sorry. The Dukes Head; it's in the square. You can't miss it. Ask anybody where it is. I'll meet you there. One o'clock."

"Okay, Scott, I'll see you there. I'm looking forward to it."

"Me too, Joanna. Me too."

He cancelled the call and sat there, his mind going back to the States and the happy times with Joanna.

***

Denny had her arm hooked into Mitch's as they walked along the precinct on their way to the Lafayette store. Mitch had suggested they go to the shop that afternoon as it would be closed and that would give Denny an opportunity to check the layout in peace and quiet. Mitch had been in touch with the security people who maintained CCTV surveillance to inform them he would be in the shop sometime early afternoon.

Denny was pointing out the changes she'd seen in the town over the last fifteen years when she saw a vaguely familiar face with a very attractive woman sitting on a bench facing the square. She stopped, still holding on to Mitch.

"Do you see who that is, Mitch?" she asked, nodding towards the two figures.

Mitch looked and frowned. Then he turned his head towards her. "Is that who I think it is?"

"Yes; it's Scott Jones."

"Are you sure?" He looked back again.

"Alesia told me he was back from the States. He was working at Monk's Farm."

Mitch gave her a puzzled look. "What, that old place his dad owns?"

"Guess so," she said. Then she tugged his arm. "Come on, let's go and see him."

As the two of them got closer, Scott, who had just said something to Joanna and laughed, caught sight of them coming over.

"Oh my God," he said to Joanna and stood up.

Denny got to him first. "Scott? Really?" She put her arms around him in a quick hug. "Alesia told me you were back. Is it for long?"

He lifted his shoulders in a small shrug. "Hello, Denny. I don't know yet," he said. Then he looked her up and down. "Wow, you haven't changed a bit."

"Liar," she said. Then she turned towards Mitch. "Remember Mitch?" she asked him.

Scott expression changed immediately showing genuine surprise. "Bugger me, Mitch, you always were a handsome bastard. I see nothing has changed there."

The two of them embraced. "Good to see you, Scott."

Scott pointed towards Joanna who had watched the exchanges with deep interest. "This my friend, Joanna."

They both stepped forward and shook her by the hand as Scott told her their names.

Denny then looked from Scott to Joanna and back again. Scott could see she wanted to ask the obvious question, so he answered it for her.

"Joanna lives in America. She's over here for a while and thought it would be nice for us to spend some time together."

Denny looked at Joanna. She could see that she was of mixed race, but her skin tone was fairly light giving her a beautiful complexion. And she was absolutely stunning too. Denny immediately thought of Alesia.

"Are you over here for long, Joanna?" she asked.

Joanna gave Scott a warm look. "That depends on Scott," she said. "I've no plans to go back yet." She reached up and touched his arm. "We have a lot of catching up to do."

Denny could see from the way he looked at her that there was hint of something unspoken, but it still managed to reveal a great deal.

"Where are you off to?" Scott asked.

Denny laughed softly. "Well, it's actually a bit of business to fill in the afternoon until we go out for dinner tonight."

"Where at?"

"Potters. Do you remember it, Scott? I think we went there with some of the others. It was after the Prom night I think."

Scott screwed his face up. "Vaguely," he said.

"Why don't you come with us," Mitch asked, butting into the conversation. "You could tell us all about your time in the States."

Scott grinned and shook his head. "I'm sorry, Mitch but we've already got our day sorted. We could catch up some other time perhaps. I'm not going anywhere just yet, so I'm likely to be around for a while."

Joanna stepped forward and gave Denny a quick hug. "Lovely meeting you, Denny. Perhaps you and I can have a coffee together some time. Without the boys," she said glancing sideways at Scott and Mitch.

Denny smiled. "Of course; I would like that." She opened her shoulder bag and took a business card out from the small pocket. "This is where you'll find me most days.

It's an Art gallery and Photo studio. If I'm not there when you ring, Alice will patch you through."

Joanna took the card and looked at it briefly, then she put it into her pocket. "That sounds good. I will definitely do that."

Scott held his hand out. Mitch shook it. "We will have to meet up soon; fifteen years is a long time, Scott. You must have a lot of stories to tell."

"We all have," Denny interrupted. "So why don't we arrange another kind of Prom night? For those of us who are still here."

"Why not at Lafayette's," Mitch put in. "When we have centenary celebration?"

"Centenary celebration?" Scott asked.

"It's a few weeks away yet," Mitch told him. "Christmas time. But I'm sure we'll get to chat before that."

Scott nodded and took hold of Joanna's hand. "Okay then, we'll grab a coffee together before that. Enjoy your evening."

They watched the two of them walk off. Denny was a bit thoughtful.

"Do you think Scott was in a hurry to get away?"

Mitch laughed. "I don't blame him. Not when you've got someone gorgeous like Joanna attached to your arm."

Denny punched him playfully. "Men, you're all the bloody same. She may be just what Scott said she was: an old friend."

Mitch just chuckled and shook his head. "Sez you."

But Denny couldn't help thinking again about Alesia.

***

Scott and Joanna spent the remainder of the afternoon together. Most of their conversation was about their time together in America and the inevitable question from Scott as to why Joanna called off their relationship. They were actually on their way to Monk's Farm. Scott wanted to show Joanna where he worked in the hope that it might put her off any plans she had to rekindle the relationship long term. She had admitted to him that she broke off their pseudo engagement because she couldn't contemplate a life with him when he was constantly on the road with the bands. And he couldn't imagine she would be happy with his prospects here in England once he'd shown her what kind of future lay in store for him.

Scott turned into the rutted lane and allowed the car to bounce around bringing squeals of complaint from Joanna. He had a big grin on his face; he could see the funny side of it. Joanna could be a bit precious at times, and this kind of treatment was not the kind she was used to.

He pulled up beside the bagging shed, turned the engine off, yanked the handbrake in and looked at Joanna with a big smile on his face.

"Welcome to my world, Joanna. Prepare to be amazed."

Joanna's face was a picture. As gorgeous as she was, she managed to make herself look ugly. "What on earth is this place, Scott?"

"Come on," he said. "I'm sure you will learn to love it."

Joanna looked across the yard at the cottage. "Is that where you live?"

He shook his head. "No, I only use it when I bring women here."

"Scott!"

He turned round. "What?"

"Be serious."

He caught hold of her arm. "Joanna, it pays to be frivolous when you're forced to work in a place like this."

"Like what?"

"You'll see," he said as he unlocked the door and led her into the small kitchen. Fortunately, he had cleaned and tidied the place up so it was presentable. Except for the lingering odour, which was something he couldn't get rid of.

Joanna immediately clutched at her nose. "Oh my God," she gasped. "What's that awful smell?"

"You don't notice it after a while. It gets worse when they've emptied a chicken shed and brought the chicken shit over here."

Her face paled in horror. "What on earth…"

He took her elbow. "Come on; well have a quick look and then I'll take you over to the cottage where we can have a cup of tea. Or coffee if you wish," he added.

He opened the door to the interior and beckoned Joanna to follow him, which she did with her hand clamped firmly over her mouth. Scott pointed to the far corner of the building.

"That's where they dump the chicken muck and we bag it using those machines there." He was pointing as he explained the basic operation. "My dad's emptying one of the houses this week, so when that's done, I'll bring you over and I can show you properly what one of the tail ends of the chicken business is used for. You can have a go at bagging up too. It's not too difficult to pick up."

Joanna stood there mortified. "Scott Jones, if you think I'm gonna…"

He laughed and stopped her. "Joanna my love, I wouldn't dream of it." He tipped his head back towards the small kitchen. "Come on, let's go to the cottage. There's no smell there, I promise you, so you won't have to cling on to your nose all the time."

She pulled her hand down. "It must be awful when all that…" She waved her hand about. "Chicken shit is dumped here."

He nodded. "Yep, you could say that, but it makes a helluva good fertiliser for nurseries and garden centres."

"Is that what you do with it?"

"Yep, and that helps to keep us from the breadline. Come on, time for a cuppa."

Joanna needed no second telling, and she practically ran out of the bagging shed, through the small kitchen and into the blissful fresh air outside.

Scott locked up, took her arm and they walked together over to the cottage.

Chapter 9

Scott held the door open for Joanna. As she stepped into the tiny hallway, he pointed towards one of the doors.

"Kitchen's through there. There isn't much room, but I can manage to make a brew, and we can sit on a couple of chairs in the lounge." He pointed to another door.

"Where's the loo?" Joanna asked.

He nodded towards the bottom of the staircase, just a few feet away. "Upstairs. Should be easy for you to find. It's clean. I'll make a drink for us while you get yourself sorted out."

She squeezed her lips together, gave him a peculiar look, slipped her coat off and handed it to him. "Perhaps you would put this in the cloakroom for me," she said.

He took it from her and draped it over the knob at the bottom of the banister rail. "Done," he said.

Joanna shook her head and hurried up the stairs.

Scott smiled and went through to the kitchen where he set about making a coffee for them both. He gave some thought to how much, or how little he wanted Joanna to be part of his life again. He wasn't convinced she could morph into an Anglophile, no more that he could become Americanised despite living in the States for fifteen years. He thought it would be best to let Joanna do all the running until she persuaded herself that this was not the way she envisaged her life turning out. He had another reason too, hich he kept tucked away in his heart; dormant for now but maybe one day…

Joanna breezed into the kitchen as he was stirring sugar into the coffees. "My, my, Scott; what a palace. I didn't realise you lived in such comfort and luxury." She took the cup he offered her.

"I usually need staff to run the place for me," he said. "But I've given them the day off."

He went through to the front room, or lounge as he'd called it earlier. The room was very plainly furnished with just a sofa, a couple of chairs and a coffee table. A stained mirror hung above an old fashioned mantlepiece. The only thing in the grate was a blackened fire basket. A thin carpet covered the floor in front of the sofa.

Joanna did a quick twirl and stopped to look at him. "And you live here?"

He shook his head. "No, Joanna, I live with my dad. I told you I only stay here —"

"I know," she interrupted. "Only when you bring women here."

He grinned and sat down on the sofa, putting his cup on the coffee table. She sat beside him.

"How long do you plan to stay here, Scott?"

He raised his eyebrows. "Truth to tell, Joanna?" He shook his head. "I don't really know. I came back to please my dad, but I can't see it working out." He waved his hand in an arc. "Managing this isn't my idea of fun either. I'm not a business man. If it was down to me I would sell the whole kit and caboodle."

"Really? Not for the money, surely?"

He gave a snappy shake of his head. "No, you know I don't need the money. But I would be tied to something I'm not convinced about, so why hang in to it."

Joanna shifted and crossed one leg over the other. As she did this, she took the hem of her skirt and flicked it, making it lift a little before tidying herself up and making herself a little more comfortable. Scott caught a brief glimpse of her thigh taking his mind back to the number of times he'd seen more than just a brief glimpse. It stirred pleasant thoughts in his mind. He coughed to clear his throat.

"So, what are your plans, Joanna?" he asked her. "You didn't really come all this way just to see me, did you?"

She picked up her cup and took a mouthful of coffee, then put the cup down. Scott thought she was giving herself a moment to phrase her response.

She shook her head briefly. "No. My company are commissioning a new line in packaging." Scott knew Joanna was an engineering project manager with a large food processing business in the States. "We have several Italian machines but for some reason our senior engineering manager has become interested in a British model that he believes will perform better and more economically. So, he wants me to have a look at it, give it some thought and see if it will come up to expectations." She shrugged. "It's subjective really."

"So, you won't be here for long then?"

"That depends, Scott," she said, making a face. "I could spin this out; I'm quite good at that. And I know my boss will allow me a few weeks. I told him I couldn't be expected to come to England and not have a chance to see something of the place. So, I have a three month work permit."

She picked up her cup and held to her lips looking over the top of the rim as though she was hiding. It did make Scott wonder if there was any truth in her explanation.

"Is it a local firm, Joanna?"

She took the cup away from her mouth. "Yes. On the industrial estate. Faradays?"

Scott shook his head. "No. Don't forget; I'm practically a stranger here myself. So where are you staying?"

"Knights Hill. It's got a Spa and everything." She looked at her watch. "I think I need to go, Scott. I have to get changed before we go out tonight."

He lifted his cup and drained it. "I'll take you home then and pick you up at seven o'clock. Sound good?"

She put her cup on the coffee table, reached forward and kissed him. "Could be quite a night," she said and flashed her eyes at him.

A warm feeling ran through his veins as he reacted to Joanna's soft lips.

She pulled away. "Best we go now, Scott; I don't want to end up on some broken bed upstairs."

He laughed and took her by the hand, and they walked out of the cottage in much higher spirits than when they first went in.

**

"Your health, Denny," Mitch said, raising his glass.

Denny smiled back at him. "Yours too, Mitch."

They were at the restaurant after spending most of the afternoon with each other. The only break was when they went their separate ways to get ready. Mitch would have been quite happy to ignore that part of the day, but he needed to freshen up and have a shave. Denny just needed to get her mind straight and make sense of what was happening. She had tried to read Mitch's body language and interpret any little asides he made as they reminisced about their college days. But trying to make sense of anything while she was in his company was pointless.

"Were you involved with anyone in London?" she asked as she put her glass down.

He licked his lips after sipping his wine. He lowered the glass carefully, placing it almost precisely between the cutlery and folded napkin.

"For a while, yes," he told her. "She worked in the office at Harrods, so I got to see her fairly regularly. Nice girl. Her name was Consuelo."

"Consuelo?"

He nodded. "She was Spanish. Had all that fiery, gypsy like temperament you find in a lot of Spanish people." He arched his eyebrows. "Cracking looking woman too."

"So, what happened?"

"Her heart was in Spain, really. I don't think she would have been able to settle down in London. Or England for that matter," he added.

"Did you love her?"

He shrugged. "I thought I did, but I was wrong."

"How so?"

He leaned closer to the table and looked directly into her eyes. It made her tingle all over. "Have you ever been in love, Denny?" he asked.

She shook her head. "No, too busy trying to build a career and a business. No time for it."

He huffed. "That is a God-awful answer, Denny: no time for it indeed," he said. "You don't have to put yourself out there to find it; love will come looking for you, and when it strikes, you're done for — that's it."

"And it has never happened to you?" she asked, the doubt clear in her voice.

"Once," he said. "But that was a long time ago."

"Not Consuelo then?"

He shook his head. "No."

Denny opened her mouth to ask him who it was, but that was the moment the waiter chose to turn up and take their order. Once they'd decided on their choices, Denny was about to put the question to him, but he stopped her.

"Can we talk about the celebration now, please Denny?"

She couldn't object to that despite wanting to know more about Mitch's love life. And the celebration was going to be an important event after all, which meant she would be in his company quite often.

"Okay," she said reluctantly. "So where do we begin?"

"Why don't we go back to the Prom night and unravel the story of the town, and the people involved."

She smiled and shook her head. "Wouldn't work; nothing has turned out for us in the way of happy endings. Our lives and dreams have come crashing down, which would turn the celebration into a tragedy and not one of excitement and hope." She stopped there for a moment. The she said, "Let's make it a theme of hope and find some of those dreams that have come true. They have to be out there somewhere."

"Okay," he said slowly, "we'll do that. So, from tomorrow, we start looking."

And Denny knew there was one dream of hers that would never come true.g

Chapter 10

Heather felt apprehensive as she stood outside Wandsworth prison in South London. She had never imagined that she would ever have a connection with an inmate in one of England's toughest prisons, or that he would be the father of her daughter, Christine.

November had announced itself with a chilly north east wind, dropping the temperature a few degrees, and although manageable, it felt a lot colder than the high temperatures they'd enjoyed during the last few months. As she stood outside the prison gates, Heather's mind went back fifteen years to the lovely warm night of the Prom. She recalled, with a smile on her face, how the ten of them had responded to the challenge. She had been drawn to remain at the table. Wally had been drawn to look after the boys' table. It was later that the two of them started to talk. They were both on their way to the toilets. Wally opened up the conversation with her about it being bad luck. Heather hadn't thought so because she didn't want to be drawn with Chicken George, but she agreed with Wally just to put a brave face on it.

When Heather came out of the toilet, Wally was waiting for her. He asked her for a dance to make up for the fact that he had been deprived of the chance to get to know her properly. They knew each other from college, but only as part of a bunch of young friends, so there was no real awkwardness between them, which was why Heather agreed.

And that was the beginning of the rest of her life.

She didn't know how long it took before she realised she was in love with Wally. He'd told her eventually that he'd fancied her for a long time, which was why he'd waited outside the toilets for her. He told her some years later he was so nervous that it was worse than serving time inside. They became lovers of course, and one week after Heather discovered she was pregnant, Wally was arrested on drugs and criminal charges.

What followed was one of the most awful periods of her young life. She refused to name Wally as the father of her child even though they'd been an item for a long time. Most of her peers assumed it was Wally, but Heather kept her mouth shut and promised Wally she would never tell anyone until he gave his consent.

One unexpected outcome for Heather was that Wally paid a substantial amount of money into her personal bank account so she and their daughter would not be in need of anything. One thing he couldn't give her though was somewhere to live, but Wally's thoughtfulness meant that she had sufficient funds to rent a small flat for when her baby was born.

Heather had to put up with rumour and gossip about her and her situation. She was ignored by many of her former college friends except Alesia and Denny, for which she was mightily grateful. Many people thought of her as a 'gangster's mole' — a ridiculous anachronism from Hollywood gangster films, but she learned to live with that too.

She didn't need to rent anywhere though because her parents wanted her to stay at the Fiddler pub. Her mother had to persuade Heather's dad that it was the right thing to do. Her dad was furious that she wouldn't name the father, which was why he was reluctant to agree. But it didn't take long for him to realise what a bonus it was to have the baby Christine there all the time because he became a doting grandfather.

And so, time passed, and she found herself outside the Scrubs waiting for Wally to be released.

When the small pedestrian door opened and Wally stepped out into the sunshine and cold wind, Heather practically squealed with delight. She was so excited that she couldn't keep her feet from running on the spot. She clenched her hands into fists and then lifted both arms and waved madly at him.

Wally was carrying a small bag over his shoulder and was wearing scruffy jeans and a jean jacket over a Tee shirt. He had old trainers on his feet, and a mop of hair that fell untidily around his ears. A big smile broke out on his face as he waved and started running over to her.

Heather looked down at little Christine whose eyes were wide at her mother's behaviour. "It's your daddy, Christine," she said. Then she turned as Wally dropped the bag at his feet and enveloped her in an enormous hug. It was so tight, Heather couldn't breathe properly, but she didn't care; it was Wally and that was all that mattered.

She started crying and pushed her head away, looked at the tears on his face and kissed him full on the lips.

"Oh, God, Wally."

She couldn't say anything else because she was kissing him again.

Eventually, Wally let her go. Then he knelt down on one knee beside the buggy. "Hallo, my little girl. Can I give you a kiss?"

Little Christine looked up at her mum, not sure what was happening. Heather nodded her head vigorously.

"It's okay, Christine. This is your daddy."

Wally was still looking at his daughter. He leaned forward and kissed her softly on her cheek. "I am so happy," he said. Then he stood up, picked up his bag and threw an arm around Heather. "Right, let's get away from all my bad memories," he said, looking back over his shoulder at the towering monstrosity of the prison gates. He grabbed the buggy. "I'll take this," he said with a grin. "Got to get used to it."

Heather took his hand and together they set off for the long walk to the railway station where they would catch a train into London and then finally home to Kings Lynn.

"I still haven't found us a place to live, Wally," she told him, "but mum and dad said its okay for you to stay," She squeezed his hand. "But we'll have to find somewhere for ourselves."

His eyes brightened. "I think I've found something temporary," he said. "A mate of mine —"

"No mates, Wally!" Heather said sharply. "You promised me you'd finished with all that."

He made a calming motion with his hand. "He's not that kind of mate," he told her. "He's never seen the inside of a prison and is as straight as a die."

She gave him a 'yeah!' kind of look. "Where did you find a mate like that?" She looked back quickly at the prison. "Not in there, I'll bet."

They'd turned into Earlsfield Road where the traffic noise notched up several degrees. "I got a phone call from someone I haven't seen for years," he told her, raising his voice a little. "Out of the blue. He said he was back in town, and someone had told him about me and you."

Heather stopped and turned towards him. "Me and you?"

A bus went roaring by and the blast of wind from it almost blew then both over. "Bloody hell," Wally laughed. "I was safer in prison." He ran his fingers through his untidy mop of hair. "Anyway, as I was saying; we had a chat, he asked how things were, and I told him I was being released on parole. Next thing I know is we're talking about me and you looking for somewhere to live, and me looking for a job."

Heather stopped walking and made Wally stop too. "And?"

"He's got an old house on a site, which is barely habitable, but liveable. He said we could stay there until we found something more suitable."

Heather was about to say something, but he put his hand up and stopped her.

"He also said he might be able to give me a few hours work a week if I needed it."

"So where is this place?"

He shook his head. "I don't know exactly, but it's at a place called Monk's Farm."

Heather's face opened up in complete shock.

"It's Scott Jones," she said. "Chicken bloody George!"

Wally's face was a picture as he stared at Heather. "You remember him?"

Heather gave a triumphant look. "Of course I do; he was part of the gang that night at the Prom."

He chuckled, his voice dark and growly. "Oh yeah, I remember alright: the Ice Queen and Scott. Quite a shock to her system, eh?"

Heather nodded. "Yes, well, she met him at Monk's Farm the other day. She was delivering fish."

His eyebrows lifted. "Fish?"

She grinned. "Never mind, Wally, another time. But yes, it was Alesia who told me. We thought he lived in America, so it was a surprise to both of us."

They turned into Garrett Lane and headed towards the station. The traffic was manic and so was the pedestrian traffic. Wally had to steer the buggy carefully making Heather laugh at his awkwardness.

"Want me to take over, love?"

He shook his head as he laughed and avoided another walker whose head was glued to her mobile phone. "No, I'll manage," he told her. "Once we're home it should be a lot easier."

"We're not going home, Wally; not yet anyway."

He looked at her sharply. "What do you mean?"

She edged closer to him. "I've booked a hotel in London. One night, the three of us. And we can let your little daughter watch her mummy give daddy lots of cuddles."

He lifted his head and had a big grin on his face. "Hallelujah!" he cried. "There is a God after all!"

She gave him a quick kiss on his cheek. "And keep your voice down; especially tonight."

Wally smiled, shaking his head slowly, thinking how he loved this girl more than life itself.

"So, you still have some money left?"

She nodded. "Yeah, but not much. It's been four years, but I've been careful. Dad paid me for the hours I put in at the pub, plus I only paid a very low rent — you know; to help out with the bills and that."

"You've got a good mum and dad," he told her.

She stopped and turned to face him. "What about your parents, Wally? Are they okay with you?"

He nodded. "They came to see me a few times. Dad found it hard, but mum…" He shrugged his shoulders. "You know what mums are like. I think once you and me and little Christine here are established, we'll be happy families again."

Heather liked the sound of that and began to feel a contentment she hadn't felt for a very long time.

***

Denny was sketching out a floor plan for the Lafayette celebration, using the photos she'd taken when her and Mitch were at the shop the previous day, when the front door opened, and Mary Dean walked in. Denny looked up from her floor plan. Her face lit up in surprise.

"Hello, Mary. I didn't know you was back. How was Australia?"

Mary came over to the large table where Denny had been working. "Oh, it was lovely; Clive and Pam really made me welcome."

Denny could see those two in her mind's eye back at the Prom. They got together not long after that night. None of the gang were that surprised, but like most courtships among a bunch of friends, no-one expected it to last. But Clive joined the Royal Air Force and got commissioned as an Air Traffic Control Officer. He married Pam (that was a surprise) and they settled down to a life away from Kings

Lynn and a career serving Queen and Country. And then they surprised the gang again when Clive transferred to the Royal Australian Air Force. Clive's mother always kept Denny informed of Clive and Pam's progress, his promotion and their children, and how happy they were living in Australia.

"Of course they made you welcome," Denny told her. "And how are their kids?"

"Ed and Josh? Typical boys. Nearly teenagers. Ed is twelve and Josh is ten."

"Will we ever get to see them again?" Denny asked.

Mary sat down on a stool beside the table. "Well, they are actually planning to come back to England for Christmas and the New Year."

Denny's face brightened. "But that will be wonderful. Wow, I can't wait to see them."

"All four of them," Mary said wistfully. "It'll be manic."

Suddenly, Denny sat up straight. "I've just had a thought," she said. "I'm helping to plan a centenary celebration for Christmas at Lafayette's." She ran her hand over the rough sketch she'd been working on. "This is part of the prep work I'm doing." She then went on to explain how Mitch had turned up and how it all fell into place.

"You know, that would be lovely," Mary said. "And you think you'll be able to get all of you together for that?"

Denny screwed her face up "I hope so, but it's a big ask. None of us know where Simeon disappeared to. Once he'd dumped Alesia with her kid, he disappeared. Not that he would be welcome anyway." Then she brightened a little. "But what the hell; with Clive and Pam here, it would be brilliant. Alesia is still here as you know. Wally…" She stopped and leaned forward a little. "Wally came out of prison today. Heather's gone up to London with her little girl to meet him."

Mary looked a little forlorn. "That was so sad; the way he went off the rails. And Heather's little girl; is Wally the father?"

Denny shrugged. "I don't know," she lied. "Could be though. But Heather has been getting so excited about Wally coming home. I feel so happy for her. So, I guess you could say they will be at the Christmas do. I hope so."

"And is that all your group accounted for?"

Denny held up her hand and started ticking the names off. "Sylvia — we don't know where she ended up. She got involved with the church and then disappeared. Probably running a mission somewhere in South America."

They both laughed at that. But when Denny had finished, she'd accounted for eight of the ten who were at the Prom all those years ago.

"It will be great," she said. "And if you could let me have a couple of photos of Clive when he was growing up, that would be good. Oh, and Pam as well? Perhaps you could ask her next time you speak?"

Mary laid her hand on Denny's. "I'll do my best," she said. "I'll pop in again later."

She got up from the stool and blew a kiss. "See you soon, Denny."

Denny returned the kiss and got back to looking at the rough floor plan, her mind on those early years and a winsome smile growing on her face.

Chapter 11

Heather looked out of the train window as the train pulled slowly away from Victoria Station. Beside her was little Christine, fast asleep thankfully. Sitting opposite, across the table, was Wally. Piled around them was their luggage, not that there was a great deal, but enough to discourage other passengers. It wasn't deliberate, but fortunate for them that no-one had asked if they could sit there.

Although Heather was looking out of the window, her mind was on the previous day and the high emotion that carried her and Wally into giddy heights of pure pleasure. Once they had locked the door of the hotel room, they both had one thing on their mind. Heather smiled at the memory because they had to make sure their daughter was otherwise engaged as they made up for four years of enforced abstinence. But the one thing that fixed the smile on Heather's face as she recalled those heady moments, was Wally, on his knees, stark naked and proposing to her. He was holding a diamond ring and looked like a lost child as he smiled and cried at the same time.

"Where did you get the ring?" she asked him after he had slipped it on her finger.

"I've had it all the time," he told her, getting up off his knees and kissing her.

She pushed his head away. "In prison?"

He nodded. "I bought it the weekend before the plod arrested me. I was going to propose. Got it all planned." He tilted his head back to blink away the tears. "God, I could have killed the bastards. I'd booked a table at Potters and..." He sniffed a couple of times. "Well, it didn't happen, did it?"

"Why didn't you say something, Wally?" Heather asked, putting her hands on the sides of his face.

He shook his head. "I couldn't, could I? They took my stuff and locked it away before putting me in that bloody jump suit." He chuckled. "At least it meant the ring was safe. It was still in its little box in the draw string bag. I remember the plod's face when he wrote down what I had. He looked kind of sorry for me."

Heather pulled him to her. "When do you want to get married?"

He pulled his underpants on and sat down on the bed beside his daughter who was engrossed in a cartoon playing on her iPad. She was wearing her favourite pink headphones and completely oblivious to the drama being played out beside her. Wally put his hand on top of her head and rubbed it gently. She looked up at him, smiled and then went back to her cartoon.

"I would like to marry you now," he said. Then he laughed softly. "If we were in Vegas, we could get married in one of those quick marriage booths. You know, hundred bucks gets you a preacher and a marriage certificate." Then he shook his head. "But that's not what you deserve, so I would like a normal wedding, me with a suit, you with a lovely white wedding dress, and our little Christine as a bridesmaid. Once I can afford it," he added.

Heather sat on the bed beside him. She splayed out the fingers of her left hand and admired the ring. "You won't keep me waiting too long, will you Wally?"

He put his arm around her. "Tell you what: if I haven't earned enough by Christmas, then we'll get married in a registry office. How's that?"

She smiled and kissed him. "Perfect."

The memory started to fade when Heather felt a nudge on her arm. She looked over at Wally.

"Penny for them?"

She gave him a lovely smile. "Oh, I was just thinking about last night. You, stark bollock naked, on your knees with a ring in your hand asking me to marry you."

He grinned. "Romantic, eh?"

She splayed her fingers and looked at the ring. "We will make it work, won't we, Wally?"

He reached across the table and laid his hand on hers, covering the ring. "Nothing is going to stop me from loving you, Heather, and nothing will make me go back to the way I used to be. I promise."

Heather knew he meant it, and she knew they would make it work despite everything. She leaned back against the seat and closed her eyes; her mind reliving the precious, happy moments, and loving the way she felt right now.

***

Denny walked into the studio, her mind on the events of the weekend. She wondered about Scott and his 'friend', Joanna, and whether Alesia knew about them. Not that it was any of her business, but she did think that maybe Alesia would prefer not to have any obstacles in the way of her progress with Scott. If indeed Alesia had any thoughts in that direction' — something Denny did wonder about.

But the time she had with Mitch was the highlight of her weekend, and all kinds of fantasies had filled her mind the longer she spent with him. As they walked around the empty Lafayette store, Denny felt she was drawing closer to Mitch than she felt fifteen years earlier. She had really fancied him in those days but there was a silly kind of peer pressure that stopped her from declaring those feelings other than admitting a 'girlie' crush would soon disappear. The evening at the restaurant was blissful. The food, the wine and having Mitch to herself made for a perfect evening, and she was so glad that Scott had turned down the opportunity to join them. The evening didn't finish in the way it could have done, much to Denny's disappointment, but it was early days, and she was sure it would happen.

She closed the studio door behind her and walked into her office calling out to April that she was in, She took her jacket off and hung it up on the coat stand, then she dropped into her swivel chair and picked up the mail that April had left there for her.

There was no junk mail there; April would have delt with that and thrown it in the bin. But of the remaining envelopes, only one intrigued her, simply because of the feel of the Crown Vellum envelope and the light pink colouring. It was addressed to Denny.

At that moment the door opened, and April walked in with a coffee and put it on the desk for her.

"That looked a posh envelope, Denny. Not opened it yet?"

Denny thanked her for the coffee. "I was just about to open it," she said, and lifted a paper knife from the desk set. She slit the envelope open and pulled out a single sheet of paper. For some reason she held it to her nose to see if there was any fragrance.

"I thought it might have been scented," she said to April. "Looks posh enough." Then she started to read through the letter. April watched, fascinated by the changing expression on Denny's face. Denny looked up and handed the letter to her. April scanned it quickly and knew why Denny's face had changed.

"The Corfe Gallery?" she said in astonishment. "That's in Duncannon Street behind the National Gallery."

Denny was grinning like a Cheshire cat and nodding furiously. "I know. And…" She grabbed the letter back from Hazel and looked at the signature. "It's only Martin Longstaff."

Now April was grinning like a Cheshire cat as well and nodding her head. "He owns the Gallery." She grabbed the letter back. "And he wants to talk to you about exhibiting there." Her eyes were bright. "This is brilliant, Denny. You'll be one of the top artists in the country. Your work will…"

Denny stopped her. "April — let's not get carried away; he wants to see me to talk about it. He won't be coming down here; I'll have to go up there."

"Well, you will, won't you?"

Denny grinned and got up from the chair. She went round the desk and grabbed April in a hug, and the pair of them started jumping up and down like a pair of schoolgirls. Just then, Isabel walked in.

"Whoa, what's going on?"

April broke off from the hug, picked up the letter and thrust it into Isabel's hand. Then she grabbed Denny again and they started jumping around again.

Isabel read the letter, banged her eyes and dropped the letter back on the desk. "Well. when you've got a moment Denny, I have finished framing that fabric you painted. You might like to see how it's turned out." She turned to go and then stopped. "Oh, and by the way; congratulations. I've met Martin Longstaff and he's an absolute dream. You'll love him."

She pulled the door to softly and left the two women to their carousing moment. But she had a smile on her face and couldn't help pumping her fists; it was a massive boost for Denny and her aspirations to become one of the top creative artists, and good for the studio to have a top-notch designer recognised by her peers in the world of Fashion and Photography.

Chapter 12

It was Wednesday and for some reason her delivery schedule was bigger, which meant it was a push for Alesia to finish and get back in time to pick up Alex from school, but she made it as Alex appeared at the school gate. He was with his friend, Mandy. Alesia liked the way the two of them got on with each other. When she'd got him home on the Sunday, he told his mum that Saturday night was 'Brill' and that Mandy's mother had made a brilliant spaghetti Bolognese for them.

She watched him as he ran over to the car, his school bag bouncing on his back as he ran. For a brief moment, Alesia felt sorry for him because he didn't have a dad, and although she was quite capable of taking him football training and trying to be two parents in one for the boy, she wished she could find time to meet someone, cultivate a friendship and bring that person into the sphere of influence she had over Alex because the boy needed an Alpha Male in his life.

She was also self-conscious about her battered Vauxhall Corsa lining up with the SUVs, EVs, Audis and BMWs. And the mums always looked smart and chic. She allowed these moments to filter through her brain until she reached the thought of Scott coming back from the States and wondering if…

Her mind was miles away as the car door opened and Alex jumped up into the passenger seat. "Hello, mum." He kissed her, wriggled out of his backpack and snapped his seat belt on.

"Did you have a good day, Alex?" she asked as she started the motor. "What did you do?"

"Just stuff," he said, which he always did.

Alesia wondered what it would be like to have a degree in just stuff. She grinned and pulled out into the road carefully avoiding the crush of schoolchildren who were unaware that there were a lot of mums in cars picking up their kids and trying to negotiate human traffic.

"What's for tea, mum?"

She glanced at him quickly. "Fish?" she said hopefully.

He wrinkled his nose. "Really?"

She reached her hand over and tousled his hair. "Not, not tonight. We'll get a Big Mac on the way home if you like."

He turned his head sharply and looked at her, a big grin on his face. "Great — much better than fish."

She knew that would please him. She was about to say something when her phone started ringing, which was clamped into a bracket on the dash. She pressed the accept button and put it on speaker. It was Heather.

"Hello, Heather. How's things?"

"Hello, Alesia. Did you manage to get Alex from school?"

"Yeah, he's with me now. Did you get Wally home safely?"

"You bet. He's standing right beside me."

"Hello, Alesia!" Wally's voice boomed out loudly. "How are you?"

"I'm fine, Wally. Looking forward to seeing you sometime."

She heard Heather's voice telling him to give her the phone.

"It's me again, Alesia. Could you do us a favour please?"

"Sure, what is it?"

"Scott wants to see me and Wally. He's at the farm and has asked us to go over there. He says its important. Could you take us please?"

Alesia felt a lift in her spirits. Suddenly she had a chance to see Scott again without having to come up with a reason.

"Yes, of course I can. I've got to give Alex his tea first. Say five o'clock? Is that okay?"

"That's great, Alesia. See you at five then. 'Bye."

Alesia smiled to herself as the call was cut off. Naturally, she was curious as to why Scott wanted to see Heather and Wally, but for her it was another opportunity to see Scott.

She wasn't aware if Alex had heard any of the conversation: he was listening to some music through his earpieces and singing to himself.

Kids, she thought. Right, Big Mac and then Monk's Farm.

***

Alesia turned into the lane at Monk's farm and the car started bouncing wildly.

"What the —"

"Wally! Language," Heather snapped at him.

Alesia smiled when she saw Wally's expression in her rear-view mirror. She also caught Alex looking up at her with a big grin on his face.

"Sorry about that, Alesia," Wally shouted as the car rocked about. "Took me by surprise."

Alesia thought back to that day when she drove her van up the lane for the first time. She did wonder if her old car could stand being knocked about as she allowed the steering wheel to roll back and forth through her hands. Then they were suddenly on to firmer ground, and she relaxed.

As she turned towards the parking area, she saw Scott walk out of the side door. He waved as she pulled up and turned the engine off. She put the window down as Heather and Wally started getting out of the car. Alesia stayed put and watched them as they hugged each other. She noticed that Heather avoided getting a kiss from Scott by holding herself at arm's length. She smiled at that, remembering those moments back at the Prom.

Scott looked over at Alesia. He said something to Heather and Wally and then came over to the car.

"Hello, Alesia. I didn't expect to see you." He winked at Alex.

Alesia nodded towards Heather and Wally. "They don't have a car yet. Heather asked me if I could bring them over."

He started to say something and then stumbled a bit. "Erm, I…" He shook his head. "I've asked Heather and Wally over because I have a proposition for them."

Alesia put her hand up. "Oh, yes, don't worry about us Scott. We're okay here. You get on with your business. I'm just the taxi driver. Don't worry."

He thanked her, visibly relieved, and walked away as Alesia closed the window and started to make conversation with Alex who had already lost interest in the grown-up stuff.

"Okay," Scott said as he reached Heather and Wally. "Let's go into the bagging shed first. Shouldn't take too long, but I want you to see it."

They went through the small kitchen and into the shed. Heather immediately put her hand to her nose. "My God, Scott, what a stink."

He grinned. "You get used to it in time." He pointed to a mountain of chicken shit piled up to about twenty feet at one end of the shed. "When we clear out a chicken house, the muck is brought over here for us to bag up and send out to our regular customers."

"Who buys the stuff?" Wally asked.

"Garden centres, nurseries. It makes for good manure and fertiliser."

"What, as it is?"

Scott shook his head. "No; we sift it first before we bag it." He pointed to the different machines. "Fairly straightforward," he said. "Once you get used to it."

Wally looked at the mountain of chicken muck and then at the rest of the equipment in there. "Is this where you work, Scott?"

"Only when I need to be here, otherwise I help out over at them main farm — the chicken sheds."

"Can we go now?" Heather asked.

Scott chuckled. "Of course. We'll go over to the house."

Heather was quite happy to get away from the smell and to what was probably the reason Scott had asked them over: to look at the house.

He led them out of the shed and passed Alesia who had her head back on her headrest, eyes closed. "It was good of Alesia to bring you over," he said as they walked by.

"She's a good friend. Loyal too," she added, hoping Scott might pick up on that laconic statement.

Scott made no comment to that and said nothing until they reached the front door of the cottage. Heather thought it looked lovely with its thatched roof and wood framed windows.

He ushered them into the kitchen first.

"Right," he said, stopping and leaning back against the worktop. "First things first. This is the accommodation I offered to Wally." He was looking at Heather because he knew she would be the driving force behind any decision they came up with. "In its present state it needs some work and certainly some TLC. Furniture too," he added. "But we'll come to that."

Heather was already imagining her and Wally with little Christine in the cottage. She done a swift survey of the kitchen as they walked in, casting her woman's eye over it. She had also noticed what had appeared to be an old, disused garden, which directed her thoughts to her allotment and how she might be able to make use of it.

"Everything works in here: the electric, the plumbing, the boiler. Everything. Could do with a lick of paint maybe, but that's for later." He pushed himself away from the worktop. "Right, let's talk a walk round the place, give yourselves time to think about it as we go round, and then I'll put my proposition to you."

Suddenly Heather felt nervous. It sounded like there was going to be some kind of proviso or certain unhelpful conditions attached to the tenancy. And because she didn't know Scott, what kind of man he was, and remembering the fact that she regarded him as a figure of fun at school, she was fearing the worst. It could be payback time for him.

They finished the tour of the house and the surrounding area even though it was dark, including the old barns and a couple of thatched sheds and were back in the kitchen when Scott put the proposal to them.

"I'll give you the details, Heather," he said to her. "I'm sure Wally will be okay with that." He glanced over at Wally who nodded. Then he looked back at Heather. "Right, rent will be two hundred a week because it's only part furnished. If you want it furnished, the rent will be increased accordingly." Heather felt her heart drop and disappointment started creeping in.

"You will have to pay your bills," Scott went on, "to the Company. That is: my dad's company. The rates will be decided by him and do not necessarily relate to the services provided in the usual way by the National Grids. The gas, water and electric meters are in the bagging shed, which means they can be read without the need to come into the house. Under the tenancy agreement which will be drawn up and signed by all parties, you will be required to maintain the fabric of the cottage, carry out any repairs that are necessary, and ensure the interior paintwork is in good condition."

Heather couldn't believe what she was hearing, and it showed on her face. Scott ploughed on.

"You cannot hold any private parties on site because it is Company land and subject to liability insurance that is peculiar to our Company business."

Heather felt her growing disappointment running through her veins again and could see themselves back at the pub living with mum and dad, and Wally driving her dad up the wall.

"Maintenance will be down to Wally of course, but I'm sure you'll be willing to help with those chores, Heather."

He stopped there, his expression showing a need for some response. Heather opened her mouth to tell him what she thought of it all and that he could shove it, when he held up his hand to prevent her saying anything.

"Oh, and there is one other thing. Whenever I come to collect your rent, you must personally bow your head to me and apologise for your behaviour at the Prom." He stopped, his face expressionless. "What do you think?"

She lowered her head and started shaking it slowly, thinking of the words that surely must come. Hiding her disappointment was easy. The truth was, she was thoroughly pissed off and wondered what on earth they were doing there. She lifted her head to say something and saw Scott grinning at her. He stepped forward and put his hands on her arms.

"And if you can persuade Wally to work for me by looking after the bagging shed and all that entails, I'll chuck in the furniture for nothing, and you can live here practically rent free. And I'll pay Wally a living wage. How does that sound?"

Heather's mouth fell open, and tears started to fill her eyes. "Scott…" She couldn't say anything. Then she looked over at Wally who was trying desperately not to laugh. And then it clicked. "Wally, you bugger! You knew, didn't you?"

He let the laughter flood out and he walked over to her and wrapped his arms around her. "It was Scott's doing," he told her. "Said he wanted to pay you back for the Prom night."

She turned towards Scott. "Really?"

He put his arm round her and brought Wally into the huddle. "We'd sorted all this out some time ago, Heather. I just wanted a bit of fun with you, that's all." He then stood back, swept his arm round in a wide arc. "Welcome to your new home."

This time, Heather flung his arms round him and gave him a smacking kiss on the lips. Then she pulled away. "Shit; I can't believe I've just done that," she said with laughter and tears. "I've just kissed Chicken George."

Then they all clung together and started bouncing up and down like a bunch of eighteen-year-olds at a Prom night.

Chapter 13

Alesia had managed to fall asleep in the car while she was waiting for Heather and Wally. Alex was absorbed with his mobile phone, which meant he wasn't pestering his mum with questions. Alesia's forty winks was suddenly disturbed by the sound of a car. She opened her eyes and glanced up at the rear-view mirror where she saw the headlights of a car bouncing its way up the lane. She released her seat belt and turned round to get a better view and kept an eye on it as it finally negotiated the lane and pulled up several yards away from her.

She frowned when she saw a gorgeous woman step out of the car. The security lights on the bagging shed threw sufficient pools of light to see that she had a lovely olive-skinned complexion and was wearing some pretty serious clothes: much more fashionable than she could ever afford by the looks of them. At that moment she spotted Scott coming out of the cottage. He was on his own, so she guessed he had left Heather and Wally behind.

The woman waved to him. He waved back and quickened his pace. Alesia lowered the window and watched as Scott came up to the woman, a look of surprise and pleasure on his face, and put his arms around her. She reached up and kissed him, putting her hand against his face and her other arm wrapped tightly around him. He pulled away.

"Joanna, you're early." He looked at his watch.

"I got bored with waiting. Thought I'd come over here and drag you out."

Alesia felt herself sagging, literally. Her body seemed to deflate when she saw the obvious connection between Scott and the woman he'd just called Joanna. She kept her eyes on them, watching and reading their body language. Then Scott looked over and held his arm out, said something to Joanna and brought her over to the car.

"Alesia, I want you to meet Joanna: a good friend of mine from the States." Alesia got out of the car as Scott introduced her. "And this is Alesia," he said and left it at that.

Joanna smiled and shook Alesia's hand warmly. "Hi, pleased to meet you."

Alesia glanced at Scott. He picked up on the look. "We've known each other for a long time now."

Alesia couldn't help feeling he was attempting to water down anything that she might regard as a serious relationship.

"Well," she said, "it's no business of mine." She looked beyond Scott's shoulder. "What have you done with Heather and Wally?"

Joanna reacted to that. "Oh, you have company? Sorry; I didn't know."

Scott shook his head. "They're going shortly. I left them at the cottage. They will be moving in once I've added a few sticks of furniture." He pointed at Alesia. "Alesia will be taking them home as soon as they're ready."

"Your tenants, then?" Joanna said to him thinking that would kill off his stories about taking women there; not that she thought for a minute that he was up to that kind of business.

At that moment, Heather and Wally came out of the cottage and walked over.

"Happy now?" Scott asked them when they reached him.

Heather nodded a little sheepishly. Wally just had a broad grin on his face.

"When can we move in, Scott?" Heather asked.

He screwed his face up as he figured out dates and timings. "It's Wednesday today, so how about, erm, next Monday? We've got some of the furniture stored over at Dad's place." He looked at Wally. "You can give me a hand, Wally. Say Saturday morning?"

Wally nodded. "You've got it. Can you pick me up?"

Scott said he could. "You can drive the lorry," he told him. "Get you used to it."

Wally's face brightened. Heather glanced at him but chose not to say nothing. It was four years since he last drove something substantial. She just hoped he could cope.

Scott turned to one side. "Oh, this is my friend, Joanna," he told them. "Flew in from the States a week ago."

Heather tried not to show what was in her mind and managed a breezy hello. Wally had trouble trying to get the word out of his mouth as he stepped forward and shook Joanna's hand. Heather chanced a quick frown as she looked over at Alesia who simply shrugged.

"We'd better go, Heather," Alesia said. "I need to get Alex home so he can get on with his homework."

"Oh, yes." She hooked her arm through Wally's. "Come on love."

Scott caught Alesia by the arm as she turned to go. "Let me say hello to your boy before you take off, Alesia."

They walked over to Alesia battered car and clambered in. Joanna remained where she was. Scott walked round to the passenger side where Alex was sitting and tapped on the window. Alex wound the window down. Scott put his hand through the opening and gave him a fist bump.

"Hello, Alex, how are you getting on with your football training."

Alex's face brightened at the word 'Football'. "Great. Mum says I'm as good as Harry Kane."

"I bet you are. Perhaps I can come over and watch you on Saturday."

Alex pulled a face. "I can't go this Saturday; mum's got a hospital appointment."

Scott's face dropped. He looked at Alesia with the unasked question on his face.

"It's routine, Scott: just routine."

"Well, let me take Alex."

Before Alesia had a chance to respond, Alex got there first. "Would you?"

Alesia touched Alex on the arm. "Scott can't take you, Alex; he's moving furniture for Heather and Wally."

"That won't take long, Alesia," Scott reassured her. "We'll be done by mid-day." He glanced at Wally as he said it who nodded.

"We leave at two o'clock," Alex said brightly. "Okay?"

Scott gave him another fist bump. "You're on. I'll pick you up at two o'clock." He looked at Alesia. "Is that okay?"

Alesia smiled and shrugged. "It looks like I don't have any say in the matter, Scott. Thanks anyway."

She started the car and backed away from the bagging shed, catching sight of Heather's face as she turned to look back, and imagined the kind of emotions and questions that were rattling around in her head. And as she surged forward towards the lane, she could see Scott and Joanna walking arm in arm looking like two people who were more than just good friends.

And that made her incredibly sad.

***

Alex was ready when he heard the sound of a car horn. He looked out of the window and saw Scott at the wheel of his Range Rover. Scott waved his hand at him. Alex jumped away from the window and grabbed his backpack, then ran through to his mother.

"Scott's here, mum."

Alesia stooped to give him a kiss and a few words of advice.

"Don't misbehave, Alex. Scott is doing us both a big favour, so be good."

"Yes, mum!" And he was gone leaving Alesia with a wry smile on her face as she listened to the sound of his footsteps disappearing fast down the hallway. She walked over to the window and watched as Alex climbed into the rear passenger seat. She wondered why he hadn't got into the front seat next to Scott. Then she caught a glimpse of Joanna. She muttered something under her breath and walked away from the window.

"Seat belt, Alex," Scott said to him over his shoulder. "Oh, this is my friend, Joanna by the way."

"Hello, Joanna," Alex said to her. "Do you like football too?"

"Ah, well, sometimes," she told him. "We call it soccer back home. We play football with an oval ball," she said, trying to make some sort of conversation.

"That's Rugby," Alex told her. "And we don't wear all that padding and silly helmets."

Scott started laughing. "Better not get involved, Joanna. He could crucify you."

Joanna chuckled and looked back at Alex. "What, a sweet little boy like that?" She turned back and looked ahead, conversation over.

The drive to the football club took a little over twenty minutes, and Alex had used that time to send a message to his friend, Mandy, and consequently begin a conversation that he hoped might lead to another sleepover at her house. He was only aware they had arrived at the ground when the car stopped, and Scott turned the motor off.

"Right." Scott started to say something, but Alex was ahead of him and already getting out of the car. "I'll see you later then, Alex. Okay?"

He looked at Joanna who was smiling. "He's keen, isn't he?"

Scott nodded. "Alesia did warn me."

Joanna studied him for a moment. "Scott, were you and Alesia ever an item?"

He frowned. "Goodness me, no. She only had one guy in her sights and that was Simeon. What made you think that?"

"I've seen the way she looks at you."

He shook his head. "No, you're imagining things."

"Am I?"

"Yes," he said, and climbed out of the car. "She has someone who she's secretly in love with," he said as he closed the car door. "Well, she told me that in the past tense, but I have a feeling she still hankers after him."

Joanna got out and followed Scott to the playing area where a lot of youngsters were warming up. Alex had disappeared into the club house, which gave Scott and Joanna no choice but to join the other mums and dads and family members standing loosely grouped close to the touch line.

The weather was being kind: a little cold but bearable. Joanna hooked her arm in Scott's and snuggled up close to him.

"So, where's all the razzamatazz?" she asked.

He leaned his head a little to one side. "This is England, honey," he said to her in an American accent. "They don't go in for all that bullshit."

She gave him a bump with her hip. "Helps make it more fun, Limey," she joked.

They didn't say much else between them, just watched at the various drills the kids were being put through. It all looked well organised and controlled. Then a game started, if you could call it a game. They were not using full size goals. Scott tried to explain why to Joanna, but she seemed miles away. Probably bored, he thought, and he couldn't blame her. He kept his eye on Alex though because he wanted to be able to give the lad an honest opinion about his game, which to Scott's inexperienced eye wasn't too bad,

When the session was over, the youngsters all disappeared into the club house.

"What now,?" Joanna asked.

"We just wait until Alex shows up, then we go home."

"Home," she said softly. "I like the sound of that. But home in America."

He looked at her as she tightened her hold on him. "You getting homesick already?"

She shook her head. "No, but I could be getting homesick for what we once had, Scott."

"What did we have, Joanna?"

"We could have been married."

Scott remembered how close they had come to that. "You stopped it, Joanna."

Joanna lowered her head and nodded. "We could go back, Scott, and start again."

"You mean we should go back to America and get married?"

As Joanna was about to answer, Scott felt something tug at his elbow. He turned round and saw a little girl about Alex's age standing there looking up at him.

"Are you Scott?" she asked.

He smiled and nodded. "Yes, that's me."

"Oh, good. I'm Mandy, Alex's friend. He said he won't be long but it's his turn to help clean the dressing room. Ten minutes," she said.

"Well thank you, Mandy. Are you going back to Alex now?"

She nodded vigorously. "Yes. Goodbye."

He watched her go and smiled. Then he turned to Joanna. "That was Alex's girlfriend — his sweetheart. Alesia told me he often has a sleepover at her house."

"Young love," Joanna quipped.

"Yeah, nothing wrong with that."

"Until you grow up and learn about the real world waiting for you out there."

"You're right," he mused. "Life can suck sometimes."

Joanna kissed him on the cheek. "We've both been there, done it and got the Tee shirt."

He laughed and kissed her. "Too right."

And then they saw Alex running out of the club house. Mandy was with him. They parted company and waved at each other, which brought a smile to Scott's face and a warm feeling he could never have expected to happen.

"So, what did you think?" Alex said a little breathlessly as he reached them.

"It's like your mother says, Alex: you're a budding Harry Kane. I thought you looked pretty damn good." He tousled the boy's hair. "So, let's get you back home and you can tell your mum all about it."

And the three of them turned and walked back to Scott's car.

***

Alesia was home when Scott handed Alex over to her. "How did you get on at the hospital?"

"Oh, fine. They'll be giving me a call if there's anything they need to look at. How was Alex?" she asked, deliberately changing the subject. "Did he behave himself?"

Scott shrugged. "I didn't see much of him, but what I did was pretty impressive."

She smiled down and Alex, a warm feeling running through her veins. Somehow there was real connection between the three of them. She wondered if Scott felt it too.

"So, what are your plans for this evening?"

"I'm taking Joanna to the pictures. Or the 'Movies' as they say back —" He nearly said 'back home. "In the States."

Alesia had hoped he would have been able to stay. "Oh, well, I hope you both enjoy your evening."

"I'm sure we will." He stepped close to her and kissed her on the cheek. "See you soon." He called out to Alex. "I'm off, buddy, take care of your mum." He winked at Alesia. "Bye."

She waited until he had gone and went in search of Alex. "Enjoy your afternoon with Scott?" she asked when she found him in his bedroom on his phone.

"Yeah, it was good." He looked up from his phone. "Mum, can I have a sleepover at Mandy's please?"

Alesia had half guessed that would happen. "I'll have to phone Mandy's mum, just to make sure."

"Great, can you do it now so I can text Mandy?"

She sighed. "Give me your phone."

Alex handed it to her and watched as she dialled.

"Hallo, Janet," she said as soon as the phone connected. "Alesia here. Alex wants to know if…"

"…if he can have a sleepover," Janet finished the sentence for her. "Of course he can. It will give me and you a chance to have a chat. When are you coming over?"

"Now?"

"Lovely. See you soon."

Alesia arrived at Janet's home thirty minutes later. Alex said hello to Mandy's mother and then went in search for Mandy.

"Janet pulled a funny face. "I think he's in love." She closed the front door. "Glass of wine, Alesia?"

"Sure, but only one because I have to drive home."

They went through to the kitchen where Janet poured a drink for them both. Then they walked through to the front room. Before she sat down, Janet called through to her daughter.

"Mandy, come and say hello to Alex's mum please!"

Mandy duly walked in with Alex in tow. "Hello Mrs. Merriman. Thanks for letting Alex come over."

"Did you enjoy your football today, Mandy?" Alesia asked.

Mandy said she did. "Who were those two people who brought Alex?" she asked.

"Oh, you saw them? That was Scott and Joanna."

"Is she American?"

Alesia nodded. "Yes."

"And are they boyfriend and girlfriend?"

Aleisa frowned and looked at Janet for some reason. Janet asked Mandy what made her think that Scott and the woman, Joanna, were a couple."

"Well, it's because I heard them say they were going back to America to get married."

Alesia dropped her glass into her lap. She caught it and just avoided getting her wine all over the place. "Shit!"

Mandy opened her mouth in shock. Janet too. Alesia stood up, brushing her wet jeans and apologising for spilling her wine and swearing.

Janet could see that Mandy's revelation had affected Alesia quite deeply. She caught hold of Mandy's arm, holding it gently.

"Are you sure, Mandy? Why would they say that in front of you?"

"They didn't," Mandy said, shaking her head. "I was behind them, and they were talking, and he said to her that they should go back to America and get married." She shrugged.

Janet let go of her arm. "Okay love, you and Alex can go back to your room. I'll call you when tea is ready."

Mandy ran off. Janet turned to Alesia.

"I guess that wasn't something you wanted to hear, was it Alesia?"

Alesia shook her head and blinked several times. "No." She looked at her half empty glass. "Could you fill me up again please, Janet. And if I get drunk, send me home in a taxi, will you?"

Janet took the glass from her. "If you get drunk, Alesia, you'll have to crash out on the sofa. But before you do, you need to tell me how come you're in love with Scott Jones."

Chapter 14

Denny stepped out of the taxi at the entrance to the Corfe Gallery in Duncannon Street and waited for the taxi to pull away before turning round and looking at the ornate Gallery frontage. She immediately pictured her own studio and imagined it looking the same with an elegance that declared culture and class. But she knew that the real beauty of the place was inside, and it was this that she was eager to see and, hopefully, learn from.

She opened the door and stepped into a world that bore little resemblance to her studio. She detected a fragrance in the air but not an overpowering aroma. It was the kind of sensation one might get when walking past someone, usually a woman, wearing an absolute joy of a perfume. Denny did wonder if it was from a joss stick but dismissed that as unlikely. There was music too; not loud but so quiet that visitors to the Gallery would soon be unaware of it.

But as Denny was taking in the ambience, she caught sight of a young woman sitting behind the ivory white reception desk. He hair was streaked in a mix of colours and piled up into a top knob. It looked like she was wearing a bib front outfit, and there was a sign of a tattoo just about visible at the vee of the open neck, check shirt she was wearing.

Denny smiled and introduced herself. "Oh, good morning. I'm Denny Brown. Here to see Martin…"

But before she could get the words out of her mouth, the young woman let out a joyful shout. "Yes! Miss Denny Brown. We're expecting you. Lovely to see you."

She got up and came round from behind the desk. Denny could now see she was wearing a pink dungaree onesie and green sneakers on her feet. The complete contrast to the chic elegance in the room that Denny had seen was stunning. She didn't think she'd seen so many colours on a woman since she was a kid at a Christmas pantomime.

"I'm Chenelle," she said to Denny and held her hand out, which Denny shook. "Would you like a coffee? Martin should be back any minute now," she said, looking at an enormous, coloured watch on her wrist. "He's expecting you."

Denny was almost too tongue tied to speak. But this was London and in the world of fashion, what could be a better place to dress than by wearing something fashionable?

"A coffee would be lovely, Chenelle," she said.

"One coffee coming up." She spun on her green sneakers and left Denny to stand in awe at what she'd just witnessed.

The door opened and Martin Longstaff walked in. Denny turned round as he closed the door behind him and walked over to her.

"I saw you get out of the taxi," he said a little breathlessly. "Sorry I was late, but I did nearly beat you to it." He smiled.

"You sound like you've been running."

"I would be a liar if I denied it. But yes, as soon as I saw you."

Martin was not as Denny expected. With the clothes he was wearing — jeans, Tee shirt and boots, he could have been anyone and not Martin Longstaff of whom she had heard so much. He was good looking too. She remembered Isabel describing him as gorgeous, although Denny thought Mitch was better looking. But she liked what she saw.

He took her hand. "Welcome to the Corfe Gallery."

Denny almost felt like curtseying, but settled for a smile, a nod of the head and a hand shake. "Thank you, Martin. I'm so pleased to be here."

He pointed towards the back of the gallery. "Let's go through to my office," he said. "I take it you've met Chenelle?"

"Yes..." Her response tailed off.

"Quite a girl, eh?"

Denny chuckled. "Yes; you could say that."

Martin took her through to his office and pointed to a small two-seater sofa up against one wall. A glass coffee table stood in front of it. The walls were covered in a wallpaper of bold colours and what looked like palm fronds.

"Would you like me to take your coat?" he asked.

Denny slipped it off and handed it to him. He hung it on a coat stand near the door. She sat down facing the desk and was able to see a number of framed certificates, photographs of well-known celebrities and important people in the world of fashion; all with Martin. She could see that some of them were signed.

Martin sat in the chair behind his desk, which was covered in paperwork and the kind of impedimenta one would associate with a busy writer's desk. He was just making himself comfortable when the door opened and Chenelle came in with Denny's coffee, which she put on the coffee table.

"Do you want one, Martin?" she asked.

He shook his head. "No thank you, Chenelle."

When Chenelle had gone, he smiled over at Denny. "I've been looking at your work again," he told her. "I'm really impressed. You have a way of conveying a kind of empathy with your subjects, which is most unusual and something I admire."

All Denny could do was smile and say thank you as she drank her coffee.

"What I would like to do for you is to give you a room to showcase your work. It would be a short-term contract initially of course, but once we have an idea of how successful it has been, we could come to an arrangement that's beneficial to both parties."

Denny knew he was talking money. There would be a free, short-term exhibition at first. If it worked out, then maybe a contract between the Corfe Gallery and Denny's Studio. It would be a good opportunity for her; one she would have to consider carefully.

"Where would you exhibit my work?" she asked.

He pushed himself up from the desk. "I'll show you."

Denny took another mouthful of coffee and put her cup down. Then she stood up and followed Martin into the Gallery.

What came next surprised Denny. There were an unbelievable number of rooms going deeper into the building. Each one had a different theme of art, photographs, framed painted fabrics, and even sculptures. It was like a miniature museum. And in one room that they were passing through, Denny saw a framed photograph of a stunningly beautiful woman posing in the only way a top fashion model could. She stopped and couldn't take her eyes of the photograph.

"What a gorgeous photograph, Martin. Who is she?"

He raised his eyebrows with a smile. "You don't recognise her?"

Denny shook her head. "No; I've never seen her before."

"It's Chenelle."

Denny's face fell open, and she turned to him aghast. "Chenelle?"

He nodded vigorously and pointed back towards the front of the studio. "That wild eclectic mix of colourful nonsense back there is one of the most sought-after fashion models both here and abroad."

Denny frowned. "I don't understand."

He breathed out slowly and folded his arms across his chest. "Chenelle studied at the Nova Accademia Di Belle Arti in Italy."

"What, the NABA?"

"You know of it?"

"Who in the world of fashion hasn't?"

He held both hands out in a gesture. "Chenelle ended up with a master's degree. But when she came back to England, she found that a master's degree did not guarantee a job at the top of the pile. So, she took to modelling as a sideline."

Denny looked back at the photograph. "But it isn't the same girl."

He laughed. "I can assure you it is. Chenelle is always in high demand during London fashion week. In France and Italy as well. They pay her good money, Denny. She doesn't need to sweat buckets trying to become head of a large fashion house. She designs clothes as well."

"Here? In the studio?"

He pointed up at the ceiling. "We have a large cutting room upstairs, You know — sewing machines, long flat tables, rolls of fabric. Chenelle will often come in when she has an inspirational moment and disappear upstairs."

"Doesn't she work here?"

He shook his head. "No. I asked her to come in and mind the shop for me today while you're here. There are two other girls here, but they're working upstairs on a fashion project; I didn't want to stop them. Chenelle's quite happy to do it for me."

Denny pointed a finger towards the front of the studio. "So why…?"

"Why does she dress like that?" he said. "It frees her from the straight jacket that top models often have to adhere to. And think on this: what you see in that photograph is the inner beauty that Chenelle has: one she can disguise in her outrageous choice of clothes. But only a clever, gifted photographer or artist can bring that inner beauty to the surface." He touched Denny gently on the shoulder. "And that is a gift that you have."

Denny tried closing her mouth again but had to make do with shaking her head slowly and accepting something that she found quite amazing.

"Come on," he said. "Let me show you where you can hold your exhibition. And then after that, we can go for some lunch and talk business."

He turned away and Denny followed until they came to a closed door. He opened it and stepped into an empty room. There was nothing in there: no furniture, no decoration, just four plain walls in a room that was almost as big as Denny's studio back home. It was an ideal place to free the mind and exhibit that inner beauty about which Martin had spoken so eloquently.

She breathed in slowly, turned to him and smiled. "Perfect," she said. "Absolutely perfect."

Chapter 15

Heather couldn't wait to get started on the house. Wally and Scott had made a decent job of putting the furniture in. Heather had wanted to supervise the operation but was disabused of that idea because both men knew she would be in the way. Consequently, they placed all the furniture thoughtfully and with care so that Heather could deal with the smaller items that had been packed into cardboard boxes when her and Wally arrived to take up residence on the Monday morning.

Scott was making allowances for them both, so consequently he didn't expect Wally to start on his new job for a couple of days. By the evening of that Monday, Heather had managed to make the place more homely than when they had first seen it while Wally had taken up the challenge of cleaning and scrubbing. They had left little Christine with her Nanny and Grandad over at the Fiddler pub, which meant they could relax in complete privacy and look forward to a new dawn.

The following morning, Heather was up early, anxious to get on, and set about getting breakfast for them both in her own kitchen. Her mind was spinning with all manner of thoughts running through her brain, particularly one that had come to her during the night. She called up to Wally to come down for his breakfast. He'd had a shower; for him it made such a difference too, knowing that he had only to share it with Heather and not an overload of prison inmates.

He came into the kitchen and gave Heather a hug, kissed her warmly, told her he loved her and sat down at the small table. Heather had put cereal and milk there, warm toast, and cooked them both eggs and bacon. She sat opposite him with a huge, satisfied grin on her face.

"Busy day today, Wally," she said. "Mum and dad will be over soon with Christine."

Wally nodded as he chewed on some bacon. "Your dad won't want to let our little girl go, will he?"

"He'll get used to it," she said with a lift of her shoulders. "We'll still be happy families." She spooned some cereal into her mouth. "And I've been thinking."

Wally frowned. "Oh — oh."

"You know I grow stuff on dad's allotment?" He nodded. She went on. "Well, there's enough land here to start an allotment of my own. I'm sure Scott wouldn't mind."

He pursed his lips. "So long as you don't encroach on anything important."

"Like what? There's nothing here. A bit of a garden that has been neglected. And there's so much space. If Scott agrees, I could start on it and have a thriving allotment by summer of next year. Maybe have my own veg stall at the market."

Wally put his hand up. "Slow down, sweetheart. I know you're keen to get on with things, but let's take it one step at a time. Scott has very kindly given me a job that may or may not work out. After all, he's already said he might persuade his dad to sell the business. And if that happens…" He left it unsaid.

"He would go back to America with that Joanna woman," Heather remarked disapprovingly.

"You don't like her, do you?"

Heather sighed. "It's Alesia I'm thinking about, Wally. I know she has feelings for Scott. I could see how disappointed she looked last week when we came out of the house and Joanna was there. You could just tell by her body language. Joanna's gorgeous, but so is Alesia. We never called her the Ice Queen for nothing, you know."

Wally agreed. "Yeah, but that was before she became a single mum and fell on hard times." He lifted up the hand holding his knife. "You know, we should be able to shape our lives, but often our lives shape us. Alesia has allowed herself to look exactly like a single mum who delivers fish for a living."

"I'm a single mum," she reminded him.

"Yes," he said. "But you have someone who loves you. And that makes a world of difference."

"And I love you too, Wally, but that doesn't stop me worrying about Alesia. I mean; what kind of future does she have? No man in her life; a son like Alex who needs an Alpha Male in his. Young boys need that."

He tipped his head a little to one side with a whimsical expression on his face. "And who's to say Alesia will find the right kind of Alpha Male for him. She screwed up royally with Simeon, didn't she?"

"That was Simeon's fault."

Wally shook his head. "That's not the way I heard it. Simeon didn't want kids, Alesia did, so she tricked him and got pregnant."

She nodded reluctantly. "I know, I know."

"Which means Simeon wouldn't have been much of a father figure for Alex, would he?"

Heather shook her head knowing how Alesia's plan had failed spectacularly and ended up leaving her as a single mum.

"And you have to think on this, Heather: Scott legged it off to America. Fifteen years later and he's back, but no wife in tow, so what makes you think he would be the right man for Alesia and the perfect Alpha Male figure for Alex?"

She shrugged. "They seemed to get on alright at football training," she said.

Wally grunted. "One swallow doesn't make a summer."

She puffed out her cheeks and sighed. "Well, perhaps you're right, Wally," she agreed. "But I'll live in hope."

Wally wiped his plate with his last remaining piece of toast. "So, what plans do we have for today?"

Heather got up from the table and gathered up the dirty dishes. "Well, we've got Mum and Dad coming over this morning with Christine," she said as she put the dishes in the sink. "They'll want a good nose around the place, and I think dad might like to see where you'll be working; so, I guess it will be a kind of 'non day' until they've gone."

Wally stood up. "Sounds good to me. I think I'll wander over to the bagging shed, see if Scott's there yet. Unless you need me here?" he added,

She shook her head. "No, you won't be far away, and I'll know where you are if I want to find you."

He came over and kissed, pinched her bum and left her there with a smile on her face and a warm feeling running through her veins.

Today was going to be a good day.

***

Alesia was well into her Tuesday morning round of deliveries when her phone rang in the van. She accepted the call. It was from Scott, which brought a smile to her face.

"Hello, Scott," she said brightly.

"Hi. What are you up to?"

"Right now?"

"Yes, right now."

"Delivering fish," she told him. "I'm almost up to my next drop off, so what can I do for you, Scott?"

"Will you be coming anywhere near the farm?"

She shook her head. "No; I haven't had any double fish orders from some silly bugger who thinks I do personal deliveries." She heard him chuckle. The sound sent a small tingle up her spine. "Why are you asking?"

"Well, Heather and Wally have moved in. Her mum and dad have just turned up with little Christine, so I guess they'll be busy. I had planned to start showing Wally the ropes today, but I decided to let them get on — bit of family time for them as well."

A smile crossed her face. "That's thoughtful," she said.

"Yes, never mind that. Can you make it?"

Alesia hesitated. There was something she needed to ask but could think of no other way than to come out with it and ask directly.

"Will Joanna be there?"

"No," he answered with a slight change in his voice. "She's in London. Something to do with her work. I've no idea what. Why did you ask?

"Oh, it just crossed my mind. No reason," she lied.

"So, you'll come by? I can get lunch if that's okay?"

She pulled a face. "Not in that kitchen, surely?"

He laughed. "No; I'll get a takeaway. I'll let you have the chair in the kitchen though.

She felt a lovely warmth seeping into her. The conversation had echoes of familiarity between two people who were on the cusp of a meaningful relationship.

"Okay, I'll be there about twelve. What will you order?"

"Chicken?"

She laughed out loud. "You bugger. Don't you have more than that?"

"There's lots more I could suggest, Alesia," he told her with a level voice. "I could order fish and chips if you like."

"Smart arse," she joked. "I'm at my next stop, Scott, so I'll have to ring off. See you later." She blew a kiss at the dashboard as she leaned forward and turned the phone off. As she came to a halt outside the next delivery, she leaned back in her seat, a warm, satisfied glow on her. She turned the engine off and clambered out of the cab and got her mind back to the reality of frozen fish and her customers.

***

Heather and Wally were already busy in the house when Her Mum and Dad turned up with little Christine. Heather was so excited at being able to show them round the home and pointing out where she planned to do particular things in order to make a loving, warm and comfortable home for Wally and their daughter. Her mother walked round with her, approving of whatever Heather had planned to do. She was on tenterhooks in a way; she so wanted her daughter to be happy with Wally, which was why she was a little apprehensive listening to Heather planning their future.

"Oh, and I'm going to start a vegetable garden," Heather said. This made her dad's ears prick up.

"Where are you going to do that?"

Heather's mum turned to him. "Outside, silly," she scoffed.

He grunted. "I figured that out myself. It's just that there's no garden to speak of, so I was wondering where. That's all."

Heather took his arm. "I'll show you."

Her mother wasn't particularly interested, so she let them go off while she went in search of Wally and Christine.

Heather took her dad round to the back of the house and closer to the old barn and sheds. "I figure I can create an allotment in this area, and maybe use one of the sheds for all my gear. It will take time," she admitted, "but I think I could have it up and running by summer next year."

"Will you be here that long?"

She frowned at him. "Why shouldn't I be?"

He shrugged. "Oh, I don't know, Heather. Your mum and I have talked about it; wondering if you and Wally will make a go of it." He made a gesture with his arm, sweeping it round in an arc. "It's not exactly Shangri-la, is it?"

"No, but it's mine and Wally's Shangri-la, Dad."

He gave her and affectionate hug. "I know, sweetheart. I know." He pointed at the sheds. "So, are you going to show me what pile of junk is in there?"

She smiled and hooked arm in his. "Let's find out, shall we?"

The first shed turned out to be an Aladdin's cave of unidentifiable farm equipment, most of which was covered in tarpaulin. Her dad carefully lifted each cover; just enough to see what was underneath. One of the covers he lifted revealed a machine that intrigued him, so he pulled back the tarpaulin until it was completely exposed. He raised his eyebrows in surprise and then called Heather over.

"Look at this, Heather!"

She came over. "What is it?" she asked.

"It's a rotovator." He had a huge smile on his face. "Perfect for getting your allotment ready."

She looked at the machine. "I wonder if it works."

"Well, you'll have to ask Scott first. Then see if Wally can't turn his hand to repairing it. That's if it needs it."

Heather shook her head slowly. "When I first thought about growing vegetables, Dad, I imagined taking a few to market." She looked at him. "With this, I could start my own stall."

He patted her on the arm. "Don't get carried away, love; you have to walk before you can run. Just be patient."

But Heather knew that was the last thing she could be. She stepped forward and pulled the tarpaulin cover back over the rotovator. "First thing tomorrow," she said, "I'll ask Scott about it. Then we'll see." She took his arm. "Come on; let's go and see if there's anything in the other shed."

She stepped out of there with a happy, confident feeling about life at Monk's Farm.

***

Alesia pulled up outside the bagging shed and got out of the van. She hadn't bothered to take the van back to the depot because she was impatient to find out why Scott had asked her to drop by. She had plenty of time before needing to pick up Alex from school too, so she was quite happy.

Scott was in the bagging shed when Alesia looked through from the kitchen. He saw her and immediately stopped what he was doing. There was no machinery running, so Alesia assumed he was doing some maintenance. He waved at her and walked over. When he reached her, he put both hands on her shoulders, pulled her close and kissed her on both cheeks.

"Thanks for coming, Alesia." He checked his watch. "Good timing, too; the takeaway should be here in about twenty minutes." He took her arm. "Would you like a cup of tea?" he asked.

"Do you have any bottled water?" She asked.

He laughed. "Don't trust the drinking water, eh?" He grinned at her. "Yes, we have Monk's Farm approved bottled drinking water, bottled here at the bagging shed when we're not bagging chicken shit."

She gave him a playful punch on the arm. "You sod."

He took her back into the kitchen and opened the fridge. He handed her a bottle of Spring water and then pointed to the only chair there. "For you, Madam." Then he pushed himself up and sat on the small worktop. "I can multi-task as well," he said.

Alesia opened the bottle and took a couple of mouthfuls. It was more to cover up her mixed feelings. She knew he was playing with her, but there was a refreshing innocence to it where in no way could she be offended. It felt so natural being there with him; just the two of them.

"So why did you want to see me, Scott?" she asked.

He looked down at his feet, swinging above the floor. It was a little while before he spoke. "I was thinking about you and your hospital appointment, Alesia." He looked at her. "I don't want to be nosey…"

"Yes you do, Scott," she said with a twisted smile on her lips.

He grinned and nodded his head. "Okay, I do, but you can tell me to wind my neck in if you want, and I promise not to say another word on the subject, but I think you was lying just to protect Alex."

That shook her, and it took a while to regain her composure. "I didn't say anything, Scott; other than it was routine."

"No, but your body language said it for you."

Alesia could feel her colour coming up. She took another swig of water. "A woman's problem," she said, taking the bottle away from her mouth. Personal," she added, looking a little sheepish.

Scott dipped his head. "Okay. So how long do you expect to be in hospital?"

She frowned. "Why are you asking me this, Scott?"

"Because I want to know what you are going to do about Alex."

"Alex?" She looked a little flustered. "Why do you want to know?"

He lowered himself off the worktop and leaned up against it. "I figured that you would want him to stay with Heather." He looked back towards the door. "But it's a different ball game now, Alesia; it isn't just Heather and her daughter over at the pub."

"That won't matter. I'm sure Heather will be okay looking after him."

"Why don't you let me look after him?"

She couldn't help pulling a face. "You. What, here?"

He shook his head and smiled. "I don't live here for goodness' sake, Alesia; I live with my dad."

"And you'd take Alex to your dad's place?"

He lifted his chin, tipping his head back. "No; I'd live at your place while you're away."

"My place?"

He nodded. "It makes perfect sense: Alex's routines would be barely disrupted, and he'd be in his own environment, which would help him."

"But you — where would you…?"

"Sleep?" he finished for her. "I'd crash out on your sofa."

"I couldn't let you do that."

"It isn't a problem for me, Alesia. Believe me, I've done that kind of thing dozens of times. And I'm sure Alex would be a lot happier. I'd take him to football training as well if you're still in hospital."

Now she was really flummoxed; here was Scott offering to sleep at her place and she was reluctant to find the right response. She knew what the right answer would be, but how to put it to him without showing her true feelings.

Scott could see it too. He held up his hand. "Okay, Alesia. Let's leave it there. Just understand that I'd be quite happy to do this for you. If you want to go ahead with it, let me know when the time comes." He went to move away from the worktop, then stopped. "Oh, and I'll take you to the hospital as well."

Alesia opened her mouth to say something, but she could see he wasn't going to brook any argument. "Thank you, Scott," she said reluctantly. "That would be helpful."

He stepped forward and held out his hand. "Come on, let's go and see how Heather and Wally are getting on before the takeaway arrives."

She got up, took his hand and allowed herself to be led out of the bagging shed. And Scott never let her hand go until they's walked the short distance to the cottage.

Chapter 16

Denny breezed into the studio; her mind full of the previous day with Martin Longstaff at the Corfe Gallery and the amazing, Chenelle. The lunch date lasted until almost mid-afternoon during which time they'd talked about Denny, her career and the exhibition she would put on at the gallery. He accepted the fact that she could do nothing until the New Year because of her existing agreement with Mitch to stage a Christmas event at the Lafayette. Martin had asked if she could delay her return to Kings Lynn so that he could take her out to dinner that evening. She'd pointed out that she hadn't planned an overnight stop, so had nothing with her. She knew she might have been tempted though; after all, he was a lovely guy, pleasant and attractive. Her assistant at the studio, Isabel, had described him as gorgeous, and she wasn't wrong. But Denny still had high hopes with Mitch, and she didn't want to jeapordise those happy thoughts.

The moment she walked into the studio; April was on her straight away. "How did it go?" she asked, her eyes wide in anticipation.

Denny took her coat off and draped it over the chair by the counter. "Let me get in, April," she said lightly, giving her a quick hug. "One coffee please and then I'll tell you all about it."

April picked up Denny's coat from the chair. "Your coffee is ready for you," she said. "In the office."

Denny blinked. "How did you know…?"

"Tracker," she said. "I knew you was on your way."

Denny nodded. They had a tracker on their phones; something they'd agreed on a long time ago. "Smart girl," she said and followed April into the office.

"Isabel was right," Denny said as she sat down and lifted the coffee to her lips. "Martin Longstaff is absolutely gorgeous." She then went on to tell April how the day unfolded, including the Chenelle revelation. "I invited her down here, so you'll get the chance to see a phenomenon of the fashion world. That's if she decides to come."

"What about Martin Longstaff?" April asked. "Did you invite him as well."

Denny shrugged. "Goes without saying," she said. "I think without him, Chenelle wouldn't bother."

April frowned. "Is she that special then?"

Denny put her cup down. "Well, you've heard about those top models who won't get out of bed for less than ten thousand pounds..."

April nodded her head slowly, and suddenly she had her mobile phone in her hand and was searching for Chenelle's name. Denny watched her remembering she'd done the same thing on the train back to Kings Lynn.

"Chenelle Jenkins," April said quietly, reading the Wikipedia post. She looked up. "Bloody hell," she said pointedly. "And she's coming down here?"

Denny laughed. "April, she's only a woman like you and me. And you might have more in that head of yours than Chenelle has."

April smiled. "Yes, but at least I would get out of bed for less than ten thousand pounds," she joked.

They both started laughing until they heard someone come into the studio as a warning sound buzzed softly in the office.

April got up. "Back to work," she said. "You'll have to tell me more later."

Denny sat there for a while, gently sipping at her coffee, her mind on April and their conversation, and thinking of Mitch and the Lafayette. Life was suddenly opening up for her in a new and unexpected way, and she could only hope it promised a brilliant future.

She sighed, put her empty cup down, booted up her laptop and got herself back down to earth and started searching for the files that she needed for the Lafayette.

And promised herself she would not open the file on the college Prom.

***

The following morning, Wally came out of the house and found Heather pacing out the ground at the rear of the cottage. Christine was sitting in her pushchair watching her mother and, like a lot of youngsters, had that curious expression on her face as she wondered what her mother was doing. It was a brand-new experience for the little girl who was used to the family routines at the pub but being too young to understand why adults behaved the way they did.

"What are you up to Heather?" Wally asked.

Heather looked up from her pacing. "I'm working out how big to have my vegetable garden." She said as she continued taking lengthy steps. "I'm trying to replicate the size of my dad's allotment."

"Ever thought of a tape measure?" he asked. "Perhaps you should buy one."

"I've got one in my sewing box," she told him. "Seemed a tad small to use. I need those big ones the professionals use."

He walked up beside her and gave her a kiss. It stopped her.

"Don't make me lose my count," she protested.

He grabbed her and twirled her around, then kissed her again. "You make me lose my mind," he said grinning at her, "so why shouldn't I make you lose your counting."

She slapped him playfully. "Bugger off; you've got work today."

"Yep, first day with Scott. Should be fun. I'll see you later then, sweetheart."

She grabbed his arm before he could walk off. "Oh, don't forget to ask Scott about the Rotovator; that would be a big help if we can get it fixed."

"Will do," he told her and then went over to Christine, leaned over the pushchair and kissed her. "Love you my precious."

She looked at her dad as he straightened up and started heading off towards the bagging shed.

Scott was already inside when Wally popped his head through the door of the kitchen. "Morning, Scott. Not too late, am I?"

Scott had told him not to turn up too early because there was a delivery due. He looked at his watch. "No, Wally; that's just about right." He looked him up and down. "Yes, that should do," he said. "You won't mind getting that lot dirty, will you?"

Wally knew that Scott was referring to his clothes. He'd been warned to make sure he didn't wear anything he might want to wear in public because his gear would get tainted and smelly despite having to wear overalls.

Scott opened a cupboard and tossed a pair of overalls at him. "Put these on, Wally, then we'll go through."

Wally slipped the overalls on, zipped them up and then put on the rubber boots Scott was holding for him. Once he was ready, Scott nodded and pushed open the door into the bagging shed.

As Wally stepped into the large interior, he was hit by an appalling smell. "Bloody hell," he said, nearly choking. "What the hell is that?"

Wally wasn't referring to the smell, though; it was the mountain of chicken shit that rose up to a height of about twenty feet and seemed to fill almost half of the floor space.

Scott laughed. "That's what we get when we clear a couple of chicken houses. That was delivered this morning, which was why I didn't want you in too early."

Wally followed Scott over to the mountain. He could visualise the chicken houses being cleared by a small tractor and bucket — scraping the muck off the floor and piling it into the back of a lorry, and then the evil smelling load being hauled over here to the bagging shed.

"Is that one lorry load?" he asked.

Scott shook his head. "No takes about four trips." He stepped closer to the mountain and pushed his gloved hand into the muck that was now beginning to steam a little. "Look at this," he said, turning to Wally and holding his hand out. He started brushing at it gently.

Wally frowned and looked at Scott in astonishment. "Beetles?"

Scott grinned. "Yeah; they love this stuff."

"Bloody hell; that's creepy."

Scott tossed the much back on to the pile and brushed his hands. "You get used to it."

"So, what happens now?"

Scott started the tour for him. "Right. You use the small tractor there to bucket the stuff into the Riddler. The trash that comes off is scrapped. The finer shit then gets conveyed up to the top of the bagging machine hopper, which is there for you or whoever is working it to discharge into the bags, stitched and stacked ready for transporting to our customers."

"Customers?"

Scott nodded. "Nurseries, garden centres and some DIY stores." He could see the astonished look on Wally's face. "It's business, Wally. You didn't think we dumped all this, did you?"

"And this is what I'll be doing?"

"For a start, Wally. It won't take you long to get the hang of it. Then I can leave you here and spend more time over at the chicken sheds keeping an eye on dad." He then put his arm around Wally's shoulder and gave him a gently hug. "Think you can handle it?"

Wally nodded still a little wide eyed though. "Think so."

"Good, so let's make a start. I'll take you through it all starting with the small bucket tractor and digging out the mountain."

And so, Wally started his first day as another 'Chicken George'.

***

Alesia had managed to get over to Denny's house after Denny had called her saying she wanted to talk to her about the Corfe Gallery and her day in London. Alesia had Alex with her, but he was playing a video game on Denny's huge TV screen, headphones on and in no need of conversation with his mother or 'Aunt Denny'.

The two women were sitting in the kitchen at the breakfast bench. Denny had a glass of wine, but Alesia was drinking coffee. Denny had given Alesia a detailed account of her Monday trip to London, waxing heavily on the gorgeous Martin Longstaff and his adorable friend, Chenelle.

"You can imagine my shock," Denny was saying, "when he told me who the woman was in that photograph. And when he said how sought after she was — well; you could have knocked me over with a feather, as they say."

Alesia smiled at the thought. Then for some inexplicable reason her mind shot back to the night of the Prom and being called the Ice Queen. She mentioned that to Denny, her eyebrows lifted by the smile building on her face. "I wonder if she'll end up delivering frozen fish like me," she said with a giggle. "Would she be dressed as colourful then, or in rubber apron and wellies?"

Denny laughed. Then she stopped suddenly. "Alesia, why don't we give you a makeover and photograph you?" Alesia was about to protest but Denny grabbed her by the wrist. "It isn't such a terrible idea," she said, her hand holding Alesia's arm firmly. "You was gorgeous then, and you're gorgeous now." She fluttered her other hand when she saw Alesia's mouth opening in protest as she shook her head. "I can use it in the exhibition. And listen," she said urgently, "when Scott sees it, he'll be knocked out by it. And he'll dump that Joanna woman if he hasn't already done so." Her expression changed to one of subtle pleading, brightening up as she did so. "Please?"

Alesia sighed and nodded. "Okay, but not because I want to impress Scott. Besides," she added, "him and Joanna are going back to America to get married."

Denny's face dropped in surprise and shock. "Seriously?"

Alesia nodded and explained how she'd found out.

"Have you asked him about it?"

She shook her head. "Good heavens, no; it's none of my business."

"But you could ask out of curiosity, surely?" Denny countered. "Make it conversational like."

Alesia looked thoughtful. "And when he says yes, what do I say? Oh, really?"

Denny leaned back on her stool. "That's a blow."

"Why?"

She gave Alesia a peculiar look. "I thought you two were actually going to make a go of it."

"What, because we went out to dinner together. One night?"

Denny shrugged. "Well, I did think it was a little bit special for you. Will you be seeing him again?" she asked.

Alesia twirled her empty cup, twisting it back and forth. "He's asked me if he can look after Alex when I go into hospital for my op."

Denny leaned forward. "You told him about that?"

She shook her head. "Not exactly, but it kind of come out in conversation. I tried to play it down, but he could see right through me. He told me my body language betrayed me."

Denny chuckled. "Easily done. So, what did you say?"

"I said yes."

"So, what will he do with Alex? Take him to his dad's"

Alesia grinned a little sheepishly. "No; he's going to crash down at mine. He said it would be better for Alex to stay at home in his own environment while I'm in hospital."

Denny reached for the wine bottle and poured herself another glass. She offered the bottle to Alesia who shook her head. "No thanks, Denny; I really have to stick to coffee. Can't afford to lose my licence." She looked at Denny who had a whimsical smile on her face and could see what was going through her friend's mind. "No, Denny," she said. "Scott will crash on the sofa — not with me! Besides, I'll be in hospital, won't I?"

Denny took a sip of wine and put her glass down. "Are you worried about the op?"

Alesia shook her head. "It's supposed to be a straightforward procedure. They said the cancer is contained within the appendix and nowhere else. It's not unusual apparently, so they are quite happy to go ahead with it."

"And you?"

Alesia shrugged. "I don't have any choice, do I?"

Denny put her hand on Alesia's, but gently this time. "My God, Alesia, you are certainly going through it, aren't you? I wish there was some way we could go back fifteen years and change everything."

Alesia smiled and chuckled softly. "Yeah, then I could have stayed on that bloody dance floor with Scott."

Chapter 17

Wally's first day at work gave Heather a sense of being complete. Even though it had been barely two days, she was happier than she had been for a long, long time. Her days without Wally while he was serving his prison term had been like a sentence for her too. Sure, she had her little Christine to care for, and she enjoyed many happy moments with her like most mums do with their children. Living with her parents was okay, but trying to cope with that kind of family life was stressful, and in those moments when she was alone, the loneliness crept in and increased her longing to have Wally back with her. The only respite she could manage were those brief periods when she could spend a couple of hours with Alesia and enjoy the kind of girlie moments while her mum and dad looked after Alex and Christine.

But today was her first day as a wife looking after her family in her own place, albeit a rented cottage on a kind of annex to a chicken farm. Today, her husband was at work and would be coming home for a meal when his day was done. And as she moved around the cottage making changes (several), she was able to role play and feed her imagination, particularly about the allotment and the plans she had when Wally had fixed the Rotovator.

Although he didn't know when he would be home, Wally did call during the afternoon to tell her that he was with Scott over at the chicken houses watching the cleaning and getting to see what a chicken house looked like when it was full of chickens. Monk's Farm had four houses; two were in use, while the other two were being prepared for hundreds of young chicks.

It was five o'clock when he called to say he was on his way home. Heather's pulse rate went up a notch as she started getting his meal ready and telling Christine that her daddy was coming home. Heather was like a kid, but it was such a new experience for her that she couldn't help getting excited about it.

Until Wally walked through the door and Heather flung her arms around him.

"Oh, my God," she said as she was hugging him. "What's that smell?"

He pushed her away gently, a beaming smile on his face. "Chicken shit," he said with a laugh. "And Scott has told me not to stand too close to a fire because the smell grows with the warmth."

She squeezed her face up into a deep frown. "Ugh! You'd better have a shower, Wally; I can't have you sitting at the table smelling like that."

He put on a puzzled look and held his arms out. "Why not? You get used to it."

She slapped him playfully on the arm. "Upstairs! Now! And throw your clothes out of the window when you're done."

He grabbed her and pulled her close. "You want to come upstairs with me, sweetheart? Could be fun."

She pushed him away. "Off you go. I'll have your dinner on the table in fifteen minutes."

"Where's my little Christine first?"

She rolled her eyes. "Sitting at the table in her high chair waiting for her daddy like a good girl."

He nodded. "Right. Christine first, then a shower."

She watched him disappear into the kitchen, heard him say hello to Christine. She thought she heard him say something about the chickens before coming out of the kitchen and going upstairs for his shower. He smacked Heather playfully on the bottom as he slid past her in the small passageway.

Heather went into the kitchen shaking her head slowly, but with a smile on her face and a comforting feeling running through her veins. Wally was home and they had so much to talk about, just like most normal, happy couples.

***

Wally sat back, his stomach full and a contented feeling swarming all over him. "That was lovely. Thank you, sweetheart."

"Now you've eaten," she said, "do you want to tell me about your day?"

"I'll wash up first."

She shook her head. "No, you won't; you've been at work."

"So?"

"So, tell me about your day."

He knew he wouldn't win against her, so he told her how his day had gone and what he believed Scott expected from him, and how he saw his own future panning out as an employee on Monk's Farm.

"I didn't realise how big it all was," he told her. "Did you know there's a road over the other side of the bagging shed?" He pointed over his shoulder using his thumb. "That's where the lorries come in from the chicken houses. Scott took me over there." He shook his head. "I didn't understand what kind of an operation it was until I saw what's involved."

"Where will you fit in, Wally?"

He leaned forward putting his forearms on the table. "Well, that's the thing; I'm not sure what Scott is planning. I have a feeling he wants me to part manage the business while he oversees everything. It wouldn't be until after his dad retires though. Unless he goes back to the States."

"Has he said anything about that?"

He shook his head. "Not yet; it could just be me reading between the lines though." He shrugged. "But for now, it will just be me working in the bagging shed I guess."

Heather started gathering up the dishes. "Well one thing's for sure, Wally; Scott won't be staying." She put the dishes into the sink. "He's going back to America — he's going to marry that Joanna woman."

Wally sat bolt upright in his chair. "America? Married?"

She nodded as she came back to the table and stood there, her hands on her hips. "That's what I heard, which means it will be you and his dad, no-one else."

He frowned, a puzzled look on his face. "So, if his dad decided to retire and sell the business, I'd be out of a job."

She picked up the remainder of the dirty tableware. "And we'd probably have to move out of this place. Unless we had squatters' rights."

He shook his head vigorously. "No; I don't think Scott would do that. We talked a lot when he came to see me in prison, Heather. He's not like that. And where did you hear about him getting married?"

Heather told him of the conversation Alesia's boy had reported to her from the training ground.

Wally snorted disdainfully. "Nah; he's only a kid. Probably got it all wrong."

Heather went back to the sink. "Well, you could always ask Scott when you see him tomorrow."

Wally grunted. "He won't be there; he's seeing Joanna tomorrow. He's asked me to clean up the bagging shed and oil some of the machinery. We're due another mountain of chicken shit later this week and Scott says it's important to start each new bagging operation with a clean slate."

"So, ask him when you see him," she said. "Tell him you need some positive idea of what role he wants you to play and if there's a long term prospect for you. If he can't come up with an answer, you'll have to start looking for a driving job."

"Which means we would have to move out."

She put the bits and pieces she'd been holding back on the table. "We're jumping the gun here, Wally, aren't we. We're putting two and two together and coming up with five, so let's cool it, play our cards close to our chests and wait and see what happens."

He could see she was right; there was no sense in getting worked up over something over which they had no control. Then he suddenly thought of something that would cheer her up.

"Oh, I spoke to him about the Rotovator. He said it was okay to have a look at it and get it running. So maybe this weekend I'll make a start on it."

She sat down on his lap and put her arms around him. "Do chickens stop for weekends too?" she asked, giving him a wicked smile.

He laughed and gave her a kiss. "I'll drag it out of the shed before it gets too dark then and have a quick look. Okay?"

She kissed him back. "And say nothing to Scott about him getting married and moving to America; it's only hearsay." She got up from his lap. "I have work to do," she said, "so why not take your daughter up for a bath and get her ready for bed?"

He watched her pick up those last few bits as he got up and lifted little Christine out of her highchair. He knew he had two people now to love and cherish, and he would make sure, despite the talk they'd just had, that he would never let them down.

Chapter 18

Denny had agreed to meet Mitch in the café at Lafayette's so they could plan ahead and, hopefully, make progress towards the Christmas exhibition, but Mitch had stalled that because he wanted to know how Denny's trip to London and the Corfe Gallery had turned out.

"Well, I was really impressed," she said when he broached the subject. "Everything about Martin's studio was exactly how I could imagine mine to look."

He shook his head. "But that wouldn't be you, Denny. Your image, your whole *raison d'etre* has to be reflected in the way in which you present yourself to the world of fashion. You are not Martin Longstaff; you are Denny..." He shook his head and fluttered his hand. "Whatever you want to call yourself."

Denny smiled. "Wow, are you into this kind of thing?"

He shrugged. "Working at Harrods taught me a great deal. Everything about style, nuance, background. Even the bloody food and the way it was displayed."

Denny chortled. "Yes, but I don't think Denny 'whoever you want to be' will sound right somehow."

Mitch bobbed his head one way and then the other. "How about an Italian name?" He pursed his lips together and screwed his face up to make it look like he was thinking hard. "How about Denise Versace?"

"That's taken, silly. Of course, I could always call myself Chanel."

His expression changed immediately. "Oh, for a moment there I thought you said 'Chenelle'. You didn't though, did you?"

That set Denny back for a few seconds. "Do you know her?"

His eyes widened. "Oh yes; she's one good looking lady. She did some fashion shoots at Harrod's. I got to know her quite well. And Martin of course," he added.

Denny couldn't help feeling a little put out at his reaction to Chenelle's name. "Well, you may get the opportunity to meet her again," she told him. "Martin said he would come and visit my studio. Chenelle said she would like to come as well. Naturally I said yes."

Mitch showed genuine surprise. "Wow; that's quite a coup. Perhaps you could ask them for some help with the exhibition. You know; cast their eye over it, see what they think."

Denny leaned closer to the table. "But then it wouldn't reflect my Denny 'whoever you wanted to be' image, would it?"

He grinned. "*Touché*. You're right, but it would be nice to see Chenelle again. And, I suppose, for you to see Martin?"

The noise in the café was beginning to build up as more and more people came in for a cup of tea or coffee and a piece of cake. Denny wanted to get on with planning the exhibition, and they weren't exactly getting anywhere with talk about Martin and Chenelle. And she did think mentioning Chenelle's name had distracted Mitch, so she suggested to him that they started on the business of how and where to begin.

"Well," Mitch said when Denny asked if they could begin. "I've decided to give you a whole window where you can showcase your business and introduce the general public to the thoughts behind the exhibition, and the tie-up between Lafayette's and the Corfe Gallery. One of the fashion shoots at Harrod's that I mentioned earlier was in one of the big windows facing the Brompton Road. It was brilliant. So many people stopped and spent time looking in, it was unbelievable."

Denny sat back in the chair. "That sounds lovely, Mitch. Let's have a look, shall we?"

They got up from the table. Mitch came round and took Denny by the arm. She looked at him quickly. Their eyes locked together for a brief second. Then the moment was gone, and he steered her away from the café and into the shop.

***

Scott was talking to Wally at one of the chicken houses when his phone rang. He put his hand up to Wally and pointed outside. Wally nodded and waved him away as he stepped through the chickens scrabbling around on the floor. There was very little room for him to place his feet, but he was managing. Him and Scott had been checking the small, moving feed conveyor that curved through the chicken house like a toy train set, and it wasn't unusual to find a chicken had managed to get a leg trapped while pecking away at the food. There was often little option but to wring the chicken's neck and dump it outside in the trash bin if they couldn't free it successfully. Fortunately, it didn't happen very often, but it was just part of the training Scott was putting him through.

Scott opened his phone and saw it was Alesia.

"Morning, Alesia, what can I do for you, my darling?"

Alesia loved it when he said things like that even though she knew it meant nothing. "I have my hospital appointment, Scott. It's on Monday. They want me in by nine o'clock."

"Right, fine," he told her. "I'll come over at eight o'clock. You have Alex ready, and we can drop him off at school on the way."

Alesia hesitated before asking him about staying. "Would you like to come over the day before? You can start your sofa surfing then,"

"I can't; I'm seeing Joanna. We're going out for a meal. Lot to talk about. But don't worry," he said brightly, "I'll be there Monday morning, first thing."

Alesia was about to say something, but Scott hadn't finished.

"I have to go now; I'm putting Wally through his paces, and I don't want him treading on too many chickens. 'Bye."

Alesia hadn't got a clue what he was talking about, but her heart had slumped when he mentioned Joanna. She turned her phone off and put it into her pocket. Then she started the van and pulled away from the fish factory to get on with her daily deliveries. She was not in the least bit happy, but that was her life, and she had to accept it. Or rather; she had to accept that Scott and Joanna were an item, and it wouldn't be too long before they had gone, and she could forget him.

Well, she could try.

***

Alesia felt uneasy about the forthcoming hospital visit. Despite telling herself repeatedly that there was nothing to worry about, she still carried that alarming thought in her head that they might find something else when they opened her up. She'd had little sleep, such was the worry, and was up by five o'clock sitting at the kitchen table nursing a cup of tea. Breakfast was out of the question because she'd been asked to avoid eating anything on the day of the op, which meant from midnight.

Another thing on her mind was the thought that Scott was taking her to the hospital and would be looking after Alex. He would be like a surrogate husband and father to her and her son, and she so wished it could be reality and not a fleeting period where she would literally have Scott's fullest attention and not have to share him with Joanna.

She roused Alex a little earlier than normal; something the Alex objected to, but she needed company. And as she literally paced up and down and checked her small case for the umpteenth time, she was aware that Alex was watching her every movement.

Eventually she sat down at the table. Alex had finished his cereal and toast and was about to take his empty plate to the sink when she stopped him.

"I'll do that," she said a little firmly and stood up to start gathering the plates.

He sat back on the stool. "Are you scared, mum?" he asked.

Alesia made a brave attempt at shrugging the question off. "Scared? No, of course not." She waved her hands about. "It's just like, well, going to the dentist. Not even as bad as that," she added.

"Mandy's mum said it was sad that you had no-one and would be in hospital on your own."

She grimaced. "Mandy's mum says a lot of things, Alex; not all true. I'll have people coming to see me. There's you, Scott, Heather will as well." She shrugged and tried to put a brave face on it despite knowing that

Mandy's mum had spoken the truth. "Now, perhaps you'd better get ready for school; Scott will be here soon."

Alex slid away from the table. "Okay mum."

He left her standing there wringing her hands together, her mind hopping all over the place. She could feel the tears stinging her eyes, not because she was about to go into hospital, but because Scott would turn up, be cheerful and would try to act as though everything was fine. But he had someone in his life; someone who loved him and was about to take him from her. She sat down, put her face in her hands and sobbed her heart out.

Chapter 19

Denny always liked Monday mornings; that was the kind of workaholic she was. Had she worked in a factory, or delivered frozen fish like Alesia, it might have been a different matter, but Mondays meant opening the studio and freshening her mind to the endless possibilities and opportunities that seem to come her way regularly. Denny would have opened on a Sunday, but her conscience would have been pricked if she opened on the Lord's Day of rest. She was not religious, but her father always cited that as the reason he remained closed on Sundays, and Denny was not about to change it.

One of the reasons for Denny to have a spring in her step was that she'd spent a great deal of time with Mitch at the Lafayette, then Saturday evening having dinner with him. Sunday, they spent some time up on the coast at Hunstanton reliving old memories of their youth when a trip to 'Sunny Hunny' was always on the cards at weekends and holidays. But the extra ingredient for Denny that morning was that she'd received a phone call from Chenelle to say she would love to pay her a visit — today if possible. What a joy, she'd thought to herself when she'd finished the conversation with Chenelle; to have a world-famous fashion model in her studio. She couldn't wait to tell Alice and Isabel.

The studio was open, as ever, when Denny arrived. Alice was there to greet her with a coffee. Denny took the coffee from her.

"Is Isabel here?" she asked.

Alice lifted her eyes and looked up at the ceiling. "She's in the cutting room."

"Can you ask her to come down to the office please, Alice? You too," she added.

Alice frowned. "Ooh, I don't like the sound of that. You're not going to let one of us go, are you?"

Denny thought she'd tease Alice. "Just come to the office," she said. "With Isabel."

Alice turned away abruptly, leaving Denny with a growing smile on her face. She went through to the office and sat down at the desk, opened her laptop and stared reflectively at the desktop image of her father, thinking how proud he would have been with the way in which she'd grown the business. He was suffering from Dementia, and sometimes struggled to understand how well she was doing.

She heard the door go and looked up as Alice walked in with Isabel. Alice had a worried look on her face, whereas Isabel's expression was one of curiosity.

"Morning girls," Denny said cheerfully. "Why such gloomy faces?"

The two women looked at each other and then back at Denny. "You're going to sack one of us, aren't you?" Alice said.

Denny laughed. "Of course not. How would I manage without you?"

"So why…?"

"Sorry, Alice, I just wanted a bit of fun, that's all. And I have some news which you might like to hear."

"Which is?"

"Chenelle is coming down here today. She wants to have a look at our studio and talk about the show at the Lafayette."

Isabel slid on to the visitor's chair. "Chenelle from London?"

Denny nodded. "On her own; not with Martin."

Alice looked a little puzzled. "You mean the expensive model who wouldn't get out of bed for less than ten grand?"

Denny nodded again, this time with a big grin on her face and her eyebrows raised. "That one," she said.

"So, you want us to get this place cleaned up or something?" Alice asked.

This time, Denny shook her head. "No, of course not; Chenelle is not coming for a fashion shoot. I couldn't afford her anyway. No, she's coming as a friend."

"Some friend," Isabel said. "They don't come much higher in the fashion world than that."

Denny looked at her watch. "She's due in at the station at twelve o'clock. I'll bring her here first and then take her out to lunch later." A thought crossed her mind. "I'd better ask Mitch if he wants to meet her," she said. If she wants to talk about the show at the Lafayette, he's the best one to ask."

"Not really," Isabel said. "It's your show, Denny; Lafayette's is just another venue. Mitch can only advise on space and timings etc, but you, you're the one who will be at the heart of it. Don't forget that."

Denny knew Isabel was right, but she still needed, wanted, Mitch to be involved.

***

Alesia heard Scott's car as he pulled up outside the old Victorian house where she lived in her rented flat. She glanced out of the window, gave Scott a quick wave and called Alex.

"Scott's here. Have you got your school things ready?"

"Yes, mum." He walked into the small kitchen carrying his backpack. "Have you got your hospital stuff ready?" he asked in a voice that almost mimicked Alesia's.

"Cheeky sod," she said and rubbed the top of his head. "Let's go."

They hurried out of the house and clambered into Scott's mud splattered Range Rover. Alesia gave him a quick kiss on the cheek and made herself as comfortable as she could beside him. Alex got himself sorted out in the back and snapped his seat belt on.

Scott let them both settle before turning and facing Alesia. "Are you okay?"

He didn't think she looked too special. He wondered if she'd been crying. He thought that maybe the prospect of the operation could be playing on her mind. He could understand if she had, particularly as she was on her own. Loneliness was something that had to be endured, and he was sure Alesia would feel that loneliness despite having Alex.

"Yes," she said brightly. "I'm fine."

He smiled and put the car into gear. "You okay in the back, young man?" he shouted as he pulled away from the house. He got no answer because Alex had already got his head buried in his mobile phone and was miles away with his earpieces in.

Scott smiled. Kids, he thought.

They said very little on the way to school. Scott didn't want to get involved in a discussion about the operation while Alex was in the car. He didn't know what Alesia was thinking, but he had a fairly good idea. When they arrived at the school, Alesia got out of the car and walked with Alex up to the school gates. Scott watched as Alesia wrapped her arms around Alex. It was a lengthy hug from what Scott could see and it spoke volumes to him.

She came back to the car after waiting until Alex was out of sight. She had her arms wrapped around her waist and a tight expression on her face. She got into the car, glanced quickly at Scott and burst into tears.

Scott released his seat belt and moved closer. He took hold of her arm and closed his hand around it. Then he reached around her shoulders and put his hand on her other arm. He pulled her in close and held her like that as she cried into his chest. He said nothing, just held her tight and let her cry out until she sniffed loudly and slowly pulled away.

As he let her go, she looked up at him. "Thank you, Scott," she said, and then she made a feeble attempt to clean his tear-stained shirt with the palm of her hand. And as she did that, she allowed herself to think of the moment he held her and took her mind back to the night of the Prom when she first realised how strong and comforting his hands felt.

She sat up and pulled a handkerchief from her pocket. Scott watched as she tidied herself up.

"I thought ladies only used tissues," he said.

She grinned and blew her nose. "When you deliver frozen fish for a living, Scott, a tissue wouldn't last five minutes."

He chuckled at that. Then he clipped his seatbelt on and started the car. "Time to get you to hospital, Alesia," he said and pulled away from the kerb.

And Alesia felt a little happier. Not a lot, but that moment in his arms lifted her spirits more than she could ever have imagined.

***

Denny finished off the conversation about Chenelle's visit and let Alice and Isabel get on with whatever they were doing before she got to the studio. Once they were gone, she pulled up the calendar on her computer and began looking at what was planned and what was forthcoming. Then she tipped her head back and swore. This day was clearly shown as the day Alesia was due to go into hospital, and Denny had forgotten everything about it. She grabbed her phone and hit the speed dial for Alesia. As the phone started calling, Denny sat there tapping out a tattoo on the desk with her fingers, hoping she could catch Alesia in time and wish her all the best; it was the least she could do.

"Hello, Denny."

She took in a sharp breath. "Oh, Alesia. I'm sorry I didn't call you earlier. Where are you?"

"We've just arrived at reception. I'm waiting to be admitted. Scott is with me."

"Scott?"

"Yes, didn't you know he offered to bring me here? He's looking after Alex too."

Denny felt her whole body relax knowing that Scott was with her. "I'm sorry I couldn't be with you, Alesia," she said. "I feel so guilty."

"Well don't be — you have a business to run. I'm fine."

No, you're not, Denny thought to herself. "Will I be able to visit you later?"

"I don't know. It's best that you phone Scott; he'll know what's happening."

"Okay, Alesia. I'm really sorry. Good luck. Love you. 'Bye."

"Love you too."

Alesia turned her phone off and looked at Scott who was sitting beside her. "Poor Denny. She's worried about me."

"So am I," Scott muttered. "Believe it or not," he added.

Alesia nodded her head briefly. "I'm glad."

"What, that I'm worried?"

Alesia laughed. "No, silly; I didn't mean it like that." She gave him a nudge with her arm. "It's nice to know you have…" She stumbled on her words and tried to unscramble them in her mind. "Well, that you like me enough to worry about me."

Scott turned and faced her. "I've always liked you, Alesia. Don't you ever forget that." His voice was stern as he said that.

She was about to say something to him when a nurse came up to them. They both looked up at her.

"Alesia Merriman?"

Scott gave Alesia a quick look at the mention of her maiden name. He thought she was still Mrs Grant — Simeon's surname.

Alesia stood up.

"Are you ready?" the nurse asked. Alesia said she was. Then the nurse spoke to Scott. "I'm afraid you can't come through, sir, but your wife will be fine, I assure you."

Scott looked confused and a little uncomfortable. He wanted to explain the situation, but before he could get the words out of his mouth, Alesia kissed him.

"'Bye darling. See you soon. And don't worry."

He watched as she walked away with the nurse and felt an immense satisfaction at Alesia's thoughtful and crafty way of helping him out of his dilemma. He shook his head and smiled, and then took himself off to the business of chicken muck and not being able to get Alesia out of his mind.

Chapter 20

Denny had phoned Mitch from the studio, and they were now waiting at the station for Chenelle to arrive. Denny wondered what outfit she would be wearing and said so to Mitch.

"I wonder what she'll be wearing," she said in an aside to him. "She looked outrageously gorgeous when I saw her at the Corfe Gallery."

Mitch grinned but kept his eye on the platform where they were expecting the London train to arrive. "She never let us down at Harrods, you know — outrageous or not."

"Did you see much of her?"

He glanced quickly at her. "Yes. I think we did about four fashion shoots with her. We became pretty good friends too. You know, hanging out with a bunch of like-minded geeks and professionals."

Denny laughed. You're no geek, Mitch. Might be a professional though."

He put his arm around her shoulders and gave her a quick hug. "Thank you, Denny."

Denny liked the feel of his arm around her, but it only lasted a second or two, and it was never meant to be a touch of familiarity — more like a response to a wisecrack.

"Here's the train," she said.

They watched in silence as the train rolled almost silently to a halt. The carriage doors opened as the passengers started stepping out on to the platform.

"There she is," Mitch exclaimed, pointing his finger. Then he put his hand to his mouth. "Oh my God, look at her. Bloody gorgeous."

Denny stared open-mouthed. Chenelle was wearing a long frock coat with a fur-trimmed collar. Her hair was straight and hung down to her shoulders. She had a white, polo-neck jumper on which emphasised her breasts, and slim, tight-fitting trousers. Her shoes were flat but, Denny assumed, would be Jimmy Choos or something equally extravagant. And she walked with a kind of languid grace as though she was on the catwalk, even though she was dragging a small suitcase on wheels behind her.

Denny shook her head slowly, her mind full of envy and amazement. "God, I could never carry that off."

Suddenly, Chenelle started waving madly when she saw the two of them. Denny and Mitch both waved back, and it was all Denny could do not to jump up and down.

Chenelle came through the waist-high turnstiles and came over to them, a huge smile on her face. She let go of the suitcase and flung her arms around both of them. Then she pushed back and looked at Mitch.

"Hello handsome. Have you missed me?" She grabbed Denny in a bear hug and kissed her on the cheek. "It's so good to see you, Denny."

Denny tried to return the hug but gave up and returned the kiss instead. "Lovely to see you too, Chenelle. You look gorgeous by the way," she said.

Chenelle made a face. "What, these old things I just threw on?" Then she laughed.

"Don't I get a kiss too?" Mitch asked.

Chenelle put a hand on her hip. "Oh, alright then; if you insist." Then she kissed him on the lips.

Denny couldn't hide the look of surprise on her face, but it shook her a little. And it made her wonder just how close the two of them had been when they hung out together in London.

But she shoved those thoughts to one side and hooked her arm through Chenelle's. "Come on then, let's get you to the studio and once we've had a coffee, we can head over to Lafayette's."

Mitch reached down for Chenelle's case. "I've got this," he said, and the three of them walked out of the station and over to the taxi rank while Denny was trying to rationalise all the thoughts now running riot though her head.

***

Scott left the hospital and drove over to Alesia's flat. He had already planned to do that because he wanted to familiarise himself with the layout and where things were generally. He knew he would have Alex to answer any questions, but he still wanted to spend some time there on his own.

He parked outside the Victorian dwelling and lifted his overnight bag from off the back seat, then let himself into the house with the keys Alesia had given him. The hallway didn't have a great deal of light coming through the front door, and the dark brown wood of the panelling and staircase didn't help either. He checked to see if there was any mail for Alesia, but her pigeonhole was empty. He then walked over to her door and let himself in.

He dropped his bag on to the floor beneath the coat hooks on which were several coats. There was a small table with an empty bowl, probably for the house keys, he thought, so he dropped the keys into the bowl. Beneath the table were several pairs of shoes. It was obvious from their sizes that they were either Alesia's or Alex's.

He looked around and then went through the first door, which led into the kitchen. The window overlooked the front garden, and he remembered Alesia waving at him from there that morning. The kitchen worktops were not as cluttered as he would have imagined; just some condiment jars, a radio, a small TV and a photograph of a woman who Scott vaguely remembered. It was Alesia's mother.

He went from the kitchen and into the lounge. He looked at the sofa, which was where he intended sleeping. He was too big for it, but what the hell, he thought, it was only likely to be for a couple of nights. A TV sat on a cabinet inside which he could see the Router and soundbox for probably SKY, or maybe BT.

He walked over to the small sideboard and picked up a framed photo. It was of him and Alesia at the Prom. They were dancing. He studied it for some time, his mind going back to that moment when he held her in his arms and wished it could have gone on for ever. He sighed and put the photo back. There was another one of Alesia holding a newborn baby and smiling like all new mums do. There was no-one else in the photograph. He assumed the baby was Alex. He sighed and shook his head. Poor Alesia, he thought, alone with just the baby. He knew her mother had died a long time ago. He had no knowledge of Alesia's father and wasn't sure if he was ever around.

He went through to Alex's bedroom and wasn't surprised at the explosion of colour and posters, most of which were of Harry Kane and Spurs footballers. There were other posters too; some of action shots from Sci-Fi films like Star Wars and Batman. It was a typical boy's room. Alex's laptop lay folded on his bed, which was made. He wondered about that. There was a TV, albeit a smallish one. And evidence of decorative lighting; none of which was switched on.

He went back into the kitchen and made himself a cup of tea. He checked the food cupboard and fridge just to make sure there was no need for him to buy anything. Then he sat down at the kitchen table with his cup of tea and thought about Alesia and the way she lived.

And the fact that the only photo of a man in the flat was the one where he was dancing with Alesia.

***

"Is Scott in this morning?"

Wally had been working in the bagging shed and had popped over to the cottage for a cup of tea. He could have made one for himself in the small kitchen, but as there was no-one else working with him that morning, he wasn't allowed to operate any machinery under the Health and Safety rules imposed by Scott. He'd been cleaning up generally, ready for when Scott put in an appearance.

He took a sip of his tea and looked over at Heather who had asked the question. She was standing at the sink peeling potatoes.

"No, he's taken Alesia to hospital. He said he would probably be in before lunch."

"I must not forget to phone her this evening," she said as she dropped a potato into a saucepan. "That's if she's okay after the op."

"Why not go in and see her? I'm sure Scott would be happy to take you."

She half turned. "Do you think so?"

"Heather, he's not an alien; he'd be happy to, I'm sure."

She turned round and leaned her backside up against the sink. "What's the arrangement between him and Alesia?"

Wally shook his head and shrugged. "I don't know. I think he's doing this as a friend, nothing more. Besides," he added, "he's got a girl, hasn't he? Joanna."

Heather looked a bit thoughtful. "Yeah, I wonder where she is then."

Wally chuckled and shook his head. "Could be anywhere. It's none of our business, anyway, is it?"

Heather mumbled something and turned around, picked up another potato and started peeling it.

"Wally?"

He could tell by the sound of her voice she was about to ask him for a favour. He had no idea what was coming but the odds were that she would get what she wanted, whatever it was.

"What." He put as much disinterest in his voice as he could.

"I want driving lessons,"

His head shot up. "What? Driving lessons? Whatever for?"

She turned round, a half-peeled potato in one hand and the peeler in the other. "I finished rotovating that patch this morning and I'm ready to start planting some vegetables. It got me thinking."

Wally uttered a long groan. "Go on then."

"Well, I was thinking about the market and the veg and stuff I take there most weeks. You know — from Dad's allotment." She shifted and making a point with the hand holding the potato. "I'll probably grow far too much for us, so what we don't need, I can take to market."

"And you think you need a driving licence for that."

She shook her head. "No, I'm thinking beyond that. I would like to have a stall of my own one day. When Christine is at school," she added. "And I would need a van or a pick-up truck." She paused and looked up at the ceiling as though imagining her vision and the fruits of her labour. "And if I make a success of it, I could open a small farm shop here in one of the barns."

Wally got up from the table, went over to Heather, took the half-peeled potato and peeler from her and laid it on the kitchen sink. He then put his arms around her and looked lovingly into her face.

"One step at a time, sweetheart. Plant your vegetables and once they start showing, you can have your driving lessons."

She flung her arms around him and kissed him firmly on the mouth. "I knew you would say yes," she said, pulling away.

He grinned at her and nodded. "I know; that's why you married me."

Chapter 21

Scott sat at the table nursing his cup of tea thinking about Alesia and that photograph. In a way it made him a little sad and reflective, knowing what the photograph was telling him. He thought about Simeon too and how everyone knew, or at least expected, Simeon and Alesia to end up as a couple. He also thought of Joanna and how she had suddenly come back into his life, which kind of muddied the waters for him. And then he thought of Alex and how that boy had no father in his life — no Alpha Male to help him negotiate those moments that can have such an effect on a boy. He smiled at the thought of Alex wanting to be as good as Harry Kane. It was never likely to happen, but with a dad, they could at least live the dream together.

His phone suddenly vibrated on the table beside him. He picked it up and looked at the screen. No number was showing. He frowned and swiped the screen.

"Hello."

"Ah, is that Mr. Scott Jones?"

"It is."

"This is Mrs Jennings at Gaywood Primary. We have Alex Merriman here. His mother gave us your number as a contact while she's in hospital."

He nodded. "Yes. Is there a problem then?"

"Well, Alex has got himself into a bit of trouble. He had a fight with another boy. He's okay, but I think in the circumstances it might be better if you could pick him up and take him home. Alex isn't usually the kind of boy who gets into fights, but I think it has something to do with his mother being in hospital."

Scott couldn't help smiling. "Sure, I'll come to the school now. Who do I ask for when I get there?"

"Thank you, Mister Jones. Ask for me at reception, Mrs Jennings."

Scott thanked her and turned the phone off. He finished his tea, washed the cup and left it on the drainer and went off to pick up young Alex.

Alex was brought to reception looking rather sheepish and handed over to Scott. He offered Alex his hand thinking that would be the right thing to do, but Alex ignored it. Scott looked at Mrs. Jennings, shrugged and thanked her, then walked Alex out through the school gates to his car.

He couldn't see any damage on Alex, no signs of cuts or bruising on his face, so he guessed it was probably the boy's ego that had taken a mauling.

"Are you okay?" he asked as he opened the car door for him, Alex simply nodded and climbed into the passenger seat. Scott decided not to ask him anything until they were home, but Alex pre-empted him.

"Am I going to get into trouble?"

Scott looked at him as he started the car. "What for?"

"Fighting."

"Not from me, you won't," Scott told him.

"What about mum?"

Scott put the car into gear and pulled away from the kerb. "Who's going to tell her? You?"

Alex glanced up at him. "She'll need to know, won't she?"

Scott shook his head. "No, Alex; your mum has enough on her plate without being told you was fighting."

"You're not going to tell her?"

"No. It will be our secret, okay?"

Alex brightened a little. "Okay."

Scott thought he could chalk that up as a 'win' in his efforts to develop a solid relationship with the lad. He let it rest there and nothing else was said between them until they got home.

When they arrived back at the house, Scott opened the door for him and watched as he disappeared into his bedroom. He allowed himself a few minutes to think about how he was going to play this, but in the end he decided it would be better to let Alex take the lead. He knocked on Alex's bedroom door.

"Can I come in, Alex?" He waited for a response then knocked again. Suddenly the door swung open. He saw Alex's back as the boy left him there and walked back to the bed and sat down.

"You want a cup of tea, coffee, lemonade?" he asked.

Alex shook his head. "No thanks."

"Are you feeling okay?" Scott asked him. "No bruises?" He sat down on a chair beside the small sideboard.

Alex nodded and then he looked up. "I hit that boy because he insulted my mum."

"Good for you, Alex," Scott told him. "I would have done the same thing."

"Really?"

Scott gave him a positive nod and expression. "Most certainly; I wouldn't let anybody insult my mum."

"Did you fight at school?"

"Sometimes."

"What about?"

Scott took his mind back to his early school years with some pleasant and some not so pleasant memories. He shrugged. "It was often about my music. I liked playing the guitar and some boys were jealous because I was pretty good at it. And some of the boys called me 'Chicken George' because my dad was a chicken farmer. So yes, I got into lots of fights."

"Did you win them all?"

"Some."

"I wish I could play the guitar," Alex said. "I asked mum if I could have one, but she said we couldn't afford it."

This pricked Scott's imagination. "Have you ever played one?"

"Couple of times."

"And?"

Alex glanced up at him. "I had a problem getting my fingers on the frets, but…" He pushed out his bottom lip. "I thought I did OK."

Scott kept his eye on Alex's face and thought he could see a wistful expression as the boy recalled those moments in his mind.

"How about if I bring my acoustic guitar here? I could teach you a few chords. Maybe learn a simple song for when your mum comes home. What do you think?"

Alex's face brightened immediately. "Really? Wow, yes please."

"There have to be some conditions though," Scott said. "You mustn't tell your mum until you can play a tune for her. And while I'm here, there will be no lessons until after you've done your homework. Deal?"

Alex lifted his fist. "Deal." He bumped his fist against Scott's, his little face a picture of excitement."

Scott grinned at him. "So why don't we go back to my house, and I'll get my guitar. What do you think?"

Alex leapt up off the bed. "Now?"

Scott nodded. "Now."

And at that moment, Scott felt a connection, a bond between him and the boy, which he hoped would bring him closer to Alesia.

***

For some reason, Denny felt nervous as she opened the door of her studio and ushered Chenelle in. Mitch wasn't with them; he still had a job to do at Lafayette's and agreed to catch up with them later that day, possibly at dinner. Since her visit to the Corfe Gallery in London, Denny had tried to implement some changes that reflected the ambience she'd experienced at the London Gallery. She just hoped it would work,

Chenelle stopped and took a steady look around her, listening to the soft, quiet music. It was Buddhist chanting but so gentle and soft it could barely be heard. She was also aware of a pleasant fragrance in the air. She turned and looked at Denny.

"I see you've learned something from your trip to Martin's gallery," she said to Denny with an approving sound in her voice. "I like it already."

"Thank you," Denny replied, having to clear her throat before she could say it. "You're right. And I think it makes such a difference." She pointed towards her office. "Would you like a coffee? I'll get Alice to make one."

Chenelle shook her head. "Not until I've seen everything, Denny." She started walking round the studio, touching some of the artwork on display and admiring the photos.

"Is this all your work?" she asked.

Denny grinned. "No, not all of it; mostly clients. My stuff is hidden away upstairs."

"Upstairs?"

"In the cutting room." She looked up at the ceiling. "That's where Alice and the girls will be."

Chenelle looked puzzled. "The girls? What, you have slave girls?"

Denny laughed. "No, Alice runs the studio when I'm not here. Isabel helps with my on-line work, while Janet and Bridget put my designs together."

"I must see this," Chenelle said.

Denny pointed to a door with the words *Staff Only* marked on it. "Through there. Be careful on the stairs though; they're quite steep."

Chenell chuckled. "You want to see some of the places I've worked in, Denny. It would open your eyes to what goes on among all those bloody frocks we have to change into."

Denny could imagine the frenetic scenes as the models changed from one outfit to another, hurrying to get out on the catwalk and trying to look as though they've had all the time in the world to get dressed.

The door at the top of the stairs opened up into a spacious area. Two women were standing at a cutting table working with some material. They both looked up as the door opened. Alice was running some fabric through a sewing machine but stopped as soon as she saw Denny and Chenelle.

Denny introduced Chenelle to them and asked where Isabel was.

"She's in the office," Alice told her. "She's doing some work on-line."

"Could you give her a buzz, please Alice?" Denny asked. "I might need her."

Chenelle edged her way towards Janet and Bridget. She was deeply curious to find out what they were working on. Denny came to the table and started to explain what the two women were putting together.

"We're working on the Spring Collection. Should be ready by December. I like to get it all done before the New Year."

Chenelle wasn't paying too much attention but was slowly fingering a piece of fabric that Janet had been cutting. She looked over at Denny.

"Cashmere?"

Denny nodded her head quickly. "Yes. I like to go for the high-end material. It's expensive, but my father helps."

Chenelle assumed Denny meant financially. "What else do you use?"

"Perhaps if I show you the collection?"

Chenelle pouted her lips. "You have it here?"

Denny pointed across the room. "Through there."

Chenelle followed Denny to a pair of double doors, which Denny slid open to reveal a walk-in wardrobe where several dresses, coats and trousers were hanging in a colourful display.

Chenelle immediately showed her surprise by the change in her expression. "Goodness me, you have been busy."

Denny chuckled almost apologetically. "Yes, me and the girls."

Chenelle put her hand on a scarf hanging indecorously on the shoulder of a beautiful cream coloured coat. She rubbed the fabric carefully with her fingers, then turned and looked in astonishment at Denny.

"Vicuña? Surely not."

"My dad," she explained. "He has a friend who gave him some fabric. There was just enough Vicuña for me to make that scarf."

"That must be worth a couple of grand, Denny. How on earth do you expect to sell it slung over a coat like that?"

Denny laughed. "No, I won't be selling it. When I launch the Spring Collection, I'll raffle the scarf off. Might make enough money to finance more high-end material."

"Raffle it off?" Chenelle almost shrieked. "For God's sake, Denny, you'll be putting stuff on a car boot sale next."

She put the scarf around her neck and purred at the luxurious feel of the South American fabric. "What other surprises do you have?"

Denny started walking along the line of clothes. "I plan to add a photographic display of where the materials come from and an explanation of how they are produced."

"Silk?" Chenelle asked as she fingered another of Denny's creations.

"And leather," Denny replied lifting a svelte looking leather jacket from it's hanger. "And denim. Mustn't forget what most people wear when they're relaxing."

"You mean working," Chenelle said with a hint of humour.

"Unlike you, Chenelle," Denny told her.

Chenelle looked away from the clothes. "At ten thousand quid a throw, Denny, I wouldn't be seen in a pair of jeans when I'm working."

Denny laughed and imagined Chenelle parading down the catwalk in a pair of ripped jeans. And she would probably charge that amount even for that.

The tour of the Spring Collection finished as Isabel came into the cutting room. She gave Chenelle a welcoming hug.

"I see you've been given exclusive access to Denny's brilliance," she said as she released Chenelle from the hug.

Chenelle agreed. "Denny's brilliance needs to be put on the catwalk, not a virtual on-line fashion shoot."

Isabel shrugged. "Money, that's all it takes. Maybe one day," she mused. "Meanwhile I'll keep updating the website and getting our stuff — sorry, Denny's stuff — in front of the paying public."

Denny put her hand on Isabel's arm. "We have to go, Isabel; I'm taking Chenelle out for lunch, then a catch up with Mitch."

And with that, Denny left the cutting room with Chenelle in tow and with a good feeling after Chenelle's good reaction after getting a glimpse of her Spring Collection.

***

Back at Lafayette's later that afternoon, Denny and Mitch were explaining to Chenelle the ideas that had been filtering through their minds as they walked around the Lafayette store. Denny had talked about the room that

Martin had shown her at the Corfe Gallery; it was where she's seen that incredible photo of Chenelle.

"I'm hoping to recreate something similar here when Mitch tells me where he's going to hold the exhibition."

Chenelle had her arm hooked into Mitch's; something which Denny wasn't comfortable with, but the two of them looked okay with themselves, so there was no point in getting moody about it.

"I have to make up my mind about the best place to hold the entire event, Denny," he said to her. "We could clear most of the upper floor, which doesn't see as much foot traffic as the ground floor, but if we went with that, it might not encourage the general public to venture upstairs."

"Ground floor would be favourite," Denny suggested. Perhaps we could merge the exhibition with your displays that are already here."

Mitch shook his head. "No; wherever we have it, the floor will have to be cleared."

"What about a fashion show?" Chenelle asked. "You could fit a catwalk in here," she said. "It doesn't have to be that long; just enough length for a few steps, a quick spin and walk off."

"And which Fashion House would you have in mind, Chenelle?" Denny asked, tongue in cheek.

Chenelle let go of Mitch's arm. "Yours."

Denny felt herself stiffen in surprise. "Mine? But I don't even have a label."

Chenelle put her hand on Denny's arm. "What I saw of those outfits upstairs in your gallery — hidden away," she added with a mock sternness in her voice, "would grace any fashion shoot, believe me. And you have a name, hence you have a label."

Denny stuttered for a moment and then regained her composure. "I would have to pay local models, Chenelle, and I'm not sure I'm ready to invest that kind of money in, well…" She looked up at Mitch. "Sorry about this, Mitch, but it would be a low-grade event."

Chenelle smiled. "Not if I agreed to model for you."

Denny's mouth fell open. "I couldn't afford you, Chenelle."

"Denny my love, I would bring a couple of friends with me. You pay their expenses. I will cost you nothing. And believe me, when the fashion world finds out we're doing a fashion shoot at Lafayette's, the Press will turn up in their droves. You'll make a fortune in orders, I promise."

Denny knew what a huge boost it would be for her fledgling fashion business with one of the world's top models showing for her. And she had no doubt that Chenelle's couple of friends would hold a very high place in that category too. It was almost too much for her to take in, and it showed.

Chenelle put her arm around her. "I want to do this for you, Denny. All you have to do is convince Mitch here to hand his ground floor over to you and we're in."

Denny looked at Mitch who had been listening with a deepening interest and concern, but he also knew what a lift it could give to Lafayette's name and popularity. He could already see the sales figures going up, and being Christmas as well… It was a no-brainer.

He gave a consenting nod. "We'll make it happen, Denny, one way or the other."

Denny almost squealed with delight but threw her arms around the two of them instead and gave them a massive hug knowing the exhibition and Christmas week would be a great success, thanks to Chenelle.

***

Alex followed Scott into his bedroom and came to a standstill. All around the room were posters of some of the top bands in the music world. Fleetwood Mac, Bruce Springsteen, Guns n Roses. There were smaller posters of Scott on stage, some on his own, others with the lead singers of different groups. He couldn't identify all the faces, but those of Scott were unmissable to him. He turned slowly to Scott.

"Did you put these up?"

Scott laughed and shook his head. "No, that was my dad. He's followed my career from the beginning. I couldn't believe it when I came home one year and saw all this." He swept his arm round in an arc as he spoke. "I didn't have the heart to take them down, which is why they are still there. Maybe when my dad has gone, I'll do it, but not yet."

"Have you shown these to your friends?"

Scott sat down on the bed. "Only Wally, but I expect my dad has shown all his friends."

"Who's Wally?"

Scott thought for a moment. "Do you know Heather? She has a little daughter, Christine."

Alex nodded his head once. "Oh yeah; her boyfriend came out of prison a little while ago." He looked a little puzzled. "And he's your friend?"

Scott put his hand on Alex's shoulder. "A very good friend, which is what I hope you and I can be." He stood up. "Now, what about these guitar lessons?"

He went over to a cupboard and lifted a guitar case from it. He put the case on the bed and opened it. Alex watched in awe as Scott pulled out an obviously well used acoustic guitar and passed the strap over his shoulder, The then sat on the bed, rested the guitar on his lap and spent a few minutes tuning it. Then he ran his fingers up and down the strings and dazzled Alex with a show of his fingers dancing wildly over the frets and producing an amazing sound. He stopped after a couple of minutes and grinned at Alex.

"So, what do you think?"

"I could never do that," Alex said, his face full of expression.

Scott pulled the strap from his shoulder. "That's what I said when I first saw someone play like that." He handed the guitar to Alex. "Just let it rest against you and pluck the strings."

Just then, Scott's phone rang. He put the guitar into Alex's lap and took his phone from his pocket. The call was from the hospital.

"I'll take this outside, Alex. Have a play; see how you get on."

He went outside the bedroom and put the phone to his ear. "Scott Jones."

"Hello, Mr. Jones. Nurse Hastings here. I just want to tell you that your wife is in recovery. The operation went well, but we may need to keep her in for a couple of days. As a precaution," she added.

"A precaution because…?

"Oh, don't worry; if your wife is well enough tomorrow, we may be able to discharge her."

Scott decided not to labour the point about Alesia not being his wife. "When can I see her?"

"Probably around five o'clock would be better. You can come in earlier if you want, but I think by five your wife will be wide awake."

"Thank you. We'll be in this afternoon; probably before five."

He turned the phone off and immediately experienced a strange sense of belonging to Alesia and Alex: of being a husband and father. It was an encouragingly pleasant thought; one which he had no wish to relinquish. As he opened the bedroom door, he heard Alex plucking at the guitar. Alex looked up as Scott stepped into the room.

"That was the hospital, Alex. Your mum is fine. We can go in and see her later this afternoon."

"She's okay?"

Scott nodded, speechless.

Alex put the guitar on the bed and ran over to Scott, throwing his arms around him. Scott held him and let the boy shed his tears. He even felt tears in his own eyes and blinked several times to stop them rolling down his face.

Alex pulled away and wiped his face with the backs of his hands. "I was scared, Scott."

Scott rubbed the top of his head. "Me too, Alex. Me too." He waited for a moment. "Now, let's get something to eat and after that we can start your first music lesson. Then we'll go and see your mum. Okay?"

Alex held his hand up and Scott gave him a high five. And at that moment, Scott felt a real connection between him, Alex and Alesia.

Chapter 22

Scott and Alex walked into the hospital and were directed to the ward where they would find Alesia. She wasn't in a ward with other patients but in a side room. The duty nurse explained it was a necessary precaution which was common practice for any patient recovering from a serious operation. This surprised Scott but he didn't want to say or ask anything in front of Alex. He thanked the nurse and let Alex go ahead of him.

Alex pushed open the door of the side room and rushed through when he saw his mum. He practically leapt up on to the bed and threw his arms around her. Scott looked on as he buried his head in Alesia's neck. Scott had the urge to reach over and pull him off in case he did any damage, but Alesia looked quite happy and tearful as she cuddled Alex.

Eventually they parted and Alex moved away so Scott could say hello. Scott leaned over Alesia and kissed her fondly on the cheek.

"Hello sleepy head, how are doing?"

Alesia smiled. "You sound like an American country cousin. I'm doing fine," she said. "The operation went well; no problems and they didn't find any nasties roaming about in there."

"I was worried. Look," he said suddenly. "Can I give you a hug?"

She nodded. "I would like that."

He reached forward and wrapped his arms around her as best he could, avoiding the attachments she had on. He squeezed her gently and as he pulled away he thought he saw Alesia's heartbeat increase on the monitor.

She wiped her eyes with the corner of the sheet. "Thank you, Scott. Now, has Alex been behaving?"

He could see that she was a little overwhelmed by the emotion she was experiencing, but for some inexplicable reason, he wondered if there was something else on her mind.

"He's been difficult and unruly; throws tantrums regularly and smashes crockery when he loses it." He looked at Alex. "Don't you boy?"

Alex nodded firmly. "Yep."

Alesia looked him fondly. "I always know when you are lying, Alex. So, how did you get on at school today."

"He was only there for half a day," Scott said hurriedly. Alex gave him a blinding look. Scott went on. "I called the school and explained the situation. I told them you were out of surgery and was asking for him. So, they let me bring him home."

She looked at him with a puzzled expression on her face. "Why would you do that, Scott?"

He shrugged. "Your apartment felt empty. I couldn't have you in it, and I like Alex's company, so I cooked up that cock and bull story." He turned away and winked at Alex. "And it worked, didn't it?"

Alesia shook her head. "He must go to school tomorrow though. No more fibbing and keeping him home."

Scott touched his forehead with the tips of his fingers. "Yes ma'am."

The conversation that followed lacked any real substance. Scott would like to have talked to Alesia about more personal and intimate things, but Alex needed to be included, which meant a lot of talk about football and Harry Kane. Guitar lessons were never mentioned.

When it was time for them to leave, Scott told Alesia that he had spoken to Heather and Denny. Alesia thanked him.

"They both phoned," she said, "once they heard. They're coming in tonight."

Alex climbed up on the bed again and gave his mum a hug. "Hurry up and come home," he said as he got down.

Scott kissed her on the cheek. "Get well soon," he said softly. "'bye for now."

He put his hand on Alex's shoulder and steered him out of the room, closing the door gently behind him.

***

Scott woke up stretched out on the sofa, if stretched out were the right words. He tossed the blanket back and swung his legs round, planted them on the floor and yawned. He ran his hands through his hair and looked at his watch. Six o'clock. He yawned again and got up, then walked through to the kitchen to make himself a cup of tea. When he'd lived in the States, coffee had always been his morning wake-up drink, but now, for some reason, he'd got into the habit of starting his day with a cup of tea.

He went back to the lounge and put his jeans on. He then glanced around briefly and thought back to the previous evening. Alex had been keen to learn a little more on the guitar, and Scott was happy to do that. Later they'd started watching a film, but Alex faded before the film was halfway through and declared his intention of going to bed. Scott wasn't sure whether he should offer to tuck Alex in or just leave him to it. Alex said he would be fine, so Scott let him get on with.

He finished watching the film and then went through to Alex's bedroom door. He stood there listening but could hear nothing. He opened the door carefully and peered in. Alex was fast asleep with just a single night-light burning. He closed the door quietly and was about to return to the lounge when he looked over at Alesia's room. He went over and opened the door, stepped through and turned the light on.

He didn't know what he expected to find, nor why he'd been tempted to look, but just being there brought a sense of closeness to her. The room was tidy, which he expected, but lacked what he believed were feminine touches. He'd seen plenty of bedrooms in his time, many of which exploded in colour and posters, decorative lighting and the pastel shades, in most cases, that were often so important in a woman's life. With Alesia's room, he could only describe it as functional — it was a bedroom for sleeping in; nothing more, nothing less.

He let his mind recall those events as he finished his tea and then went through for a shower. When he was dressed and ready to face the day, he started getting ready for Alex. Alesia had warned him that, like most youngsters, Alex would have all sorts of reasons for not wanting to get up. Scott smiled to himself as he opened Alex's door with Alesia's words running through his mind.

He turned the light on and called Alex in a loud voice.

"Morning, Alex. Time to get up. Got a cuppa here for you. I'll get your breakfast ready for you…" He stopped and watched Alex turn over, grumble about something and pulled the covers over his head. Scott walked up to the bed, lifted the covers back and poked Alex on the shoulder with his fingertip. "And if we have time, young man, we can get a couple of guitar lessons in before you go to school.

Alex sat up immediately. "Really?"

Scott put the cup on the bedside locker. "There's your tea. The rest is up to you. I'll be in the kitchen."

He came out of the room and allowed himself a soft punch of triumph. "It's just knowing how to persuade them, Alesia," he said to himself. "That's all."

Alex had performed miracles by the time Scott brought the guitar through. The boy was washed, fed, dressed for school and champing at the bit for another dive into becoming a budding musician. And when Scott dropped him off at school, he felt they had cemented another brick into the wall of their developing relationship.

Before he pulled away from the school to head over to the farm, Scott phoned Alesia. It took just a few seconds for her to come on the line.

"Morning Alesia, how are you doing?"

"Scott? Oh, I'm fine. A little bit anyway."

"What do you mean — a little bit?"

"Nothing, it's just that they think I'll have to stay in until tomorrow. I feel okay, but they said it would be better if we wait for another day."

Scott thought that kind of news would be a problem for him, but ironically he felt pleased that he would need to be with Alex, and consequently retain the umbilical between him and Alesia.

"Well, I hope everything is fine, especially you."

"How are you getting on with Alex?" she asked.

"We're getting on okay. Getting to know each other really well. He likes to hear about my time in America."

"I hope you kept all the sordid details to yourself, Scott."

He grinned. "Would I do anything different? But don't worry, Alesia; your boy is safe with me. He's at school right now and I've got to get to work. I'll call at lunchtime and we'll both be in to see you after school. Okay?"

"Yes please, Scott; I would like that."

They said goodbye to each other, neither of them wanting to be the one to hang up first. Then Scott pulled away from the school and set off for Monk's Farm and a chat with Wally and Heather.

***

Denny and Chenelle were having breakfast with Mitch at Lafayette's cafeteria. It was Mitch's suggestion because, as he reminded them, he still had a store to manage and could only devote a short time to plan the exhibition. In effect, he'd passed that on to the two women despite the fact that Chenelle would soon be returning to London.

"How was Alesia, Denny?" Mitch asked.

Denny had excused herself from their company the previous evening because she'd gone to the hospital with Heather.

"She seemed okay. But you can imagine what it must be like after an operation. Anyway, she seemed lively enough. She should be home tomorrow."

"We missed you," Chenelle said. "But it was important for you to visit your friend."

"My best friend," Denny reminded her. Her mind then began to focus on the fact that Mitch and Chenelle had gone out for dinner together the night before. She didn't like that, so she shut the thought away. "We grew up together. Friends for life," she said as a way of diverting her own dismal thoughts from Mitch and Chenelle's blossoming relationship. "But she's going to be fine, I'm pleased to say."

"And Scott is looking after her boy, I understand," Mitch put in.

Denny's mind flashed back to the conversation she'd had with Heather had after their visit. They had both come to the conclusion that Alesia would like to have that connection with Scott become more permanent, but the elephant in the room was Scott's American girlfriend, Joanna.

"Yes, Scott."

Mitch looked at his watch. "Sorry about this, ladies, but I have to go. Catch up tonight?" He got up from the table and gave them both a quick kiss on the cheek, then disappeared into the interior of Lafayette's.

When he'd gone, Chenelle reached over the table and put her hand on Denny's arm. "Denny, I may be wrong, but I got the impression that you weren't too happy about your friend, Alesia, and Scott."

Denny's expression widened. "Goodness me, no. Quite the opposite in fact." She reached down for her handbag and lifted it on to her lap, then took her mobile phone out.

Chenelle watched as Denny kept swiping the screen up. Then Denny said something and held the phone towards her. Chenelle took it from her and found herself looking at two young people holding each other, obviously on a dance floor.

"My goodness," she said softly. "These are your friends?"

Denny took the phone from her. "That was taken fifteen years ago at the College Prom. Scott and Alesia."

"But they look so…"

"In love?"

Chenelle nodded. "Yes." She frowned. "So, what happened?"

Denny turned the phone off and slipped it back into her bag. "Scott disappeared off to America, and Alesia married someone she thought she was in love with. She's now divorced and a single mum."

"What about Scott?"

"He was into music. Became something of a Rock Star. Session musician more like, but he toured with a lot of the supergroups: Fleetwood Mac; Springsteen; Supertramp. He's written and recorded songs. Done well for himself apparently."

"So, what's he doing back here looking after your friend's son?"

"He came back because of his father's business. I'm not privy to all the details, but it looks like a wasted journey for him."

"Because of your friend, or because of the business?"

Denny shook her head. "I don't know; it's difficult to figure out. I'm not sure what Scott wants to do since Joanna reappeared. They were almost married back in America. I think she wants to rekindle the flame and marry him."

"Why didn't they marry then?"

"She dumped him."

Chenelle laughed. "And she's back?"

"Hmm. And that might spoil everything for Alesia." She leaned forward. "We think Alesia is in love with Scott and has been since that photograph was taken, and if she isn't careful, Scott's ex, Joanna, is going to steal him away."

Chapter 23

Scott and Wally were leaning on the fence that overlooked the small, uncultivated paddock that bordered the lane. They had a mug of tea each in their hands. They had been discussing the future of the business.

"So, do you think your dad will sell up?" Wally asked.

Scott sniffed and shrugged his shoulders. "I would think so. Especially if I decide not to stay."

"You planning to go back to the States then?" The surprise was evident in his voice.

Scott frowned. I'm not sure, Wally; I may, I may not. It may not even be my decision; fate will decide, I think."

"And if you do decide to go, and your dad sells up; that means he'll sell the cottage as part of the business."

Scott turned his head and looked at him. "No; it's not part of Monk's Farm. It belongs to dad."

"The cottage?"

Scott pointed across lane. "See the other paddock? That patch of land from the road and up to the house, plus the sheds at the back used to be a smallholding. Dad bought it; thought he might develop it as part of the business, but his health started to fail, then we lost mum and…" He sighed heavily. "It was a big blow. That's why he asked me to come back from the States. I couldn't come back; I was touring, had a short-term contract." He heaved his shoulders in a single shrug. "So, when I did finally come home, it was all academic; I was never going to take over the business anyway."

"Does that mean your dad will want to move into the cottage when he's sold up?"

Scott shook his head. "Shouldn't think so. He's got a lovely bungalow, all mod cons, and some land."

"What about you?"

"Me?"

"Where are you going to live?"

"If I'm still here, I'll live with my dad."

Wally tutted and lifted his chin. He felt a bit slow. He drained his cup and let it swing on the crook of his finger. "Would your dad sell now and not wait until he sells the business?"

Scott frowned. "What, the smallholding? Why, do you want to buy it?"

Wally grinned and nodded. "Yep!"

Scott threw his head back and laughed. "Wally, you'd never get a mortgage with what I pay you. And even if my dad did want to sell it, where are you going to get the money from?"

Wally raised his eyebrows with a tell-all expression on his face.

Scott pushed back from the fence and turned, facing him. "Wally, you haven't been —"

Wally cut him off. "No, Scott. I haven't. What I have is legit, I promise you."

Scott puffed his cheeks out. "Well, it's nothing to do with me where you got your money from, but I can have a good guess."

"When I was driving," Wally told him, "I owned my own Arctic. I also put a lot of money away before I went inside where the law couldn't get hold of it. Believe me,

Scott, I was making money hand over fist. Everything I got was cleaned up too."

"You mean laundered," Scott said. Wally didn't comment on that. "All legit?"

Wally nodded his head thoughtfully. "I was dead lucky, Scott. If the Old Bill had figured it all out, I'd have gone down for a ten or a fifteen-year spell. And when I was in the nick, I realised how much Heather meant to me, and fifteen years would have crucified me. I made myself a promise then that once I'd done my time, I would marry Heather and go straight. And by God, I intend to."

"And how do you know you'll have enough money?"

Wally shrugged. "Well, that's the rub — I don't. But if you can come up with a price, whether your dad wants to sell or not, it will help me to either make your dad an offer or write the whole idea off as a bit far-fetched."

Scott wrinkled his brow. "Why do you want to buy it?"

Wally straightened up and turned towards him and rested him arm against the fence. "For Heather," he said.

Scott's expression widened in surprise. "Heather?"

Wally nodded and glanced down at the ground. "She doesn't know that though, so don't say anything." He then told Scott of Heather's plan to start growing vegetables and wanting to drive. "She has some pretty big ideas, Scott, that's one of the reasons I love her. Most of them are just fanciful notions. But she loves that cottage. She has all sorts of ideas about refurbishing it." He chuckled. "I don't know where she thinks she's going to get the money from though."

Scott pointed a finger at him. "She doesn't know about your secret cache then?"

Wally shook his head. "I didn't want to tell her while I was in the nick. I was afraid that she might find someone else and…" He shrugged. "Well, you know." He brightened. "But we're engaged now and hope to get married before Christmas." He turned round and leaned over the fence gazing across the uncultivated paddock. "It would be my dearest wish if I could give her the cottage as a wedding present." He didn't add anything to that.

Scott studied his friend and was seeing a person he didn't recognise. Or one he had more or less taken for granted. Now he was looking at a man with a heart filled with love for the woman who had stood by him, believed in him and loved him back. He put his hand on Wally's shoulder and gave it a gentle shake.

"I'll talk to dad, see what he says. And I promise not to say anything to Heather."

***

Scott left Wally and headed over to the chicken houses where he expected to find his dad. On his way over there he gave some thought to how he would broach the subject with his dad on selling the smallholding which included the cottage. His dad was at home though, which suited Scott. He drove over to the bungalow and let himself in. His dad was in the kitchen preparing some vegetables.

"Morning, dad."

His father turned round. "Morning, Scott. How was your night?"

"Fine. Slept on the sofa."

"Must be weird for you," his dad said. "Not to have female company when you spend a night away from home."

Scott chuckled and gave his dad a hug. "Doing a favour for an old friend. And she's in hospital so it might have been difficult to share a night of passion with her."

His dad laughed. "How's the boy?"

"Alex? He's fine. He wants to learn the guitar and play football for England."

"Sounds like my kind of man."

Scott sat down at the breakfast bar. "He wants to know if I'm going back to America."

"And are you?"

Scott shrugged. "Depends on whether you sell the business or not, I suppose."

His dad stopped chopping vegetables. "I probably will, son. I know you're not interested in carrying on with it." Scott went to say something, but he stopped him. "It's okay; I don't expect you to turn your life round to suit your old dad. And besides, I think it's time for a change in my life."

"What about the cottage, dad? Would you keep it?"

His dad shrugged and waved his hand around the kitchen. "I don't need it. I've got this place." He pointed towards the window. "And a decent patch of land out there to keep me busy. And who would want to buy a rundown cottage anyway?"

"Someone might. How much is it worth?"

His dad pulled a face. "How long is a piece of string? The cottage is a teardown really, unless someone wanted to spend money on it. And the smallholding has to be worth something. It's about two acres."

"And how much is land in Norfolk?"

"Good arable land is expensive, but for something like that? Ten thousand an acre — say twenty thousand. Throw the cottage in at, what, 250,000? Probably three hundred grand would cover it, but I wouldn't pick a figure without a professional valuation." He studied Scott briefly. "Why, do you want to buy it?"

Scott laughed and shook his head. "No dad, not me, but I do know someone who could be interested."

"Do I get to know who?"

At that moment, Scott wondered if by revealing Wally's desire to buy the cottage, his dad might baulk at the idea. But at the same time, he might be persuaded to sell at a low price. He decided to bite the bullet and tell his dad.

"Wally and Heather," he said.

"Really?"

"You seem surprised."

His dad nodded. "Well, I suppose I am. Why would they want to buy something like that?"

So, Scott explained the conversation he'd had with Wally and asked his dad to say nothing to anyone, not even Wally and Heather.

"It would be best if you make up your mind and then get a professional valuation before we say anything."

"You really want this for them?"

He sighed, puffing out his cheeks. "Once you've sold the business, there's no guarantee that Wally will have a job. If that happens he'll have to find something else. Probably go back on the road."

"Would he get a driving job with his criminal record?"

Scott shrugged. "I don't know, but let's take this one step at a time. You're the one who will be leading this, not me."

He agreed. "Okay, but don't rush me on this. Give me a while to think about it."

Scott got up from the breakfast bar and gave his dad a gentle pat on the back. "Thanks, dad. Now, I've got to get back and to speak to Wally and Heather. Not what we've been talking about though. Then I promised Alesia I would phone her, and once I've picked up Alex from school, we're going on to see his mum. So, my day is planned."

And then his phone rang. It was Joanna.

***

Scott looked at his phone and cut the call. There was no way he wanted to deal with Joanna at that moment, but within seconds the phone started ringing again. He sighed heavily and frowned, then swiped up.

"Hi, sorry about that; I cut you off," he lied. He looked at his dad and pointed at the phone mouthing Joanna's name. He walked out of the kitchen and into the lounge. "So, are you back? Where are you?"

"I'm on my way to Norfolk, Scott. Be at Kings Lynn at twelve. Can you pick me up?"

He shook his head. "No, sorry, Joanna; it's not possible. You'll have to get a cab. We'll catch up later."

"Why can't you pick me up?"

"Not today, Joanna. I'm looking after Alesia's boy, Alex. Alesia's in hospital and I'll be going over there shortly. Then I have to pick Alex up from school, feed him and take him to see his mum." He'd lied about seeing Alesia going to the hospital shortly.

"Well, that's okay, Scott; I can come with you."

There was no way Scott was going to have Joanna tagging along. It would mean she'd want to come to Alesia's flat, go to the hospital with him and basically foul up the growing connection he was having with Alex and his mum.

"No, Joanna; that doesn't work for me. I need to concentrate on Alex for now. Alesia should be home tomorrow, so you and I can catch up once she's back and I've handed Alex over to her. I'll ring you; I promise."

"Well, okay honey, I'll get a cab. But don't forget — we have something important to discuss."

Scott's eyes hooded over as he closed the call. He thought a lot of Joanna, but Alesia was his priority at that moment, and it was a responsibility he was beginning to enjoy. He went back into the kitchen and told his dad he was going back over to the bagging shed and would see him the following day.

"You having trouble with that Joanna woman?" his dad asked.

Scott wagged his finger at him. "Nothing I can't handle, dad."

"Well, you be careful. You seem a mite happier when you're dealing with Alesia and her boy, so you don't want anything or anyone to queer that pitch."

Scott smiled at him. "Thanks for the fatherly advice, dad. I think I'm old enough to handle it."

"Scott!"

His dad's change of tone surprised him. "What?"

"How does that song go? How to handle a woman? You've got two to handle, so just make sure you don't mess it up. Choose the one that you know you love. That's all I'm going to say."

It was a sobering thought for Scott, that his father could pick up on the signals he was putting out. "I'm off, dad. See you later."

He left the house and clambered into his car, but before he started it, he sat there and thought about where he was in life and what it was he really wanted to do.

And with whom.

Chapter 24

Scott and Alex walked into the hospital together and it was all Scott could do to stop Alex running on ahead. He managed to collar the boy as they got to the nurses' station where Scott asked if it was okay to go through. Alex was gone the moment he saw the nurse nod her head. Scott watched him go, thanked the nurse and went off to be with his other family.

Alex was cuddling his mum when Scott pushed open the door. He walked over to the bed and kissed her gently on the cheek.

"How are you, Alesia?"

She looked good. She had colour in her cheeks and her eyes looked bright and clear. "I'm fine. They said I can come home tomorrow."

He liked the way she said that, but he couldn't help feeling just a little disappointed that it signalled the end of his commitment, although maybe not immediately. He knew he wanted to look after them both until Alesia was well enough to be left with Alex, but he had the thought of Joanna in the back of his mind, and he needed to deal with that; it wasn't something he could easily shove to one side.

"That's good news, Alesia. I'll stay at the flat with you until I know you're back to normal."

Alesia was about to tell him that it wasn't necessary, that she would be fine, but she knew in her heart that she wanted him to be there for as long as possible.

"Okay, Scott. Maybe for a day or two, but I'm pretty sure I'll be okay."

He sat on the edge of the bed and took her hand in his. She immediately thought back to that moment when he had taken her hand at the College Prom. The memory warmed her heart and the feel of his hand in hers was a sensation she wanted to treasure.

"I'll stay overnight as well. On the sofa," he added. "And I'll sort this young man out, so you don't have to." He looked at Alex and winked. "And I'll carry on giving him guitar lessons."

Alesia's mouth sprung open in surprise. "Guitar lessons?"

Scott then explained how it had happened. "We weren't going to tell you, but the truth is, there's no way we can carry on without you knowing anyway."

Alex leaned forward, laying almost full length on the bed. "Scott's going to teach me a Christmas Carol so I can play it for you at Christmas."

Alesia's felt tears coming. She brushed them away. "That's so sweet of you, Scott, but I can't afford to buy Alex a guitar."

Scott shook his head. "It's not a problem; we're using an old acoustic of mine. Alex is doing fine with it."

Alesia looked at Alex and wrinkled her nose at him. "You're a lucky boy."

He glanced at Scott and then back at his mum. "I'm lucky because I've got you and Scott now, ain't I?"

"Aren't I," she corrected him and rubbed the top of his head. "That's the three of us then."

Just then the door opened, and Denny was standing there with Mitch. "Can we come in?"

Alesia's face brightened as Denny came over and kissed her. Mitch looked on, not too sure of himself. Alesia gave him a wave. "Hello, Mitch."

He nodded and said hello to Scott and Alex. "I hear you're playing carer for these two." He was smiling when he said it.

"Not really carer; more like chief cook and bottle washer," Scott joked.

Mitch grinned. "Excuse me," he said and pointed to Alesia. "I need to say hello."

Scott looked on as Mitch tried to muscle his way in between the two women. He managed to give Alesia a peck on the cheek, then relinquished his place so Denny could carry on chatting. He went over and stood beside Scott.

"They get on well, those two. How are you coping with her boy?"

"We're good. He's no trouble. Just an enthusiastic kid. I'm giving him guitar lessons to keep him occupied."

"You going to make him a Rock Star?"

Scott laughed. "It's not that easy. Besides, Alex wants to be another Harry Kane, so I reckon that will come first."

"Is your friend, Joanna still around?"

Scott almost gave his disappointment away with a 'hmmm' emanating from his throat. "She's back in Kings Lynn. Got in yesterday."

"Have you seen her?"

Scott shook his head. "No. I had to stand her up." He fluttered his hand towards the bed. "I've got these two to look after. Joanna will just get in the way."

Mitch gave him a querying look. "Does she know that."

Scott nodded sharply. "Well, if she didn't, she does now. I'll be seeing her in a couple of days though."

Mitch opened his mouth to say something when the door opened, and Heather walked in with Wally.

"Surprise!" she sang out.

Denny looked round as Alesia threw her arms up in the air. "Heather. Wally. Lovely to see you."

Heather looked at everyone. "I'm afraid the nurse said only four visitors. Do you want us to wait outside for a while?"

Scott touched her on the arm. "No need; me and Alex were going anyway." He made his way over to the bed and gave Alesia a kiss. "We'll see you tomorrow. Bring you home. Give me a ring, okay?"

Why didn't he say give me a call, was the thought on her mind instead of 'give me a ring'? She nodded. "Yes, of course. As soon as I know." She reached for Alex and gave him a big hug. "Be good. See you tomorrow."

And as Scott and Alex got to the door, Alesia suddenly realised that there were six people in that room who were in the group back at the College Prom. It brought a warm, pleasant feeling inside her as those moments came flooding into her mind.

Then the door closed, and Scott was no longer there.

***

The noise level rose as they all tried to say something to Alesia. It made her laugh. She put her hands up. "Not all at once, please!"

"Let Heather and Wally say hello first," Denny suggested. Heather took that as her cue and edged her way closer to the bed.

"Well, now we've got you laughing, we know you're feeling a lot better. You seemed okay last night as well, Alesia. Are you ready to go home."

Alesia nodded excitedly. "Yes, of course. I'd go home now if they'd let me."

"Home to Scott and Alex?" Heather said, the innuendo clear in her voice.

"He'll only be there for a day or so. I should be able to manage after that. And let's face it, you're all on the end of a phone if I have any trouble."

"Well, you won't see too much of Scott," Mitch said. "Joanna's back and he says he'll be seeing her in a couple of days."

Heather and Denny both turned and faced him, surprise registering on their faces. Alesia looked stunned. "I'd forgotten all about her," she said.

"Well, clearly Scott hasn't," Mitch said bluntly. He could see the disappointed expression on Alesia's face. "Does that bother you?" he asked.

Alesia tried to shrug it off with a slight lift with her shoulders. "Not really. They're planning to get married anyway, so I can't see Scott staying much longer."

"Getting married?" Denny asked showing the surprise in her voice. "How do you know that? Has he told you?"

Alesia shook her head. "No. It's none of my business anyway."

"So, how do you know?"

Alesia explained the conversation between Scott and Joanna at the football ground. "Alex's friend, Mandy, was standing behind them when she heard Scott say it."

Denny straightened up. She looked at Heather. "You're closer to Scott than any of us. Have you heard this."

Heather simply nodded and looked a little forlorn.

"Look," Alesia said holding her hands up. "This has got nothing to do with any of us; it's Scott's business between him and Joanna. After a couple of days, he'll get back to normal and we're not likely to see much of him again." She glanced up at Heather. "Except you and Wally."

Wally held his hand up. "Don't drag me in; it's all a guessing game anyway." Wally needed to avoid any talk and speculation about Scott's future for fear of leaking something of his own plans. "I just work for him — nothing more."

Heather gave him a blinding look which no-one noticed. He gave her a weak smile back and an almost imperceptible shrug of the shoulders. She turned back to Alesia.

"When you're home, you must let me know if you need anything. After all, if Joanna's back on the scene, you're unlikely to see anything of Scott." She glanced over at Wally. "And Wally will drive me over if it's urgent."

The conversations continued, mainly between the three women. Wally edged over to Mitch and started talking about the event he was planning with Denny.

"It's going to be spectacular," Mitch told him. "Denny's brilliant."

"You like that girl, don't you?"

Mitch nodded. "Whoever ends up with her is going to be one lucky guy."

Wally looked at the three women and then back at Mitch. "Then make sure you're the lucky one."

Chapter 25

Scott brought Alesia home the following day feeling really pleased with himself at being able to help her. It was decided not to bring Alex out of school, which gave them both an opportunity to enjoy each other's company without any interruptions from anyone. He made a fuss of her once they were in the flat. Alesia kept telling him she was fine, which in truth she was, but Scott was in denial about that, and it showed.

He made Alesia sit down and stood in front of her.
"You've got your tablets."
"Yes."
"Are you hungry?"
"No."
"Thirsty?"
"Yes."
"Do you want tea, coffee or water?"
"A pint of Guiness, please."
His face fell and his mouth dropped open. "What?"
Alesia started to laugh. "For goodness' sake, Scott, I'm okay. And no, I don't want a Guiness. Maybe a cup of tea?"
"Yes, sure, okay."
He darted away into the kitchen and left Alesia shaking her head and grinning. She could see he was at sixes and sevens and not really sure how to cope with the responsibility of caring for someone. Not that she needed the care but was happy to have Scott showing his concern for her.

He came back a few minutes later with a cup of tea in his hand as Alesia's phone rang. She lifted it from her lap and opened the call. It was Denny.

"Are you home yet?" she asked.

"Yes, and Scott is spoiling me rotten."

"That's lovely," Denny told her. "Do you need me to come over?"

Alesia shook her head. "No, I'm fine. I'll give you a call if I need anything. I promise."

She hung up and took the cup from Scott. "That was Denny," she said. "Wanting to make sure you're taking good care of me and not letting me wait on you hand and foot." She had a crooked smile on her face as she spoke.

Scott kind of winced. "What? Never."

Alesia's grin turned into a chuckle. "Scott, you are so nervous. You weren't like that when we danced together at the Prom."

He sat down beside her, his mind going back all those years. "I was in control then," he said.

"You are now."

"For a little while. Then back to reality."

She reached over and took his hand. "What is your reality, Scott?"

He wanted to tell her that his reality would be for these moments to be permanent; but with a fit and well Alesia, a buzzing, guitar playing Alex who was still dreaming the dream of becoming another Harry Kane, and for himself to be a cornerstone in their lives. He wanted tell Alesia that was his dream of reality, but he knew it was impossible because of her confession to him that she was in love with someone who was unavailable.

"I think my reality must be to return to my old life; one I know and am comfortable with and can live on my own terms." He was being untruthful, but under the circumstances he felt he was left with no choice.

She sighed and let go of his hand. His words had pierced her soul, and she knew there was no longer the chance of a future with him. His reality was to go back to America and, although he hadn't mentioned her name, complete the union with Joanna.

***

Scott had planned to put in an appearance at the farm before picking Alex up from school, but a phone call from Joanna forced him to ditch the farm and head over to the hotel where she was staying. She had sounded a little tense on the phone, which set alarm bells ringing, which was the reason he changed his plan.

He parked the car close to the hotel and called Joanna to say he would come up to her room, but she asked him to wait for her in the hotel lounge. This surprised him, but he agreed and made himself comfortable in a quiet area of the room. He'd ordered a coffee, which was on the table beside him. He sent Joanna a message to say he was waiting. Five minutes later, Joanna appeared. Scott thought she looked as lovely as ever and stood up to give her a warm hug.

"Do you want a drink?" he asked.

She shook her head. "No thanks."

Scott studied her face as they sat down. He tried to read her expression, which suggested some anxiety. He just hoped she wasn't going to tell him she was pregnant. Not that he could be blamed if she was because they hadn't been together in that way since he last saw her in America.

"So, what's on your mind, Joanna?" he asked her.

She drew in a deep breath and then fidgeted, making herself comfortable in the chair. "I need to ask you a question, Scott, and I want a straight answer."

He smiled. "Be my guest."

"When we were together in America," she began, "you asked me to marry you."

He nodded once. "Yes."

"But you never proposed, did you? Not in the old fashioned, on your knees, way."

"You mean I didn't put a ring on your finger."

"Yes." She glanced down at her hands. "I have to tell you now that I would have turned you down."

He frowned. "You did. Well, at least you dumped me, which is as good a way of saying no."

She looked up from her hands. "The truth is, Scott, I was seeing someone else at the time. Secretly of course."

"Of course," he repeated.

"I regret that," she said. "But we were going nowhere, Scott, which is how I kind of drifted into a relationship with someone else. But when you told me you wanted to get married…" She left it there with a shrug. Then she shook her head.

Scott thought she looked downcast. "And now?"

She looked up, her face brightening just a little. "My business will keep me in England until Christmas. I would like to spend most of that time with you. And maybe you'll ask me again."

That surprised him; he thought Joanna was about to end their friendship, not literally ask him to marry her, which is the way it looked to him.

He sighed heavily and took her hand. "I'm not going to make any promises, Joanna. I have an important decision to make about my future either here or back in the States. I need to focus on that."

She smiled. "I'll settle for that. For now, anyway. But we can still spend time together, can we not?"

"Of course." He looked at his watch. "But for now I have another responsibility: I have to pick young Alex up from school and take him home. I'll have a better idea of when I can relinquish him to his mum, which will probably be a couple of days from now. I'll give you a call and we'll have dinner together. How about that?"

She reached over the arm of the chair and kissed him on the lips. "Don't make me wait too long, Scott."

"I won't," he said, and got up from the table.

And as he walked out of the hotel, he blew air out from his puffed cheeks and wondered what the bloody hell he'd gotten himself into now.

***

Wally came out of the bagging shed, looked up at the overcast sky, shivered, and climbed into the pick-up truck that served as a runabout for the farm. He glanced over at the cottage and pulled away, hoping that Heather hadn't seen him, and headed off to where Scott's father, Alf, lived. He knew Scott wouldn't be there, which was why he'd contacted Mr. Jones and asked if he could pop over and see him. There was no work to be done in the bagging shed, which eased his conscience about taking time off.

He pulled up at the beautiful, detached bungalow, and got out of the truck. Although he'd been there before, he couldn't help admiring the place and the beautifully kept garden area. It didn't take long for Alf Jones to come to the door. He looked an older version of Scott. He was going thin on top but still had a presence about him. He was taller than Wally, but then most men were. He was wearing a cardigan.

"Hello, Wally. Come in."

He stepped back and let Wally into the hallway. He closed the door and pointed towards the kitchen. "Do you want a cup of tea? Coffee?"

Wally shook his head. "No thanks, Mr. Jones."

"It's Alf, son. No need to be formal."

Wally nodded briefly. "Alf then." He rubbed his hands together. "It's getting chilly out there," he said. "Can't believe Autumn's nearly over."

"Christmas soon," Alf replied. "But at least it's warm in here." He sat down at the large kitchen table and pointed at an empty chair. "Have a seat."

Wally sat down wondering how he was going to start the conversation. He wasn't sure if Scott's father welcomed the idea of having an ex-con planning to buy the cottage. He wasn't too sure if Scott had explained it fully to his dad either, but he had no choice; this was something he wanted to do for Heather. He opened his mouth to say something but stopped when he saw Alf put his hand up.

"I know why you're here, Wally; Scott told me. You want to buy the smallholding."

Wally relaxed and breathed a sigh of relief. "That's the general idea, Alf. I know it isn't part of the farm, but Scott say we can't do anything about the smallholding until we know your plans. If you don't sell up, the status quo remains as it is now. So, have you made up your mind yet? Do you think you'll sell up?"

Alf nodded briefly. "Yeah; Scott more or less persuaded me to sell the business. He doesn't want any part of it, which is why I agreed to let it go. I'm getting too old for this anyway. And it looks like Scott is planning to go back to the States once we've sold up."

"He's definitely going then?" Wally asked.

Alf nodded. "I think so." He got up from the table and went to the fridge. "You want a beer?"

"Don't mind if I do," Wally said.

Alf took a couple of lagers from the fridge and handed Wally one. He gave him a glass as well. Then he sat down and poured his own drink. He lifted the glass. "Cheers."

Wally lifted the bottle and tipped it slightly. "Cheers."

"So," Alf said after taking a mouthful of beer and putting the glass down. "You want to tell me why you want to buy the smallholding?"

Wally grinned. "It's not my idea, Alf. Heather has some fanciful idea about growing vegetables for market. She's even talked about opening a farm shop."

Alf raised his eyebrows. "Bit ambitious."

Wally agreed. "She loves that cottage; she has great plans for that too, but if you decide to sell the smallholding with the business…" He left the observation unsaid.

"It's not mine to sell, Wally; it belongs to Scott."

"I thought it belonged to you."

Alf made a kind of bobbing motion with his head and shoulders. "Well, technically, yes; I own it. But I told Scott years ago that it was his, no matter what. So, any decision about the smallholding will be his."

Wally shrugged and took a sip of his beer. "But if he goes back to the States, like as not he'll want to sell up."

Alf shook his head slowly. "I can't say one way or the other what he'll do, but he could be planning on getting married. Joanna's back," he added.

Wally sighed. "Well, it's all conjecture, so can we talk about the smallholding and what kind of price you'll be looking for?"

"I need to have the property valued professionally of course, but I think a ballpark figure would be around £350,000. Give or take." Wally showed no reaction, which surprised him. "You don't seem fazed by that."

Beneath Wally's expression was a sense of satisfaction; he knew he could manage that figure. "The point is, Alf, Heather doesn't know what I'm up to. I want to make it a Christmas present for her."

Alf smiled and nodded his head up and down slowly. The grin widened. "That's some bloody Christmas present, Wally."

"That's why I don't want her to know. She doesn't even know I'm here talking to you."

Alf twisted his glass back and forth on the table. "So, what will you do with Heather when Scott arranges for a valuation."

Wally opened his arms up. "That's easy: I'll arrange a day out for her. Maybe a shopping trip somewhere. Probably London. But it would have to be when there's no work on for me."

Alf laughed. "I'll arrange for the chickens to have a day off and stop shitting then."

Wally laughed with him. The bagging shed would always have work on because of the speed with which they emptied a chicken house in order to get it cleared and cleaned for the next batch of day-old chicks.. Wally had already experienced what it was like to 'catch chickens' when they cleared the chicken house — it was manic.

"So, can we get this done before Christmas, do you think?"

Alf opened his hand in a helpless gesture. "That's down to Scott, I'm afraid, but I'm sure he'll do his best to help. So long as he hasn't eloped," he added with another helpless gesture.

They talked on until they'd finished their beers. Wally glanced at his watch a couple of times, concerned that he might get back late. They chatted about Scott's uncertain future, Wally's time in prison and Alf's plans for retirement. When Wally took his leave, him and Alf had cemented a great relationship, which put a smile on his face as he parked the pick-up truck at the bagging shed and hurried home to the cottage.

He opened the door and called out. He heard a squeal as little Christine came running through to get a hug from him. She was followed by Heather.

"Where have you been?"

Wally frowned. "Working, where do you think?"

"I phoned you, but you didn't pick up."

Wally's mind went into overdrive. "Ah, that's because I was called over to the farm. Something Mr. Jones wanted to talk to me about. And you know what the noise is like in those bloody sheds, Heather. I left my phone in the truck." He stepped up to her. "Do I get a kiss now?"

She affected a show of reluctance and put her arms around him as he kissed her. Then she pulled away. "I didn't know what you wanted for dinner, so I've done Spaghetti Bolognese."

He patted her bum gently. "That's why I love you, sweetheart; you never let me down."

She made a noise in her throat and turned away, the smile broadening on her face. "Get yourself cleaned up," she said. "Dinner in ten minutes."

Wally allowed himself a moment of relief as he realised he was going to struggle to keep his secret from her, which made it all the more important to him. He lifted little Christine up into his arms and kissed her on the cheek. "Come on love, let's go and get something to eat."

Chapter 26

Autumn had given way to winter as December heralded the beginning of the Christmas season and promises of a white Christmas were springing from peoples' lips as they watched the weather deteriorate in typically English fashion. Heather was sitting at the kitchen table putting the final touches to her Christmas card list when the doorbell rang. She put her pen down and went through to the front door where she found Alesia there looking cold and shivery.

"Alesia, what a lovely surprise," Heather exclaimed. "Come in, come in. Social call?"

Alesia stepped into the hallway and gave Heather a hug and a kiss. "No, I just thought it would be nice to catch up. I finished my round early, which means I've got time before picking Alex up from school."

"Let me take your coat," Heather said as she held her hands out.

"Do you mind if I keep it on for a while?" she asked. "I need to get warm before I take it off."

Heather glanced over at the bagging shed and could see Alesia's car parked alongside it. She closed the door and ushered Alesia into the kitchen.

"How come you're so cold?" she asked.

Alesia sat down. "Bloody heater's packed up in my car."

Heather put the kettle on. "Time you bought yourself a new one," she said, tongue in cheek.

Alesia chuckled. "What with, buttons?"

Heather took two cups from the cupboard. "You'll have to wait until your Alex has signed forms for a Premier League club; then he'll be able to buy you a new one."

Alesia grinned. "I tell him he will be a good as Harry Kane because that's his dream at the moment."

"Is he good enough?"

Alesia shook her head. "No, of course not. It's just a dream, but I think he knows anyway."

Heather poured milk into the cups. "We all have our dreams, Alesia. Mine is to own a farm shop. Wally says I have too fertile an imagination."

"Nothing wrong with that. We all dare to dream, don't we?"

"And what's your dream, Alesia?"

Alesia pulled a face but didn't answer.

"It's Scott, isn't it?" Heather ventured. "You'd like to spend the rest of your life with him, wouldn't you?"

Aledia grunted. "That's not likely to happen, is it? That boat has sailed I'm afraid; he's planning to marry Joanna."

Heather lifted the kettle and filled the teapot. Then she gave it a stir for a minute and filled the cups. She brought them to the table and sat down. Alesia thanked her and wrapped her hands around her cup to get them warm.

Heather took a sip of her tea. "That's what I've been hearing. But you see Scott a lot, don't you? At football training?"

Alesia nodded. "Yes. He loves taking Alex. Well, more like being with him actually."

Heather gave her a knowing look. "Are you sure it's not because he likes your company and is using Alex as an excuse?"

Alesia put her cup down. "He's giving Alex guitar lessons as well."

"Hmm, like father and son, eh?" Heather suggested.

Alesia shrugged. "You can make of it what you will, but he's spent a lot of time with Joanna recently too, so that connection hasn't gone away." She shook her head. "No, he'll go back to the States with her I think."

"When?"

Alesia wrinkled her brow. "He told me she would have her business finished by Christmas, and the chances were she would want to be back in America with her family by then. With Scott in tow."

"Are you resigned to that?" Heather asked.

"Yes, unfortunately. A Christmas wedding though," Alesia pointed out. "Perfect for them." Her manner changed suddenly. "I envy you and Wally, you know. You two are so good together."

Heather lifted her cup and looked over the top of it as she took a sip. "I've got to tell you something, Alesia, but you must keep it to yourself."

Alesia expression darkened as an awful thought came into her head. "He's not…"

Heather stopped her before she could say it. "No, no, nothing like that; it's just that he's been acting a bit weird lately. I've caught him making phone calls when he thinks I'm not around. Sometimes I phone him when he's at work and…" She shook her head and put her hand on Alesia's. "I'm scared."

Alesia frowned. "Scared? Of what?"

"What if he's going back to his old ways? He's up to something, Alesia, and I'm terrified he'll end up in prison again." She brushed the tears away from her eyes.

"Have you spoken to him about it?"

She nodded. "Yes, but you know what Wally's like. He dismisses everything as if it isn't important. Tells me I'm imagining things. I want to believe him, Alesia, but what can I do?"

"Would you like me to talk to him? Discreetly of course."

Heather straightened up in her chair. "No, goodness me, no. At the moment everything is going okay, we're still madly in love with each other, but we were when he was making big money shifting drugs on the driving job. And I didn't know anything about that, did I?"

"Well, he can't be dealing drugs in the bagging shed, can he? Unless he's dealing in stolen eggs."

Heather burst out laughing at Alesia's irreverent take on the problem. "You silly sod, perhaps that's the best way to look at it. Wait until I tell Wally he's been found out."

Alesia was glad she'd been able to bring some humour into the conversation. She wished she could have done something similar in her own case, and with that on her mind she was determined to not let the conversation come back to her and Scott's futures, particularly that of Scott and Joanna.

***

Denny hurried out of the studio into the biting wind, one hand on the collar of her winter coat to hold it fast against her neck, and the other hand dragging a suitcase behind her. She was on her way over to Lafayette's to see Mitch and talk over the final details of the Christmas show. As she walked briskly through the pedestrian precinct, she bumped into Scott and Joanna.

"Hello, Denny," Scott said. "Leaving home?" He pointed at the suitcase.

"Hello, you two," she said to them both. She looked back at the suitcase and laughed briefly. "No. I'm on my way over to see Mitch. I have the final proofs of the photograph collection I've put together for the Christmas display."

"When will that happen?" Joanna asked.

"We're hoping to open it up to the public in a couple of days' time. But the big event will be Christmas Eve."

"What event is that?" she asked.

"We're having a fashion show. I'll be showing my Spring Collection."

Joanna turned and looked at Scott and then back at Denny. "Wow, that sounds ambitious. Good for you."

"Will you be able to make it?" Denny asked. "There will be some highflyers there."

Scott pointed at Denny. "Ah, you mean that Chenelle model."

Joanna turned. "Chenelle? Not…"

"Yes, that one," Denny said a little triumphantly. "They don't come bigger than her."

"How can you possibly afford her?" Scott asked. "Or will Lafayette's be paying?"

"No; she's free. A Christmas gift no less," Denny answered. "I hope you can you make it. Should be fun."

Joanna shook her head. "We're planning to be back in the States by then." She paused and looked expectantly at Scott. "Well, I am, but we haven't quite fixed our plans, have we Scott?"

He lifted his hands. "Not yet. Anyway, we have to run; got lot to do and it's bloody cold standing around here, Denny. So, we'll see you later."

Before he had a chance to move away, Denny put her hand on his arm. "Oh, Scott. Did you know that Clive and Pam are planning to be here over Christmas."

He looked at her in surprise. "Really? From Australia?"

Denny nodded. "Yes, so don't go off to the States until you've seen them. They would be so disappointed to have missed you."

He bobbed his head up and down. "Right. If you see them before me, tell them to give me a call and we'll catch up. That would be great."

She took her hand away. "Will do. I'll speak to you later. Goodbye."

And she hurried off, head down, dragging the suitcase behind her.

***

Heather pulled on her thick winter coat, bundled little Christine up in hers and went out into the garden. She was in planning mode and wanted to figure out the planting she intended doing after Christmas. There was precious little she could do anyway; the ground was too hard to work, and she couldn't buy the vegetable plants she needed until they were available at her chosen nursery. And the truth was she just liked to be out there when Wally was working. She liked those moments when he would suddenly appear at the door of the bagging shed and she could wave at him. Christine too.

Her meandering thoughts were suddenly distracted when she hear the sound of a car engine. She turned round as a Range Rover Evoque manoeuvred it's way up the lane, bouncing around like a ship on choppy seas because the ground was now quite hard. She watched as it came to a halt outside the bagging shed and three men got out. Alf Jones was one of them. Curious now, she watched as the three men went into the bagging shed. Then she realised it was nothing to do with her, and she could always ask Wally when he came home from work.

She got back to the task of considering the best way of fencing off her garden, where to plant what, and the best way to install a water supply and hose, and how she would incorporate Christine's small, but precious plot, when she heard the men's voices again. She stood up and looked over, watching as the men started walking around the bagging shed, waving their arms about and pointing at different places, including the cottage. Alf Jones saw her standing there and waved at her. She waved back, half expecting him to walk over and tell her what was going on. But again, she realised it was nothing to do with her and put her hand down.

Then she saw one of the men holding something in his hand and started aiming it at different places. That's when she realised he was using a laser measuring device. She opened her mouth and gasped because it could only mean one thing: they were measuring the land around the bagging area, which made it look as though Scott's dad was planning to sell the farm.

She scooped little Christine up and hurried indoors, peeled off their coats and went through to the little play area she'd set aside for her daughter and left her there with her toys. Then she went through to the kitchen, slumped down at the table with her head in her hands. What she'd seen meant the farm was going to be sold after all, Wally would be out of a job, and they could end up back at the pub with her mum and dad. Her dream of starting her own fruit and veg business, and maybe a farm shop, would be just that: nothing more than a dream.

And there was nothing her and Wally could do about it.

Chapter 27

The two men had finished work early and Wally had asked Scott if he would like a drink back at the cottage. Scott was quite happy to do that, which found the two of them sitting in the kitchen at the small table with a beer each. When Scott asked about Heather, Wally told him her mother had taken her out shopping and wouldn't be back until later that afternoon.

"Do you think you'll be happy here, Wally?" Scott asked.

Wally nodded sharply. "Bloody hell, yes. I've got Heather and Christine, and a job."

Scott stared down at his glass as he twirled it back and forth with his thumb and finger. "Must be nice to be that content," he said with a softness in his voice that surprised Wally. "I wish I could settle down."

"I thought you had that chance with Joanna," Wally said.

Scott looked over at his friend. "It nearly happened, but she pulled the plug on it."

"And now she's back."

Scott grinned and started twirling the glass again. "Looks like it."

"Was there anyone else, besides Joanna?"

Scott made a sound in his throat. "There was, but it was never likely to happen." He waited for Wally to ask the question, but it never came. He picked up his glass and took another mouthful of beer, putting his glass down sharply after he drained it.

"Alesia," he said.

Wally tipped his head back and breathed out harshly in a long sigh. "Bloody hell, Scott. Alesia?"

Scott grinned as he looked over the table. "You sound surprised."

"I am," Wally answered sitting upright again. "I remember the night of the Prom after you'd danced with her. You told me you loved her." He chuckled. "I said it was infatuation but no; you wouldn't have it."

Scott watched as Wally tried to grasp the reality of what he'd just been told.

"What you have to understand, Wally, is that I was the figure of fun, the no-hoper, Chicken George. No girl would look at me; probably some sort of Peer pressure I guess. But I knew I could never hope to win Alesia because of who I was and her perception of me. And she was going to end up with Simeon anyway, so what chance did I have?"

Wally sat forward and peered at Scott. "Have you been carrying a torch for her all these years?"

Scott nodded his head, slow movements up and down. "One of the reasons I went to America, was because I hoped I could get Alesia out of my system and lose myself in music. But it didn't happen. I thought I could make out with women and lose all feelings about her. I slept with dozens of women, Wally, believe me. It was like trying to flush a stain out of my system; one that was stopping me from having a fruitful, loving relationship. When I heard that Alesia had married Simeon, it didn't surprise me, and in some ways, it helped. She was no longer available and had done what we all knew she was bound to do." He gave a kind of whimsical look at Wally. "You know, when I heard that she'd divorced Simeon and was left with a kid, it simply resurrected my feelings for her. I couldn't believe it; I thought I was going mental. I wouldn't mind, Wally, but we were separated by three thousand miles and had never had any connection at all — nothing."

"I didn't realise you felt that way," Wally told him.

Scott nodded. "I'm a sad sod, aren't I?" He chuckled as he said it.

"But what about Joanna?"

Scott brightened a little at the mention if her name. "Yes, I thought that was it. I finally had someone with whom I could see a future. I genuinely believed that I had the kind of feelings for Joanna that I had for Alesia. It was as though Joanna had become a substitute." He stopped and looked at Wally. "Am I making sense?"

"In a way. I know how I felt about Heather, but she felt the same way about me thank God."

Scott grinned. "Lucky sods, the pair of you."

"So, come on then — what about Joanna? The rumour is that you and she will be going back to America to get married. Is it true?"

Scott lifted his head and was about to say something when the kitchen door burst open, and Heather walked in.

"Hello you two. What's this? A session?" She kissed Wally. "No work then?"

Wally shook his head. "We finished early, so I asked Scott if he fancied a drink. And what about you? What have you been up to?"

"Me and Christine started to prepare her little allotment this morning." She gave him a big grin. "We're going into competition," she said, spinning round. "Then I went shopping with mum, but you knew that, Wally. Now I'd better get on with your dinner." She looked at Scott. "Do you want to stay for dinner, Scott?"

He shook his head and pushed himself up from the table. "No thanks, Heather; I promised dad some father and son time. So, I'd best be getting off." He came round the table and kissed her on the cheek. "I'll see you later. He winked at Wally and put his finger to his lips.

Wally smiled back knowing that Scott wanted his feelings about Alesia kept under wraps, but he couldn't help feeling sorry for him. He put his hand up as Scott left the kitchen.

Heather watched him go and then turned to Wally. "He looks a bit solemn. What have you done?"

Wally got up and put his arm round her waist. "Nothing; I think he's a bit tired," he lied. "We've had quite a busy day."

"Who were those men at the site this morning, Wally?" she asked. "Is Scott's dad selling up?"

He shrugged, not sure what to tell her. Then he came up with a big lie. "Oh, that? No, he wanted the farm reassessed for tax reasons. It seems that this smallholding has always been included as part of the farm. His dad wanted it put right, that's all." He held his breath hoping he'd get away with it.

Heather stared at him for a moment, and he wondered if she'd sussed him out. Then she nodded her head slowly.

"Oh, that's good. When I saw them I thought…" She shrugged. "Well, it doesn't matter now. I'll go and get Christine in."

"Where is she?"

"Showing her planned garden to mum."

Wally picked up the two empty glasses as Heather left the kitchen. He washed them under the kitchen tap and put them on the draining board to drain and thought again about Scott and Alesia. Then thanked his lucky stars and went off in search of his wife and daughter.

But not before he made a quick phone call.

***

Scott and his dad had finished their evening meal. It was a little after seven o'clock and Scott had agreed to see Joanna that evening for a drink. He'd promised his dad some father and son time and figured that he'd done his filial duty and need not feel that he was neglecting that duty having spent the last couple of hours talking about this and that, and avoiding the one topic of conversation that he knew would surely come — him, Alesia and Joanna.

"I had a call from Wally earlier," he said to his dad. "Heather asked him what those men were doing this morning over at the bagging shed."

"Yes, I saw her. Gave her a wave. So, what did Wally tell her?"

"He cooked up a yarn about you having the farm reassessed for tax reasons. Told her you was keen to get the legal position straight because the smallholding was still included in the details on the land registry and that had to be resolved. Load of bullshit of course, but Heather was afraid you'd be selling up and Wally would be out of a job. He swung it, thankfully, and Heather's okay now."

Alf nodded. "Well, at least they won't have to move out, will they Scott?"

Scott gave his dad an enquiring look. "You sound sceptical. Am I right?"

"You could be. I know you've had your smallholding valued now."

Scott grinned. "Yes, that was like a covert op. Had to wait until Heather was at her dad's allotment before I could smuggle the valuers in."

"But won't the situation with you and Joanna change that?"

Scott frowned. "Why should it?"

His dad leaned closer to the table and looked at Scott with an earnest expression on his face. "If you get married, she may want to move into the cottage with you."

Scott laughed at that. "Joanna in the cottage? Don't be daft. She's going back to the States where she belongs. England doesn't suit her, and that's the truth."

"Which means you'll go back there with her."

"I haven't said I'll marry her. Not yet anyway."

"Have you proposed?"

Scott grinned and shook his head. "No, she proposed to me; gave me an ultimatum."

His dad straightened up in the chair. "What's the real reason you haven't proposed, Scott? Is it Alesia?"

Scott stared at his dad briefly. "Alesia's in love with someone else. She's not interested in me."

"Who?"

He sighed deeply. "I don't know. When I asked her, she wouldn't say except it was someone who was unavailable."

"What, married?"

Scott shrugged. "Who knows. But that's the reason I'm giving serious thought to marrying Joanna."

"But you don't love her, do you?"

"I know I could be happy with her."

"You're not afraid she'll dump you again?"

"No, not this time."

"When are you going to make up your mind?"

Scott looked at his watch. "Well, I'm seeing her tonight. Could be the right time," he suggested. "We could sell the smallholding to Wally and I could marry Joanna all before Christmas."

"Have you told Alesia of your feelings for her."

That made Scott feel a little uncomfortable. He'd tried several times but there had always seemed to be some kind of interruption which stalled the moment and let it slip by. Not to mention his own ineptitude.

"I've tried, dad, believe me, but it just hasn't happened." He pushed himself up from the chair. "I've got to go now. I promised Joanna I'd meet her at eight o'clock."

His dad got up too and started clearing the dirty dishes away from the table. "You know, Scott, you're my son and I want what's best for you. But in this case, I have to admit I want what's best for you and Alesia."

"I know, dad. I'll see you later. Don't wait up."

"Do I ever?"

Scott laughed. "You might this time," he said, "but nothing's likely to happen. See you."

He left the house five minutes later with his dad's words ringing in his ears and knew where he wanted his future to lie, but only Alesia could do that for him, and she was in love with someone else.

Chapter 28

Denny was at the station by mid-day to meet Chenelle and her two friends off the train. The snow had made an early pre-Christmas appearance and was falling without too much threat, although with maybe a promise of a White Christmas. Chenelle stepped off the train slipping on her winter coat and turning her head to laugh at something her companions had said. They too were wearing winter coats, and none of them looked like internationally famous fashion models.

Denny waved at them as they hurried to the platform exit turnstiles and gave Chenelle a hug when she got through. "I'm so pleased you're here," she said. "Sorry about the weather."

Chenelle laughed and then introduced her two friends to Denny. "Jolene and Eloise."

Denny embraced them both. "Thank you for coming; I really appreciate it."

They air-kissed Denny. "So, what's the plan?" Jolene asked.

"We'll get you booked in at the hotel, than take you to lunch. After that we are due over at Lafayette's to meet Mitch and to go through the routine for tomorrow."

They made it to the hotel as the snowfall thickened. Eloise had made a remark on having to give up a fashion shoot in the South of France. Jolene pushed her on the shoulder. They laughed together as the idea of missing a chance to enjoy the relative warmth and comfort of

Antibes or Monte Carlo. Chenelle looked at Denny and wrinkled her nose.

"Ignore them," she said. "They're just two out of work beauty queens who think Norfolk is beneath them." She was laughing as she said that, and Denny knew it was just high spirits; they were all professionals and knew exactly what they were doing.

Lunch was a source of wonder for Denny. She found the two girls were funny as well as strikingly beautiful. Beneath the winter coats and the banter, they really were like two diamonds among precious stones. It made her wonder how Mitch was going to react when he saw them. And as that thought crossed her mind, she felt a momentary weight on her heart.

Mitch's reaction when he was introduced to Jolene and Eloise was exactly as Denny had imagined. She could tell by the look in his eyes and the expression on his face he was in awe of the beauty in front of him. It took him a while to get his words sorted out as he asked if there was anything they needed before they started work in earnest.

Chenelle looked on with the glimmer of a smile on her face. She caught Denny by the elbow and whispered in her ear.

"He doesn't know what's hit him. He's drooling."

Denny felt that momentary weight on her heart again, but she put on a brave smile as she responded to Chenelle's remark.

"Like a kid in the sweet shop," she said. "Doesn't know which of the sweet jars he wants to dive into."

"Don't you worry, my darling. I've seen how those two girls operate, and believe me, Mitch is in no danger."

It was a small relief for Denny, but Mitch had no idea of how the two girls operated. She just hoped he would remain professional too.

Mitch led them into the ground floor area in which the exhibition had been set up. The Christmas decorations literally exploded around the area with all manner of typical Christmas themes including popular stories from the Carols, the Bible, Olde England and a wonderful display of lights and a beautifully lit, Christmas tree. It was almost like a Fairy-tale Grotto. The girls were held there in a moment of wonder and opening memories that went back to their own childhoods. It was pure magic.

A catwalk had been built for the fashion show. The two girls immediately hopped up onto the walk and sashayed their way along the short length. Denny imagined them wearing her Spring collection and immediately had a funny feeling in her tummy.

Mitch explained carefully the reasons for the show and pointed out the unravelling of the years through the display of framed photographs that between them they had put together. Mitch was particularly proud of the way in which he and his staff had turned Lafayette's ground floor into a magnificent, walk-in exhibition for the public.

When the tour was over, Denny asked Chenelle if they would like to see the Spring collection, which she had brought over to the store and was now under lock and key. They girls jumped at the chance. Mitch said he had to leave but promised to meet them for dinner that evening. He gave them all a quick kiss on the cheek, maybe lingering a little longer with Jolene and Eloise, and left them there. It was another small, heart dropping moment for Denny, but there was precious little she could do about it and tried not to let the dismal thought linger.

***

Alesia sat at the kitchen table holding a cup of tea in her hands and staring into space. Alex was sitting opposite her eating his breakfast. While he was eating he kept looking up at his mum, wondering why she was sitting there looking miles away.

"Mum."

Alesia jumped as Alex's voice broke into her train of thought. "What? Oh, sorry, Alex. Miles away. What do you want?"

"Can I buy Mandy a Christmas present?"

She put her cup down. "You got any money?"

He shook his head. "No, but I can borrow it from you, can't I?"

She laughed softly. "Did you never think of saving some of your pocket money then?"

"I did, but that was for your present."

She could have hugged him. She smiled warmly instead. "Why do you want to buy Mandy a present."

Alex looked down at his breakfast bowl and slowly stirred the remaining contents with his spoon. "Well, I like her; she's special."

Alesia raised her eyebrows. "So are a lot of your friends."

He stopped stirring his bowl. "But not like Mandy."

"And how special is Mandy then?"

"Mandy's brother says I love her."

She lowered her gaze a little. "And do you?" She was trying not to smile.

He gave a negative shrug. "I don't know. Mandy's mum told her that love is something for grown-ups, not for kids like us."

Alesia chuckled at that. "Which grown-ups often mess up big time." She muttered to herself.

"Can I, Mum?"

"Why have you waited until now?" she asked, looking up at the calendar. "It's Christmas Eve tomorrow."

"I was scared you might say no."

"And now you're not scared?" Her smile was trying desperately to break into a soft laugh.

"Well, Mandy's mum said that you should never be too scared to ask for what you want because you're not doing anything wrong. And they can only say no."

Coming from a little boy like Alex, even though he was repeating what Mandy's mum had said, it gave her an unsettling moment — one that he wouldn't have been aware of or even understood. She lapsed into silence and started staring at the wall again, her mind on two adults who had messed up, and one in particular who would live to regret it.

"Mum!"

She blinked. "Sorry, Alex." She sighed heavily. "Yes, okay, but we'll have to wait until I've finished work before we go to the shops." A big grin spread across Alex's face until Alesia said, "Or maybe Scott would want to take you?"

The grin disappeared. "He can't."

"Why?"

"He's going back to America with his girlfriend. You know the one."

"Where did you hear that?" Alex was about to answer when Alesia put her hand up. "I know, don't tell me. It was Mandy's mum."

He shook his head. "No; it was at football training. Someone asked me where Scott was, and I said I didn't know. Then someone behind us said he was going back to America tomorrow." He looked down at his fingers and counted. "No, it's today."

Alesia stared open-mouthed. "Today?"

He nodded. Yes. So, can we buy Mandy's present today? Please?"

Alesia slumped in her chair and fought back the tears that were threatening to break out and roll down her face. Then she pulled out a tissue from her pocket and pretended to blow her nose because she didn't want Alex to see her wiping her tears away. She got up from the table.

"Okay, Alex, tomorrow, as soon as I've finished my deliveries. It won't be too late; I'll probably be done by eleven o'clock." She gathered the dirty dishes up from the table and took them to the sink. "As soon as I've washed these things up, we'll get off to Heather's. She'll be looking after you today."

Alex slid away from the table and went to get ready, leaving his mum there to contemplate an empty future, but with her son's word ringing in her ears.

'They can only say no.'

Chapter 29

Alesia finished the last of her deliveries. It was relatively early and still snowing. She would normally have taken the van straight back to the warehouse, picked up her car and got on with the rest of her day, which today meant getting over to Heather's place and taking Alex Christmas shopping. But because she was close to Monk's Farm and the cottage, she decided to drive there in the van, pick up Alex and get back to the warehouse for her car. But before doing anything, she took her phone out of her pocket and dialled Scott's number. It was to be a forlorn attempt to tell him how she felt about him before he left for America. She could feel her heart beating as she waited for him to pick up. She had no idea how this was going to go, but felt she had no choice. The call went to voicemail.

"Bugger!"

She tried again but it still went to voicemail. She tossed the phone onto the passenger seat and started the van. The only person she could think of who might know where Scott was, would be Wally. It was a slim chance, but one she had to take. She pulled out on to the road and headed over to the farm trying her best not to hurry because of the falling snow and the usual risks when driving in a hurry with something on your mind.

She reached the farm and parked at the end of the bagging shed, clambered out of the van and hurried over to the cottage, her head bent against the falling snow. Heather opened the door to her knocking and ushered her in, closing the door behind her as she stepped into the hallway.

"Is Wally here?" she asked without saying hello first.

Heather frowned. "No, he's been sent out on an errand for Scott's dad. He's in town somewhere. Do you want me to call him?"

Alesia shook her head. "No." She sounded a little puffed out. "I need to speak to Scott, but he's not answering his phone."

"Why do want to speak to Wally then?"

Alesia shook her head and flapped her hands. "Oh, I'm sorry, Heather; my mind's all over the place." She sagged visibly. "Scott is leaving for America today." She lifted her chin and looked at Heather with tears in her eyes. "I have to tell him how I feel about him, Heather." She shrugged. "I have to tell him I love him."

Heather took hold of Alesia's arm. "Oh, Alesia. And you think that will stop him? Make him change his mind?"

"I have to know but I can't tell him if he won't answer his bloody phone." She was getting frustrated and angry.

"Call his dad; he might know where Scott is."

"Do you have his number?"

Heather pointed to the kitchen. "In there."

Alesia suddenly remembered Alex. "Oh, where's Alex?"

"He's over at the bagging shed. One of the women is showing him how it all works."

Heather picked up her phone from the worktop in the kitchen and called Scott's dad. She handed the phone to Alesia.

"Mr. Jones?" Alesia said when she heard him answer. "This is Alesia. I'm at the cottage. Is Scott with you?"

"No, sorry, Alesia. He's with Joanna."

"Have they gone?"

"They're due at the station. They're catching the twelve thirty to London."

"Scott's not answering his phone."

Alf Jones grunted. "No, the silly sod left it here. But if you want, I can bring the phone over to you. There might just be enough time to get to the station and give it to him."

Alesia thought that was a bit weird. Then she realised. "You know, don't you?"

"I know he loves you, Alesia. And if you don't stop him from getting on that train, you'll lose him."

"Sod the phone, Mr. Jones. He can get it when I bring him back. Goodbye."

She cancelled the call and handed the phone back. "He's at the station," she told Heather. "I'm going."

Heather watched open-mouthed as Alesia went running out of the cottage as climbed into her delivery van, turned it around and went bouncing and careering down the lane in her quest to drag Scott back and tell him she loved him. She sighed, shook her head and closed the door.

***

Alesia drove away from the farm as the snow started piling up on the windscreen giving the wipers a hard time and making her curse the weather and the road conditions. Her mind was in a complete spin as she contemplated the chances of finding Scott and being able to tell him how much she wanted to spend the rest of her life with him, but the fear was she wouldn't be able to detach him from Joanna.

The journey into town and the railway station was slow because of the weather, but her frustration reached boiling point when she came to a temporary set of traffic lights at roadworks where no-one seemed to be working. She banged her fist on the steering wheel and shouted at the hold up.

"Come on, come on!"

The lights changed but nothing moved. Then the queue shifted, and the lights went red again. Alesia wanted to burst into tears but had to bear the pain and wait until the snarl-up had cleared. Then suddenly she was through and into the town driving, creeping more like, with the traffic towards the next set of traffic lights that wouldn't help her at all.

She looked at the clock on the dashboard. 12.29.

"No, no!" she shouted in her frustration and anger. "Please, no."

She pulled up at the station and stopped on double yellow lines, turned the engine off and leapt out of the van. She didn't bother to lock it, just ran into the station and on to an empty concourse.

She came to a stop and looked around. She saw a staff member in uniform and ran over to him.

"London train, please?"

He pointed. "Just pulled out from platform one, ma'am. I'm afraid you've missed it."

She turned her face away, and looked over to where he had pointed, and then started walking slowly towards the platform. She stood at the turnstile and watched as the tail end of the train was almost out of sight about half a mile down the track. Then it was gone.

She sagged and slumped forward on the turnstile, her world collapsing around her, tears rolling down her cheeks and having to accept it was all over.

"I didn't think you was going to make it," a voice said behind her.

She turned to see who it was.

"Scott?"

He stepped forward. "Hello, Alesia. My dad said you was on your way."

"But your phone…?"

"He called me on Joanna's phone."

She automatically turned and looked back at the empty platform. "Joanna?" she said, looking back at him.

He looked beyond her. "She's on the train. She's going home."

Alesia turned and faced him. "I need to tell you something."

He put a finger on her lips. "You don't have to, Alesia. Scott took her hands in his and closed his fingers around them. Alesia felt her heart beat a little quicker. She blinked several times, but kept her eyes fixed on his.

"Do you remember when you first saw me up at Monk's Farm with that silly fish order?" Alesia gave a quick nod. He went on. "You gave me a hug; something I will never forget because it told me something — more than I could possibly have hoped for."

"What —"

He stopped her. "And later when we went out to dinner, you asked me why I went away?"

She gave that quick nod again.

"I told you then that there was another reason why I left, but it was personal to me, which was why I couldn't say anything."

Alesia heart rate increased.

"You was that reason, Alesia."

"Scott..."

"Don't say anything, just know this. I've always loved you. From the moment I took you in my arms at the Prom, there was never anyone else but you. And when you told me you was in love with someone who was unavailable, I believed you, which was why I couldn't reveal my true feelings."

"When did you know it was you?"

He grinned. "Heather. She already knew about your pretence at having someone else but couldn't say anything to me because she thought there was a chance I would go back to the States with Joanna. She phoned my dad just after you left the cottage. He told me when he made that phone call to Joanna's phone."

Alesia moved closer to him and put her hands on his arms. "Scott, can we stop talking for a moment please?"

"Why?"

She reached up, standing on tiptoe and kissed him on the lips. He responded by pulling her in closer and hugged her as tightly as he dared. When they finally parted, Alesia smiled.

"I've parked my van on a double yellow line," she said. "I can't let them tow it away."

He grinned. "I'll buy you a new one if they do."

She laughed. It was a soft laughter, gentle, warm and affectionate. "Scott."

He stopped again by putting his finger on her lips. "Alesia, will you marry me?"

She tried to say yes but started sobbing so much she couldn't get the words out of her mouth.

Scott wiped her tears with his thumbs, stroking them gently across her cheeks. "I'll take that as a yes," he said. Then he kissed her and pulled away. "Now, let's go and save you from a prison sentence and shift that van of yours."

Alesia put her arm around his, her tears flowing down to the huge grin that was spreading all over her face, and together they walked out of the station, their lives now bound to each other and both as happy as they could ever wish to be.

Chapter 30

Heather was upstairs putting her makeup on ready for their evening out at the Lafayette's Carol Service that evening when she heard a car coming up the lane. It was late afternoon, the nights had been drawing in, and what with the weather and snow, there was a deathly stillness and quiet around the place. She frowned and hurried downstairs. Wally was sitting in the front room watching a children's programme on TV with their daughter.

"You haven't ordered the taxi this early, have you love?" she asked as she walked in.

He turned his head. "What? No."

She went through to the front door and opened it. In the gloom she saw the headlight beams bouncing up and down as the car cleared the lane and came over towards the cottage. She had to wait until the car stopped and the lights had been extinguished before she realised it was Alesia's car. Her heart dropped because she hadn't expected to see Alesia until that later at Lafayette's, and she feared there was only one reason why she was there.

She stepped back and held the door open as Alesia and Scott came running into the house, both blowing a bit as they came to a stop inside the hallway. Heather closed the door and just stared at the two of them.

"Is Wally here?" Scott asked. He was holding something in his hand.

Heather simply nodded and pointed towards the lounge. "He's watching TV with Christine."

Scott went through on his own leaving Alesia standing there with Heather.

"What happened?" Heather whispered as though there was a need for secrecy.

Alesia grabbed her hand. "He was never going to America," she said. "He was waiting for me at the station." Suddenly she kissed Heather on the cheek. "He got your message."

Heather pointed a finger at herself. "My message?"

Alesia nodded her head. "Yes, that I was in love with him."

It clicked. Heather opened her mouth wide. "His dad? Of course." She put her hand on her chest. "Oh, my goodness, Alesia. So, what did Scott say when you got there."

Alesia couldn't hold it back any longer. "We're getting married, Heather. He's always loved me — no-one else."

They threw their arms around each other and started jumping up and down and laughing like a couple of kids. And as they were jumping around in the hallway, Wally came running in with Scott behind him.

"Congratulations, Alesia," he called out, and joined the two of them in a huddle. Scott just stood there with a big silly grin on his face.

When they calmed down, Heather took them through to the kitchen and offered them a drink, but they both declined.

"Plenty of time for that tonight," Alesia said. "But I had to come over and tell you, Heather. I'm so excited." She wrapped her arm around Scott. "I got my Christmas present early," she said. "I'm so happy." She still had tears in her eyes. Scott as well. "We'll go now. See you tonight?"

Heather had both her hands tight together in an attitude of prayer although she wasn't praying. "You bet. Oh, I'm so happy for you both. You must tell us all the details tonight. It'll be brilliant. We love you both."

As Scott and Alesia turned to go, Scott mouthed something to Wally and winked. Then he followed Alesia out of the door.

Heather turned towards Wally. "What was that about?"

Wally put his finger to his lips. "I've got something for you. Wait there." He disappeared and came back less than a minute later with a parcel wrapped in Christmas paper. It was neatly tied with a ribbon and a card had been attached.

"I've bought you two Christmas presents," he began. "One which is under the Christmas tree and this one." He handed it to her. "I wanted you to have it now, before we go to the Carol Service."

Heather's expression deepened as she took the parcel from him. It was fairly slim and about the size of a large manilla envelope. She read the small card and smiled. Then she pulled the wrapping off and let it drop onto the kitchen table. She was now holding a slim folder. She glanced at him quickly and opened it up. Inside were what looked like a bundle of official papers. She frowned and as the meaning of the words started filtering through, she realised she was looking at the deeds of the smallholding of which she was now the title holder.

She gasped and looked up at Wally, and then back at the papers, flicking through the few pages that outlined the legal stuff and rights etc. Then she looked back at him.

"What have you done? You've bought the cottage?"

"The smallholding," he said triumphantly waving an arm around in an arc. "It's yours."

"But we can't afford this, Wally." She flapped the deeds. "Goodness knows how we're going to pay the mortgage." She dropped the papers on to the table. "Please don't tell me you've gone back to your old tricks again." She let out a groan. "Oh, Wally, what have you done? You'll have us out on the streets, and you'll end up in jail."

Wally smiled and stepped forward. He put both arms around her and pinned hers to her side. The he pulled her in a little closer. "I do love it when you get angry with me." He kissed her.

Heather looked at him with tears in her eyes. "Wally."

He shook his head. "There's no trick to this, sweetheart. The smallholding belongs to you, and you can throw me out for trespassing on your property. It's all legit, I promise. Paid in cash with my own money. It's my Christmas present to you because I love you." Tears started rolling down his cheeks. "You don't know how much I've wanted to do this for you. Scott was in on it of course. So was his dad. Scott had to go into town to pick the deeds up. The girl in the office wrapped them for me."

"So, that's what all those secret phone calls were about?"

He nodded.

"I thought you were seeing someone secretly," she said.

He pulled her close. "Oh, my God, if I could have done it any other way, I would. But I wanted it this way. I'm sorry love."

She clung to him and held him so tightly as she sobbed. She loved this man so much, it almost hurt. Then she pulled away.

"Now look what you've done to my bloody makeup. And the taxi will be here soon."

He gave her a gentle smack on the bum. "Well, you'd better get cleaned up and I'll get our daughter ready for the Carol Service. Oh, and you can thank me properly tonight."

She kissed him again and left him standing there with a huge smile, a strongly beating heart and a sense of satisfaction he had never felt in his life before.

***

Chenelle made the decision for Mitch when he asked them about dinner that evening. She told him the girls would prefer the hotel, which was where they ended up after a very satisfying afternoon planning the fashion show and its final stages.

They enjoyed the meal. Mitch had ordered wine, but Chenelle and the two girls chose spring water. Jolene had joked about turning up for an event hungover and looking a little worse for wear. "Not very professional," she told him.

Mitch was surprised, but then he had learned much about the unseen world of fashion through the unaffected behaviour of the three women. Apart from inside jokes to each other, their approach to the planning was completely professional, and between the three girls they had managed to suggest ways of improving what was going to be a truly magnificent event.

As the evening wore on, Mitch could see that Jolene and Eloise were getting tired. Chenelle too. Denny had been quiet, which was unusual for her, and Mitch began to wonder if it what she had seen and experienced over the last few hours was all a bit overwhelming for her.

Eventually, Jolene and Eloise declared their intention of turning in for the night. They both gave Mitch a warm, affectionate hug and kiss, which made Denny feel quite invisible. Chenelle said she would follow them in a little while. The girls said goodnight and went up to their rooms.

Mitch put his hand on Chenelle's. She covered it with her hand and wrinkled her nose at him. Denny looked on as the two of them smiled at each other. At that moment she'd never felt so alone; it was as though they were the only two people at the table. She coughed gently and picked up her clutch bag.

"Excuse me," she said getting up out of her chair. "I need to spend a penny."

Mitch and Denny uncoupled their hands, the moment between them broken. Chenelle watched her go, and when she was out of sight, she looked back at Mitch.

"You know she loves you, Mitch."

Mitch's face blanched and his eyes widened. "What?"

Chenelle leaned forward. "Denny — she loves you. Can't you see that?"

Mitch turned his head away and looked over at the door through which Denny had disappeared. He looked back at Chenelle and shook his head.

"No, not Denny. She's not like that."

"Like what?" Chenelle asked, her expression darkening.

Mitch started to fluster. "Well, you know…" He struggled to finish the sentence, not wanting to say what he thought. He shrugged. "I don't think she's interested in men."

Chenelle sat bolt upright. "You think she's gay?"

He waved both hands in a dismissive motion. "Ah, well, maybe not gay — just not interested in men."

Chenelle looked at him exasperated. "Oh, for goodness' sake, Mitch, if I thought Denny was gay, I would have been on her in a flash."

Mitch knew that Chenelle's sexual preferences were towards women only and could understand why she would have been drawn to Denny.

"So, what makes you think she's in love with me?"

Chenelle shook her head gently. "She gives out the vibes, Mitch — every time she's in your company. Can't you see that?"

"No," he said lamely. "I can't."

Then Chenelle leaned forward and looked at him in earnest. "Do you love her Mitch?"

He flicked his eyes up at her, then nodded. It was a short, sharp couple of nods as though he was owning up to something embarrassing.

"Yes, I do."

She straightened up. "Then tell her you bloody fool. Tell her!"

He put his hands up, cupping them round his cheeks, supporting his chin. "I can't, Chenelle. I've tried but…"

"Mitch, if you won't tell her, then I will."

He dropped his hands and looked horrified. "No, please don't do that, Chenelle. I will, I promise."

She took his hands. "Then please do."

At that moment, Denny walked back in. She saw Mitch and Chenelle holding hands in what looked like an intimate moment. It made her feel quite sad and simply reinforced the notion that the two of them were lovers.

She reached the table, smiled as best she could and sat down. "Phew, I needed that."

Chenelle pushed her chair back and got up. "My turn," she said, and as she started to walk away from the table, she leaned close to Mitch and whispered in his ear.

"Tell her you bloody fool. Tell her!"

Denny watched her go and then turned to Mitch. "Tell me what, Mitch?"

Mitch breathed in deeply. He could feel his nerves screaming out at him. His tongue seemed to swell and fill his mouth.

Denny frowned, worried now that Mitch was struggling over something, and she thought she knew what it was.

"You're in love with her, aren't you?"

Then suddenly, all of Mitch's anxiety melted away when he saw in Denny's eyes the disappointment she was expecting to come, and that was when he realised Chenelle was right. He beathed again and smiled, then shook his head.

"No, Denny; I'm not. I'm in love with you." He reached over the table and took her hands. "Chenelle believes you are in love with me." He laughed softly. "She threatened to tell you if I didn't."

Denny's mind was spinning. "I thought you two were…"

He shook his head. "Denny, she's gorgeous, lovely and fun to be with, but she's not you."

Denny blinked her tears away. Her heartbeats made her chest feel hollow as the realisation of what Mitch had said began to settle on her heart.

"I can't expect you to tell me you love me, Denny," he said, "but if you can find it in your heart —"

She stopped him. "Mitch. You men can be so blind at times. I've loved you from day one, whenever that was." She smiled at him as she said it. "So why don't you give me a kiss?"

He looked round the restaurant, not sure. Then he knew what he had to do and got up from his chair, came round to Denny and kissed her. And they were still in a clinch when Chenelle came back to the table.

Chenelle tapped them both. "About bloody time, too."

Mitch and Denny both felt a little self-conscious. They laughed as Chenelle threw her arms around them both in a strong hug.

"Well," she said, "I'm going to bed, and I think you two should as well. Goodnight."

She left them standing there, grinning happily. Then Denny turned to Mitch. "My place or yours, Mitch? I don't think I can wait."

He glanced up at the ceiling. "A hotel room would be closer," he said. "And I'm sure they'll have an empty one."

Denny took his hand. "Let's find out," she said and led a submissive, excited man-child to a world of unimaginable bliss.

***

The fashion show had been brilliant. Mitch had hired an Events team from a local company to set everything up. They had expected a large gathering of important people from the world of fashion, simply because of Chenelle and the two girls. Word had got round very quickly on the relevant social media platforms, which meant several magazines would be represented in the crowd. Mitch knew he would not have been able to cope with the seating arrangements without the expertise of the Events Company.

Denny's Spring Collection had been a monstrous success and was hitting the virtual fashion world in time for the early morning digital editions which would inevitably be followed by the printed editions. It was an amazing experience for both Mitch and Denny. Mitch thought all his Christmases had come at once after his blissful coupling with Denny following their declaration of love for each other. Each time he caught Denny's eye, she gave him a knowing wink and a smile. Chenelle had cottoned on almost immediately and was so happy for the pair of them.

The fashion show ended late afternoon, which meant a pause of two hours while the Events team repositioned everything and removed the catwalk so that the area could accommodate about the five hundred people who were expected to attend. The Carol Service was to be performed by the choir from the local St. Paul's church, led by the wife of the new vicar.

Denny and Mitch had to supervise the setting for a special table which was to accommodate her old Prom college chums for the celebration after the Carol Service. She'd been so pleased to meet Clive and Pam who were on their home visit from Australia. There was precious little time to catch up with the missing years, but they promised to meet up after Christmas before Clive and Pam returned home.

There was just enough time for Mitch and Denny to dash home and change for the Carol Service which was due to start at seven o'clock. They both wished they could have shared that small slot of free time together, but patience was the order of the day for now, and they had to be content with simply being in each other's company.

Denny made sure she was back at Lafayette's well ahead of the start time. Heather had arrived with Wally and their daughter, Christine. Alesia had turned up with Alex and Scott. That raised a few eyebrows for those who were not aware of the developments between the two of them. Alesia had dragged Denny to one side and told her the good news. Denny wanted to know more, but that evening was going to be about promises to catch up later.

As seven o'clock approached, the hall was almost full. There was the usual hubbub of noise as people chatted. At their VIP table, Alesia was in earnest conversation with Clive and Pam, but there was no way she could impart the impact of what her and Scott had been through. Then suddenly the sound of Christmas music came over the speakers. Very soft at first making the bubble of conversations die away as the choristers appeared at the far end of the room. They were led by their choir leader, and all of them were wearing matching outfits which befitted the occasion.

Then Clive's wife, Pam leaned over to Alesia. "Isn't that Sylvia?" She was pointing at the leader, the choir mistress. Clive's mother leaned over too.

"I believe it is," she said. "She's the wife of the new vicar. Been there a couple of weeks. She's done a marvellous job with the choir apparently. Oh, there he is — her husband."

Alesia looked over at the handsome looking vicar who was walking behind the choir. She reeled back in shock, stood upright from her chair and almost fainted.

It was Simeon.

Chapter 31

The shock of seeing Simeon left Alesia feeling quite unwell for a while. But coupled with that was the joy of seeing Sylvia and the fact that the wheel had come full circle — all ten of them from the Prom night were now together in the same room, and that in itself was something of a miracle.

Simeon wasn't immediately aware of the slight disturbance at the table, his attention was focussed on the choir in front of him, so it took a little time as he settled into his reserved seat at the front to have a look round at the people around him. And that moment came when he was asked to bless the Carol Service. As he stood at the microphone and began to address the assembly, he saw his old friends sitting at their special table. He smiled and nodded towards them, then opened the service with a blessing. As he took his seat, he looked in Alesia's direction, lifted his arm and tapped his watch.

An hour later, as the choristers left the hall, Simeon came over to the table. Alesia felt nothing like that moment all those years ago when he came to the girls' table with the challenge but greeted him without malice as she gave him a light hug, then turned to Sylvia and wrapped her arms around her closely. But before he moved on to say hello to the others, he asked Alesia if they could talk. It was inevitable of course and something Alesia needed. Fifteen minutes later they were sat together on a couple of chairs in a quiet corner.

"It's really good to see you, Alesia. I mean that." Alesia said nothing. "I know this will come as a shock to you…" He pointed at his collar, "but it wasn't planned. I never intended it to happen, but God found a way and I have no regrets."

Alesia was still struggling to get over the shock of seeing him like this. "You don't regret leaving me with a child?"

"I do regret that, of course I do, but I need to explain, and I need to ask your forgiveness."

She gave a single shrug. "I don't think that's necessary, Simeon; and you know why."

"Because you deceived me?"

She blinked away the tears. "I couldn't see any other way. I wanted a child, and you didn't, which is why I stopped taking the pill and never told you."

Simeon thought back to the moment Alesia told him she was pregnant and how he'd reacted to the news. And when Alesia confessed to deliberately getting pregnant, he wanted nothing more to do with her or the child. Just remembering his own behaviour appalled him, but that was the kind of man he was then. The most important thing to him at the time was the image the two of them conveyed to their friends and family: a perfect couple, totally in love, so he thought.

"I can understand now," he said. "But not when it happened." He smiled briefly. "My ego suffered." He reached out and put his hand on hers. "But if you hear me out, it might help you to understand why all this happened."

She picked up her drink and nodded. "Go on then; I owe you that at least."

He closed his eyes briefly. Alesia wondered if he was praying a silent prayer. He opened them and shook his head.

"When you made me sign that ridiculous document promising to surrender all rights and ownership to our son, I couldn't have been happier."

Alesia's mind went back to that day Simeon had become the worst person on earth. She hated him: the love she believed she had at the time for him had been shorn of any meaning, and she came to despise him.

"You freed me," Simeon went on, "from a burden I never wanted and was so pleased I'd got away with it, because believe me, I had." He took a sip of his non-alcoholic drink. "My life returned to youthful abandon — girls, drinks, parties." He lifted his head a little. "I didn't believe in God then, but I thanked Him for rescuing me from what I believed at the time was a fate worse than death."

Alesia's expression darkened just hearing him gloat. Simeon could see it in her face. He held his hands together in an attitude of prayer. "Please, let me go on, Alesia. I need to."

She forced herself to remain calm and nodded grim faced.

"One evening I found myself in a bar, on my own, wondering why life seemed so irritatingly boring. I had no wish for a fling, no desire for female company, no reason to want anything out of life." He tapped his finger on his knee. "And that was the moment it happened."

"What?" Alesia snapped scornfully. "You found God?"

It made him smile. He shook his head. "No, that was the moment Sylvia walked into the bar with some of her friends. I saw her look over at me, so I waved. She waved back and said something to one of her friends and came over. She looked at me and she knew." He made a flat handed, waving motion. "She knew I was in trouble. She asked me what was wrong and, naturally, I said I was fine. Then she sat down and started talking to me. And I suddenly realised I wanted to be with her. Not in the normal boy/girl way, but just to be with her. And I'm ashamed to say this, but within minutes I was crying."

Alesia's expression changed. This was not the cool, calm, Simeon that she used to know; no, this was completely unexpected.

"You cried? Why?"

He squeezed his lips together and shook his head. "I don't know. But when Sylvia put her arms round me to console me, I knew I only ever wanted to be with her, right back to that silly dance challenge at the Prom."

Alesia couldn't help but show her complete shock at such a revelation. "You two were drawn together. I remember. Sylvia thought all her Christmases had come at once." She even managed a smile at the thought. "So why did you end up with me?"

"You was the Ice Queen. I was the handsome Simeon." He shook his head slowly. "God, when I think of how arrogant I was, it makes me shudder."

Alesia affected a kind of forgiving gesture. "Well, none of us girls thought so."

Simeon laughed at that. "It worked a treat. But believe it or not, I couldn't get Sylvia out of my head after our dance, but you came as an eminently suitable substitute." He put his hand on hers. "And I'm sorry to say that,

Alesia, but like I said: you was the Ice Queen, and you were there to be conquered."

"Well, you certainly did that," she admitted grudgingly. "Then what?"

"When I was able to stop crying, Sylvia invited me to sit with her and her friends. Under any other circumstance I would have been too embarrassed, but somehow it just seemed right. Turns out they were a bunch of Christians."

Alesia gasped softly. "Sylvia?"

He nodded. "Surprised me too. But from there it was like I had no control; I had to be with her. I went to church, became a born-again Christian, got baptised — all within the space of a month. And that September..." he held his head up in thought. "... eight years ago, I enrolled in Bible College." He sat back. "And there you have it: my transformation."

"Don't you miss the way you used to be?" Alesia asked.

He shook his head. "For me, being born again means becoming a new man in Christ. I wouldn't want it any other way. And the bonus was, I got to marry Sylvia."

Alesia leaned forward and lowered her voice. "Simeon, this isn't one of those fancy-dress things, is it? You know when you surprise someone at a birthday party or something. You rip off the costume and expose most of your body parts."

He started laughing and rocked back in his chair. "No, Alesia, I promise you. What you are seeing is a new man."

Alesia had a worrying thought. "Simeon, does this mean you'll want to claim time with your son?"

He shook his head. "I won't go back on a promise even though it was a legalised promise. I've no wish to come into your life and disturb it any way. No, but if you feel you need maintenance for our son, I will agree to pay something."

Alesia touched his hand. "I've coped this far, Simeon, and it was my fault. Mea Culpa. And I don't think vicars get paid a fortune, do they?"

He grinned. "Not quite impoverished though, but you're right; not quite a fortune." He sat forward. "This may not sound right, but I don't believe it will be of any benefit for me to claim any access to Alex. If you want to keep this from him, I think it will be best. I've no doubt he will learn the truth when he's older, and he can make up his own mind."

Alesia smiled. "Thank you, Simeon. So, for now you'll just be an old acquaintance from our school days as far as Alex is concerned." He agreed. Alesia stood up. "Can we go back to the table now? There are a lot of our old friends there, Simeon, and they will all want to talk."

He laughed. "It will be nice to restore my name and perhaps my reputation."

And so, the evening moved on, and the focus of attention was on Simeon, Sylvia, Clive and Pam allowing them to help fill in the years and the lives they'd lived since that fateful night at their College Prom.

Epilogue

Wally and Heather got married on New Year's Eve. Christine was a bridesmaid and Scott was Best Man. Simeon conducted the service. In the year that followed, Heather established her position in the market place with her vegetables, while Wally continued working as Manager at Monk's Farm under the new owners.

Mitch and Denny moved in together. Mitch gave up his job at Lafayette's to bring his Harrod's skills to bear on Denny's booming business. Her Spring Collection had been an outstanding success which was followed by another glorious fashion shoot at Corfe Gallery. Naturally, Chenelle, Jolene and Eloise were there. Denny's exhibition had an extended run at the Gallery, which helped her name and reputation grow into a "New Name" in the world of fashion.

On Christmas Day, Alex played a Carol for his mum on the new guitar that Scott had bought him for Christmas. Alesia couldn't stop crying. He also bought Alesia a brand-new car, although she had to wait a few weeks for it to be delivered, but the waiting time was filled with the two of them looking for a new home for them. And Scott had persuaded Alesia to give up her job. And more good news for her was a complete clearance by the hospital after her post op examination.

So, as they settled into their new lives, they were all able to reflect on what had been and have a hope for what was to come. And on the sixteenth anniversary of the College Prom, Scott and Alesia were married. Alesia had been given the makeover that Denny had promised so many months earlier. She looked gorgeous. And as Scott and Alesia danced they both reflected on the dream they had on that fateful night, sixteen years ago. Now they could look ahead and dare to dream once again.

THE END.

Note from the author.

I do hope you enjoyed *Dare to Dream*. Emma Carney is the pen name of established writer, Michael Parker, who has been a multi genre writer for a good many years. You can see all his books at www.michaelparkerbooks.com. His book titles follow:

Fiction Thrillers

North Slope
Shadow of the Wolf
Hell's Gate
The Eagle's Covenant
The Devil's Trinity
A Covert War
Roselli's Gold
A Song in the Night
Where the Wicked Dwell
No Time to Die
A Dangerous Game
The Boy From Berlin
Past Imperfect

Emma Carney Romances:

Happy Lies The Heart
The Girl With No Name
Chapel Acre

Non-Fiction:

My Pat, a Love Story
What Happened After
A Word in Your Ear

If you like any of Michael or Emma's stories, the most helpful thing you can do is to tell people, either by word of mouth or a written review. Thank you.

Michael Parker

Printed in Great Britain
by Amazon